The

The Road to Gettysburg

Book 3 in the Lucky Jack Series

By

Griff Hosker

The Road to Gettysburg

Published by Sword Books Ltd 2014
Copyright © Griff Hosker First Edition

A CIP catalogue record for this title is available from the British Library.

Contents

Part 1

The Road to Chancellorsville

Chapter 1

April 1863

We had spotted the Yankee patrol just after dawn. One of the advantages of having been a Partisan Ranger for so long was that you never forgot the lessons you learned. We had discovered that if you did without a little sleep you might have the edge over the enemy. We needed all the help we could get. Despite Antietam and Kelly's Ford, the Army of Northern Virginia was still on the back foot. The coming of spring accelerated our need for victory. We were running out of resources but the Yankees were increasing theirs. It was not a fair world.

"Sir?"

"Sorry, Sergeant Major Mulrooney. I was daydreaming." Cecil or Irish as he was known had come a long way since the belligerent and pugnacious Irishman who had tried to take on the whole regiment. He had matured and had been the obvious choice as Sergeant Major now that old Sergeant Major Vaughan had retired. He was right to quietly remind me that I had a job to do. I was now Captain Jack Hogan and that meant that I commanded a troop. It was, admittedly, a small troop. Our numbers were always being whittled down and we had to work and perform like a full troop.

I liked the dawn. It suited both me and my men. We were used to going without sleep and the blue-coated Union soldiers were not. We used the land and the time to aid us in our attacks and ambushes. We were not afraid of the soldiers we faced. Our equipment might have been scratched together but we were not. I would trust my troop with my life. I knew I could rely on them to work and act as one. They had been moulded by be.

The Yankee patrol outnumbered us. There were a hundred of them and only sixty of us. However, from the colour of their uniforms, they were new to the front. They were dark blue. Veterans soon acquired a faded look to their uniforms. New regiments meant easy pickings. They would have to learn as we had done, through the blood of our friends.

The deep blue uniforms were reassuring. As for our uniforms… we wore whatever we could lay our hands on. If we found any Yankees whose blousons had faded to grey we took them. In the CSA, beggars could not be choosers. The majority of us had Yankee weapons. They were more reliable and better than ours. I had three US Army Colts and they had saved my life on more than one occasion.

None of this helped me to reach a decision. How best to knock the Yankees about a little bit without losing too many men? The Connecticut cavalry obviously felt safe; they were north of their own front line. They were just showing that they owned this land. We felt as comfortable north of that invisible barrier as south and we knew every crossing both large and small. I made my decision. "Sergeant Major. We will make two columns of fours, you lead one and I will lead the other. We charge through with pistols blazing. You turn and take the rear of the column and I will take the front."

He nodded seriously, "And then sir?"

I almost smiled but Sergeant Major Mulrooney took everything seriously. "Then we high tail it back to the Potomac and tell Jeb Stuart of the new regiment they have sent."

Cecil nodded just as seriously. "Yes, Captain Hogan."

The Union cavalry trotted along the pike heading for General Lee at Fredericksburg. They had not seen us secreted in the woods above the road. Our grey uniforms blended in well with most backgrounds. As Irish rode off to tell his company I turned to the men behind me. "We charge down yellin' as though we are a brigade. Nobody fires until I do. When we turn, we will be heading for the head of the column and then back up here. Clear?" They knew well enough not to make a sound and they nodded but they were grinning. This was what they enjoyed; catching Yankee cavalry with their pants down. "We won't be able to stop for wounded. Nobody is to get wounded without my permission. Check your weapons and then we ride."

I gave them a second or two to check their guns and, after nodding to the Sergeant Major who had just returned, I waved the troop forwards. We were uphill and about four hundred yards from the strung-out column of twos. When we were two hundred paces away I waved the charge and the troop let out a collective, "Yee-haw!"

The smartly dressed cavalrymen froze. I had seen it before with green troops. The officers were either at the front or the back with their sergeants. The ones in the middle were troopers and they waited for an order which never came. At fifty yards I blazed away with both pistols. Copper knew me well and I had dropped the reins to guide my horse with my knees. The Army Colt is like a large shotgun or small cannon and two troopers were thrown from their horses immediately. The smoke from the guns meant aiming was impossible and I just pointed both of them down the column as I passed through. I holstered one pistol and wheeled Copper to the left. I took out another Colt and I fired at the column of soldiers as they tried to fend off an attack on both sides. They outnumbered us but the column of twos meant that we had a greater firepower. Most of my men had acquired two pistols and they used them both with great efficacy. When I saw the officers draw their swords I knew that they were lost. I headed for the cluster of gold at the front and fired, almost blindly at the huddle of gold-braided officers who were trying to regroup and organise their men.

"Ride you Wildcats!" We had not been Wildcats for some time but they always responded to that battle cry and they followed me as I headed obliquely through the head of the column. A captain's face loomed up and I fired my Colt. He disappeared. I felt the swish of a sabre as I emptied my first Colt but I kept firing with my second and then I was in the open.

I slowed Copper and shouted, "Sergeant James, regroup the men up the hill."

I had not seen the trusty troop sergeant but I knew that he would still be behind me. He was as reliable as the sun in the morning; he was always there.

"Sir! You be careful now sir."

He was also like an old woman who always worried about me. I smiled; I had no intention of getting wounded again. I turned Copper and took out the Colt I had holstered. It still had three balls left. I saw a corporal detach himself from the column and charge me with his sabre held forward; he must have thought he was a knight in armour. He was wrong, he was brave but it was the wrong thing to do. I aimed my Colt and fired. He was thrown backwards from his horse which continued to hurtle up the hill. I saw the last of the troop pass me and I followed. The column of blue-coated soldiers was now a shambles. The officers were either wounded or dead and the ones who weren't were desperately trying to reorganise their men.

When I reached the rest of the troop I said, "Well done. Sergeant Major, take a roll call, Sergeant James collect those spare horses." Some of the Yankee horses had followed us. They were worth money to us. The Confederate Government did not supply horsemen with their own horses we had to buy our own.

"Just one man missing sir, Trooper Rae."

It would have had to be one of the newer ones. We had found that if you could survive a couple of encounters then the odds of survival rose rapidly. Still, it was not a bad result. I did not know how many of the enemy we had killed but we had prevented a patrol from scouting our beleaguered Army of North Virginia and we had damaged their morale again.

"Corporal Jones, take a couple of men and make sure we aren't being followed." I thought it was unlikely that we would be followed but it paid to be careful.

We headed back to Kelly's Ford where we had recently defeated the Yankees but at a great cost to ourselves. We now controlled the crossing but it was just three guns and our depleted regiment which did so. The rest of the Army of Northern Virginia was at Falmouth and Fredericksburg. As we approached the Rappahannock Trooper Grey rode up. "Corporal Jones said the Yankees ain't following sir."

"Good. Rejoin the rearguard."

The Sergeant Major joined me. "It seems there's more Yankee cavalry than fleas on a dog."

"You're right but I am more concerned with the fact that there are so many new cavalry units. There is something up."

"We keep whupping them sir so we needn't worry."

I waved a hand behind me. "Look back there, Sergeant Major; is that a full troop?"

"Well, no sir but..."

"And where will we get a replacement for Trooper Rae?" He had no answer to that. I felt bad that I had snapped at him. "The thing is, Sergeant Major Mulrooney that we are bleeding slowly to death. We need to end this war once and for all and we need to do it quickly before we run out of men."

"But we never lose."

"I know. We have the best men, the best horses, the best cavalry bar none but they have the better weapons and the greater numbers of men. It is simple mathematics. They can afford to lose four men to one of ours and we will run out of men sooner or later. I even heard that they have a darkie regiment now."

"They've armed the slaves? That is madness."

"I think it is quite clever. The former slaves hate the south and there are thousands of them. Who will worry when they all get killed? No, that is the most worrying thing of all. It gives them an unlimited supply of men." We headed across the river depressed, despite our victory.

The sentries were alert as we rode across the shallow ford. The Yankees had tried to infiltrate our camp before and with so few of us, we could not afford to be caught in our own camp.

"Major Murphy just got in, sir."

"Thanks, Kershaw."

We only kept a skeleton garrison in the camp. Our job was to annoy the Union forces whilst finding out their strengths. It was what we were good at.

When we had dismounted at the picket lines Irish said, "I'll get one of the lads to walk Copper. Major Murphy will need your report."

"Thanks." We only had half a dozen officers and our mess tent was smaller than most but I knew that it would be where the others were. As I had expected Danny Murphy, the major and adjutant of the regiment, was already there and had a mug of Irish whiskey in his hand. He was talking with Captain Harry Grimes; we had been the first of the men from Boswell's Horse to be promoted. Lieutenants Dag Spinelli and Jed Smith were also there. The sixth officer, Lieutenant Dinsdale would be seeing to his patients. Our seventh was hundreds of miles away. Colonel Boswell was recuperating from a ball in the back courtesy of an English traitor, Colonel Beauregard. He would not rejoin us until the autumn.

"Ah, Lucky Jack; did you have good hunting?"

"We surprised a troop of Union cavalry on the other side of the Rappahannock. They looked, from their uniforms, like they were Connecticut boys. We cut them up a bit and then skedaddled back here." We had become experts at identifying who we were fighting. We found that it helped.

"Lose any?"

"Just one of the new boys."

"It's always the way."

I sat down and poured myself a small beaker of the powerful liquor. "The trouble is, sir, that this is the third new regiment we have seen in the past five days. Something is up."

"I know. Well, you won't be surprised that the three of us have been summoned to Fredericksburg to see the general. Dago and Jed you are in charge."

"When do we leave?"

"Now. We were just waiting for you to return." He looked at Dago and Jed, " We'll be back before nightfall."

My immediate concern was Copper. When I reached the horse lines I found the Horse Sergeant, Carlton James. "Has Apples been out today?" I had captured the Appaloosa last year and given her to the sergeant. He loved horses.

"No sir. Why, are you going out again?"

"Yeah. Gotta meet the general."

"Then take Apples. Copper looks plum tuckered out." She didn't but I knew that our horse whisperer would want nothing to hurt one of his horses; least of all me.

The Appaloosa was the second-best horse in the regiment. She was not ridden as much as the other horses and was in perfect condition. She positively pranced as we headed east.

I turned to Danny. "Any news of the colonel?"

"No, Jack. The last letter I had from Jarvis was at the end of last month. So there is no change so far as I know."

That was all that we could have expected. It had been touch and go when we took the ball from his back. He could have been crippled for life. "And any more recruits?"

"I am afraid they go to the glamorous regiments. The 1st Virginia Scouts is not the most popular." We had been cobbled together by Jeb Stuart from the remnants of three regiments. I liked to think that we were the best but then I was biased.

The pickets on the pike stopped us and asked us to identify ourselves. The Union soldiers had taken a leaf out of our book and were now trying to operate behind our lines. Mosby's Rangers and Boswell's Wildcats had had a disproportionate effect on tactics. So far they had been remarkably unsuccessful but things could change quickly. When they saw Apples they smiled and waved us through. There was just one Appaloosa in this part of the world and she belonged to the 1st Virginia Scouts.

We held on to the south bank of the Rappahannock, but only just. General Hooker's forces loomed large just north of the river. We knew, from experience, that there were many areas where the river could be forded. General Lee had other regiments watching them but it was not an easy task. Of course, we would not be meeting the great man himself. We would be meeting General Stuart, the cavalry commander. We had performed services for the general in the past and he held us in high esteem. We hitched our horses outside the general's headquarters. It was festooned with flags and was clearly the flamboyant general's temporary home. It was filled with cavalry officers. Jeb Stuart was full of life both on and off the battlefield. His aide, Lieutenant Geraghty, greeted us. Stuart was always changing his aides as he did favours for his friends but we had known the lieutenant for a month or so.

"Come along gentlemen. The general is in the rear parlour with General Jackson."

"Stonewall?" Harry admired the stoic general.

"None other. I believe he has a request to make of you." The lieutenant realised that he had been indiscreet and he shut up as he ushered us through.

There were just the two generals. They could not have been more different. Jeb Stuart was small and almost delicate with more gold and decoration on his uniform than Joachim Murat. General Jackson, in contrast, was a bear of a man who wore a plain blue frock coat. Colonel Boswell had once had the effrontery to ask the famous right hand of General Lee why he wore a Union uniform. He had been told, quite curtly, that he had always worn it. He could be quite blunt. I always thought it dangerous. He might not be the bright target that was Jeb Stuart but he was a big man in a blue uniform.

Stuart was always ebullient and he greeted us warmly. He immediately poured us three generous glasses of his favourite whisky. "And how are my favourite scouts faring? Keeping the Yankees on their toes I bet."

"General Stuart, if we could keep to matters in hand these gentlemen would be able to get back to their billets tonight."

General Stuart cocked his head at General Jackson, "Always has his mind on military matters does Stonewall." Jackson began to open his mouth and Stuart held up his hand. "Point taken, Tom." He pointed to the map on the wall. "Now then boys, as you can see the Yankees have us holding this river. There are at least five fords where they can cross upstream of us here: Ely's Ford, U.S. Ford, Bank's Ford, Germanna Ford, Scott's Ford and, of course, your camp at Kelly's Ford. Now we can hold them at those crossings but we want you to stop them getting close. We want you to divide your command into five columns and do as you did when you were Partisan Rangers. We want you to spend the next two weeks harassing them in the rear of their lines so that they spend all their time looking for you and don't try to cross the river."

Danny frowned; this would be a hard task. "Why two weeks sir?"

"A good question, major. We will have all of the crossings protected by then. You need to buy us some time."

General Jackson stood. "I know I am asking a lot of your men but we are heavily outnumbered and General Lee and I need time to reorganise our forces and defeat this new general, Joe Hooker. He has a large cavalry force and we have been getting reports of lots of new regiments appearing. Cavalry in southern Virginia and the Shenandoah Valley would be a disaster. You have to keep them occupied."

Danny nodded firmly, "In that case, General Jackson, my men will buy you that time." He stood and tossed off his drink, "Although I am not sure how many of my boys we will be bringing back."

Stonewall's face softened, "Please God you bring all of your boys back safely, Major Murphy."

We left the building and I knew that all three of us were worried in equal measure. We would each be patrolling with less than forty men each. That was a small number when you might run up against a full troop or even regiment of Union cavalry. We rode in silence for a while. Harry was always the pragmatic one. "How do we divide the men up then? The troops have different numbers of recruits and experienced men."

"I will just divide them up again and the non-coms."

"And David?" David was our doctor but he could also fight.

"I'll keep him with me and you, Jack, can have Irish." He laughed. "I don't think anyone else will want him in their troop. Take Carlton too. You two seem to understand each other."

"It's lucky that you captured those horses, Jack. At least we can all have a few remounts."

"What about food and ammunition? We will have to hit and run. We can't be trailing around with pack mules."

Even in the dark, I could see Danny's shoulders sag. "It looks like we revert to being thieves in the night."

"At least we are good at that."

Dago and Jed, the other two officers, were both past masters at acquiring Yankee supplies. The problem was it increased the risk of getting caught. Those of us with Union guns would have less of a problem. "And what about Kelly's Ford? If we are not there then who will guard it?"

"I assume that someone else will have worked that one out."

I laughed, "Don't count on it. I have not seen much evidence of intelligence so far in the generals and their thinking. Stonewall Jackson is the only one I would trust."

When we reached the camp Dago, Jed and David were more than a little interested in what we had been told. Danny surprised all three of them. None were worried but they, like Harry and me, had concerns. David, in particular, was worried about injuries and wounds. "If I had known that this would happen then I would have trained up some men to be medical orderlies."

Danny shrugged, "I guess that will have to be us. We have all watched you work and we know what to do." He took a map and placed it on the table. "I will take the middle section, as far north as Gainesville. Harry, you take the next section; north to Centreville, Jed, the rest from Manassas Junction to the Potomac. Jack, you have the area to the west; as far north as Upperville and Dago, as far as the Blue Ridge."

That was a tall order. I could see that Dago and I had the largest area and the one with the fewest settlements. I felt like complaining but then I realised that none of us had an easy time. At least it would be Dago who would be guarding my flank. We would have to work something out.

Jed sat back and asked. "When do we start?"

"Tomorrow!"

Chapter 2

As I led my thirty-eight troopers across Kelly's Ford I wondered just how many I would bring back. The Sergeant Major had managed to acquire as much food, ammunition and spares as he could, and we had four remounts laden down with the precious cargo. He made it quite clear to the four men leading the remounts that if anything was lost they would answer to him. He was a force of nature and I could leave that side of it safely in his hands. The other sergeant, Sergeant James, would make sure that all of our horses were in the best possible condition. I think he preferred horses to people.

As soon as we stepped on the northern bank we were in Union territory. It was unlikely that we would see any this close to the ford but we had to be diligent and cautious.

"Corporal Stewart, take three men and scout out the land ahead of us. I want to be as close to Upperville as we can manage by nightfall."

"Sir!" The four of them took off and headed north.

We knew the area north of us quite well but what we didn't know was where the Union forces were bivouacked. That was our first job. "Corporal Jones, take Trooper Connor and see if the Yankees are in Warrenton. Head north to Upperville and we'll meet you there."

As Davy galloped off it struck me that this was why our small numbers put us in danger. I only had thirty men left now. I hoped that we would not run into another full troop of new cavalry eager to show off their new weapons. I took my Colt out and checked that it was loaded. I knew it was but it showed me how nervous I was. The last time I had been on a patrol like this there had just been Dago and me to worry about; now I was responsible for thirty-eight men. Their lives depended upon my decisions. We kept on heading deeper into Union territory while my scouts closed with the enemy. They were adept at seeing and not being seen.

All six of my troopers rode in at almost the same time. They reined in and both corporals saluted. Corporal Stewart had arrived first and he spoke hurriedly. "There's a big Yankee camp yonder sir. Just south of Warrenton. It looks like a regiment of infantry; about twelve guns and some cavalry."

"Yes sir," Corporal Jones added the vital information which had been missing from the first account. "There is a regiment of Maryland cavalry and there is a troop heading in this direction."

Sensibly Corporal Jones had decided to return with the news of the juicy target so close to us. The targets further away could wait. We learned to make decisions fast in the 1st Virginia Scouts. I looked around and saw a small wooded hillock. "Sergeant Major, get everyone in those trees. Dismount and hide the horses."

I had expected that the road would be patrolled but I had hoped that my famous luck would hold. We made the trees and one man in four took the horses to the rear. We grabbed our carbines and Sergeant Major Mulrooney spread them out in a skirmish line. I risked leaving the woods to look back; I could not see the enemy. Once back in the woods, I said, "No one fires until I give the order." The two sergeants were close by, "I would rather damage the whole camp than just one troop of cavalry. You two take the two ends of the line and make sure no one gets trigger-happy."

We heard the jingle of metal on metal as the troop of cavalry trotted down the road we had so recently vacated. My heart sank when I saw the slightly faded uniforms. This was the 2nd Maryland and we had fought them before. They were good and were not to be underestimated. I made sure my carbine was cocked and took off my hat. I peered through the leaves of the bush behind which I was hiding. They were more spread out than the boys from Connecticut had been. They had more confidence and more skill. I also noticed that they were all checking the land around them. Worryingly a couple of their horses were sniffing the air and neighing. They could smell our strange horses but fortunately, the troopers ignored those warnings and they disappeared south towards Kelly's Ford.

"Get them mounted Sergeant Major. Corporal Jones you and Trooper Connor hang back half a mile and watch for those Yankee boys coming back." I hoped that they would be on patrol for the rest of the day. We had a chance to scout out their camp and plan an attack.

We left the road a mile or so before Warrenton. We had to cross some open fields first but we eventually found some cover. "Rest the men here Sergeant Major. I want one trooper to come with me."

Cecil flashed me a look which suggested he would argue with me but thought better of it. "Trooper Cooper comes from these parts." He whistled, "Ben, get over here."

Ben was a young trooper. I had not recognised the name which meant he was one of the younger men. He had a slight frame and looked as though a strong wind would blow him over. I had, however, learned that it was a mistake to judge someone on appearances only. I rummaged around in my saddlebags until I found what I was looking for. I slipped my deer hide jacket over my uniform and donned the old black slouch hat I had stolen last year in Fredericksburg. I tossed a union kepi at Trooper Cooper. "Sergeant Major, give him your Yankee greatcoat."

The veterans all had Union uniforms in our saddlebags. We had found that disguise was a handy thing. The coat was too big but that didn't matter; he looked like a Yankee.

"Take the men to Upperville and camp in the woods to the north east." He nodded, we had used them before. We should be back before nightfall."

"You be careful sir."

I grinned, "I always am, Irish. The Lucky Jack name is because I am so careful."

We mounted and trotted off through the woods. "Irish tells me you come from these parts."

"Yes sir. My folks have a farm on the other side of the town." His face darkened. "Leastways we did until the Yankees come through and accused my pa of being a southern spy. They shot him and my poor ma died of a broken heart. I joined up the day after I buried her."

I knew what he meant. My parents had both been killed unnecessarily and had prompted me and my sister to make a new start. As soon as this war was over I would find my sister Caitlin. "I am sorry for your loss. Don't let it make you bitter. You are a young man." We had reached the road. "Is this the best way into town?"

"It's the main road but I think there will be a checkpoint just before Main Street." He pointed to a little track leading off the main pike. "The locals use that road to avoid dumb questions. It brings you out in the middle of Main Street."

"Then that is the way we will go. If anyone asks we are from the 10th Illinois Volunteers."

"Is there such a regiment sir?"

"I have no idea but I am guessing they won't know either. Just have the confidence to bluff. Hopefully, no one will ask us anything."

We were half way along the track when I saw the Union camp to our right. It looked like it spanned the pike. The artillery and the infantry were camped on the west side and the cavalry to the east. Cooper had done well to bring us this way. We could not risk close scrutiny. I saw that they had used the fences from the farms to make their perimeter. The artillery pieces were neatly parked as were the limbers. The powder looked to have its own guards and was a sensible fifty yards from any other tents. The guards looked to be relaxed. I suspected they felt safe here so far from the Confederate front lines. Major Mosby and his Partisan Rangers were operating well to the north of here.

"There sir, that is Main Street."

There was a small avenue of apple trees leading into the town. "Right let's dismount. We want to find out which regiments are here and how many men. Keep your eyes and ears open."

We walked our horses along the trees. A few people were walking towards us from the town. They had obviously been shopping and were returning to their farms; it was well past noon. We touched our caps and said, "Morning," as we passed them; our smiles disarming them. When we reached Main Street I could see that it was a busy and bustling little town. We walked to the grocery store and hitched our horses to the rail. We walked along the street identifying the buttons and cap badges of the soldiers we passed. I saluted everyone as though I was just a trooper. We crossed the street and came back the other way. We had just reached our horses when a troop of cavalry came along the street heading for the camp.

"Let's mount. We'll follow these boys."

Cooper shot me a look of fear. "But sir, the Sergeant Major said we ought to be careful."

"And we will be. The others will think we are part of this troop. No one will look twice at us."

We followed ten yards behind the last pair. I had seen that these were the same Connecticut cavalry we had bested a few days earlier. I hoped that we would look like their scouts. The sight of cavalry must have been commonplace for no one gave us a second glance. When we reached the camp we were waved through by the guards at the end of Main Street. The cavalry headed left to their tents and we just trotted on. The guards had forgotten us and were eyeing up the wagon which was heading their way.

"Slow down, Ben, and count the sentries and locate the horse herd." I could see that the two guard points were the ones with the most guards; it was to be expected. I glanced over my shoulder and saw that the wagon was being searched. "Stop here." I dismounted and pretended to examine Copper's hoof. As the wagon came abreast of us I mounted and we followed. As we reached the next guards we were stopped again. While we waited I saw that the horse herd was close to the tree line where the ground began to rise. They wanted the smell as far away from them as possible.

I heard the driver arguing with the guards. "Goddam! We were stopped and searched by the numbskulls at the other end. Do you think we have picked up contraband in your camp?"

"Just doing my job, mister. Where are you boys headed?"

"Taking some uniforms to Fredericksburg."

"Carry on then sir. Sorry for the delay."

In reply, the teamster spat over the side of the wagon and flicked his whip. The wagon lurched through and we followed. The two guards looked at us briefly but then went back to their conversation. Half a mile from the camp, we turned off and headed across country.

"Sir? Weren't you scared?"

"Not really, Trooper. If we had been stopped I would have pulled my Colt, shot them and been away before they could raise the alarm." I tapped the Army Colt. "Close up, these are much more effective than a rifle. I would bet you that neither of those men had a ball in his musket. As a weapon, they would be about as effective as a stick. I would back a Colt against a stick any day of the week. Wouldn't you?"

We headed across the open fields to get to our rendezvous. We would attract less attention that way. I hoped that Irish had avoided attention. We could both see many blue uniforms travelling up and down the roads. As the afternoon faded into dusk we kicked on. I knew that we would be eating cold rations; we could not risk a fire and I regretted not eating in Warrenton. Then I realised that I would not have enjoyed it because I believed in sharing the hardships of my men.

Copper told me that we were close to our men when her ears pricked and she snorted. The sentry at the edge of the woods silently waved us through. The two sergeants had done well and the troop as well spread out in the woods. Our tents were no longer white but a dirty grey colour. They might not be clean but they kept us hidden better than pristine white new ones. Sergeant James had risked a small fire protected by rocks and we had hot coffee at least. He handed me a cup as he led Copper off.

"Well done Trooper. You did well today."

Surprised at the compliment he grinned, "Thank you, sir. It was a learning experience that is for sure."

Cecil wandered over, "Any problems, Irish?"

"No sir. We kept off the roads."

"We'll raid them tomorrow night. It will give us a day to let the horses recover. You can take a dozen of the boys out first thing to scout Upperville. We might as well hit them the day after."

Our camp would have to be left unguarded. We had too few men for that. It would be a small price to pay; a few tents against the damage to the Union.

Cecil returned just after noon. "They have a large presence in the town sir. I saw no artillery but they had a few different regiments of cavalry and infantry. I think they are using it to control the area."

That made sense. It would be where they had the intelligence and planning officers. The cavalry and infantry would be detachments from some of the other regiments. They would be the soldiers delivering orders. A captured courier was as valuable as fifty dead horsemen. We had enough work for the next three or four days. "Well done. You and your men get some shut-eye. We will leave after dark."

We had the most success when we operated after dark. Our grey uniforms made us almost invisible. The Yankees called Mosby and his men the Grey Ghosts and it was appropriate. We use the same idea.

After our frugal meal, I gathered the non-commissioned officers around me. "We are going to do two things; one, blow up their powder magazine and two, drive off their horses. Sergeant James, you take the two corporals and half the men. You will capture or drive off the horse herd. If we can capture any then so much the better. If you think you can capture them then just head on back to Kelly's Ford. The regiment will need those horses. Irish, you and the rest of the boys will come with me and we will blow up the powder and, hopefully, some of the guns and limbers." Cannons without limbers were useless.

"How do we coordinate the attacks, sir?"

"You take Cooper with you. He knows where the herd is. We will wait until we hear the commotion near you and then we will strike."

I suppose to a regular army unit on either side that would have sounded ridiculous but we had fought together for enough time to build trust. I knew that the sergeant would do his job; he would ensure that he had minimal casualties and he would capture the maximum number of horses. He knew that we would do the same.

We waited until the sun had set before we left. We had plenty of time to reach our destination and we moved slowly, carefully and silently though the fields and woods. We separated well north of the camp and I led my detachment well to the west to approach the hidden lane from the south west.

Leaving five men with the horses, Irish and I led the others towards the artillery park. We had slow fuses with us and flint to make a spark. Before we could even think about destroying the powder we had to eliminate the guards. There were just two sentries and they were standing close by each other, both men were smoking pipes. We all had small leather bags filled with sand. We had found them quite useful for incapacitating sentries. Cutting a throat was riskier and definitely messier. The Sergeant Major assigned two men to each sentry and they crept along the fence line. All that I could see was the shadows and the glow from their pipes as the two Union artillerymen smoked away, oblivious to their danger. When the glow stopped we moved forwards.

The two guards were trussed up by the time we reached them. "Irish keep those pipes going; they will be better than the flint." He grinned and handed them to two of the troopers who kept them alight. We ran to the barrels. "You two take one of the guard's pipes and two of the barrels and put them near to the limbers." The two men raced off and I gestured another two over. "You two take these two barrels to the cannon."

Irish had already opened one barrel and was laying a trail of powder around the outside of the barrels. Trooper Smith was cutting the slow fuse and inserting it into the opened barrel. "You finish up here. Keep the other pipe and I will taker the flint. Have the men keep a watch for any other sentries."

The camp was pitch black and as silent as the grave. They had placed this dangerous ordnance as far away from their men as they could and that worked to our advantage. I reached the limbers. "Open one barrel and spread some of the powder around the limbers then put the slow fuse in the open barrel. When I give the signal then light it."

I ran to the guns. I knew we were running out of time. All too soon all hell would break loose. "Open a barrel and spread it around the guns." As they started to do that I saw that the guns were breech loaders. When the two men had finished I said, "Take as many of the breech blocks as you can and dump them in the stream yonder." I cut the slow fuse and plunged one end into the open barrel. I took out the flint and waited. This was the nerve-wracking time. Had Sergeant James been able to reach the horses unseen? I suppose I would have heard a commotion if they had been caught. Just then I heard the pop, pop of muskets in the distance and then a fusillade.

"Now!"

I chipped the flint. It took four goes to light the fuse and I blew on the end until it glowed and then fizzed. "Let's get out of here!"

I ran towards the fence line. I could hear the commotion in the Union camp. I hoped that they would not have noticed us and that their attention would be drawn to my other detachment. I heard the thunder of distant hooves. The sergeant had, at least, managed to make the horses move. I was the last to reach the horses as I had the furthest to go, I was just about to mount Copper when the sky lit up and a wave of air almost knocked me from my feet as the first of the barrels exploded. The Sergeant Major's anxious face looked down at me. "Sir! Come on. Let's go."

I think that any other horse but Copper would have run at the noise but I had the best horse in the regiment and he calmly waited for me to mount. As soon as I was mounted we rode back the way we had come.

Sentries along the other side of the camp began to fire blindly at the sound of our hooves. It would be a disaster if we were shot by accident. We all rode low to the saddle. Suddenly there was the flash of a rifle ahead of us. I saw the lane leading to Main Street and I yelled, "Go right!"

I wheeled Copper's head around and drew my Colt at the same time. We would have to risk Main Street. If we headed left we would only have the one guard post to deal with. I knew that Sergeant James would have headed in the opposite direction and so we would be splitting the enemy. As I had expected there were no civilians on Main Street but there soon would be. I could hear more explosions from the artillery park where the charges in the limbers were now exploding. The cannon would not be of any use to Joe Hooker.

"Draw your pistols! There's a guard post at the end of the street.

The dark street, the grey uniforms and the confusion all helped to hide us from the sentries at the end. It was the drumming of our hooves which alerted them. "Open fire!"

I knew that we were beyond effective pistol range but buzzing balls would keep the sentries' heads down. I saw the flash of a rifle and then heard the crack as one of the sentries tried to hit the horde of horseflesh which was hurtling towards them. There was a whizz above my head. He had aimed high. The guard post was a mobile barrier. I emptied my gun at the four huddled soldiers and then Copper sailed over the barrier. I heard the crack and pop of the pistols of those following. I risked a glance over my shoulder and saw that my troopers were close behind me.

I heard a few 'Yee Haws!' as the younger troopers cleared the barrier. I slowed Copper a little; there was little point in exhausting our mounts.

Cecil rode next to me, his face filled with excitement. "I think we did just what the general wanted there sir."

"I think that you are right. We had better halt the men and check for casualties."

"Troop halt!"

I began to reload as I turned to see if there were any empty saddles. Our horses herded together; if any men had fallen we would still have their horses. There were no empty saddles. I felt a wave of relief wash over me. Just then, ironically, it began to rain. Although we would have an uncomfortable ride home it would afford us some protection.

"Just three men wounded sir. Two are slight but Trooper Muldoon has taken a ball to the leg. He's bleeding a little."

"Form a perimeter and I will look at him. Make sure that they have all reloaded."

The ball had struck Trooper Muldoon below the knee. It had missed all the vital bones and arteries but it was bleeding heavily. He tried to get off his horse. "No, Trooper, stay there it will be easier for me to work on it." I took out the knife I had been given when I had been a sailor. It was razor sharp. I cut the leg of his breeches down the side. "Give me your bandana." I took his bandana and tied a tourniquet above the wound. I took the whisky from my saddlebag and poured it down the wound. He winced. "Now take a slug yourself. Just the one to numb the pain a little." As he did so I used a clean dressing to bind the wound and I tied a bandage around it. It was not as good as David would have done but he would live and, once in the camp, I would be able to deal with it better.

"Right, Trooper Davis, you keep an eye on Trooper Muldoon. Loosen the tourniquet every time we stop and then tighten it again."

"Yes sir. We sure whipped them tonight sir."

I smiled, "Let's wait until we are back in camp before we start crowing eh Trooper?"

He was unabashed, "With you leading us sir, we'll get back."

I shook my head; the Lucky Jack name was like an albatross around my neck. "Sergeant Major, put two good men at the rear. I don't want any surprises."

Cecil and I led the way home. We headed along the road and then cut across country. The rain was just getting heavier and heavier. We would all be soaked but it would discourage any pursuit. Every time we passed close to a farm or a house my heart was in my mouth. I wanted us to be invisible and just disappear. I was counting on the fact that they would not think to look north of Warrenton for us; at least not yet.

It was dawn by the time we wearily rode into the camp. "Sergeant Major, we'll risk a fire. The boys need something hot inside them. Just use dry wood." We had a supply of dry wood in every tent.

"Yes sir."

"Wounded men! Come to my tent." When the four men arrived I said to Trooper Davis. "Well done Trooper, now see to Copper for me. There is an apple in my saddlebag." He looked nervous. "Don't worry he won't bite as long as you have given him an apple." I cleaned Muldoon's wound first. Luckily it had passed through the leg. It must have been fired at close quarters. "You have been lucky, Trooper but check your horse. The ball might have creased him too. Just clean up the wound if it has." I then stitched his leg up.

"Thank you, sir."

"All part of the service Trooper, now go and get some rest."

"Right after I check my horse sir."

Every trooper knew how valuable his horse was. The other two just needed their wounds cleaned and bandaged. We had been lucky. I just hoped that Sergeant James had been as lucky. Cecil came along with some coffee and a piece of salted ham between two stale pieces of bread. It tasted as good as any food I had ever eaten.

"Divide the men into two. You and your half sleep now and I will wake you at noon." He looked as though he was going to object. "I have my reports to write out and I am still wide awake. The wounded are excused duty."

"Yes sir."

I finished my coffee and began to write the report for Danny. We had learned to do this when serving with Colonel Cartwright. He was old school and he told us that it was important to record what you had seen as soon as the incident was over. Intelligence was about the little details. I spent the next two hours painstakingly writing down all that we had seen and done. Then I took a turn around the sentries. Although we had no other non-commissioned officers we were such a tight unit that I knew that none of them would slack off. They all saluted as I walked the perimeter. They had donned their slickers but, as it was still raining, I knew that they would be soaked to the skin.

"Well sir, if any Yankee manages to follow us in this then I will be a monkey's uncle."

"I think you are right but it makes for a miserable time in camp eh trooper?"

"You have to be alive to be miserable sir."

With that attitude, my men could do anything. I woke Cecil. "It is still raining cats and dogs, Sergeant Major. I think we will feed the men and rest them tonight and then head on over to Upperville tomorrow night."

He looked relieved. "I know that Carlton wouldn't be happy if the horses had two hard nights back to back." He looked away to the south, hidden in the sheeting rain. "I wonder how they got on?"

"It will do no good to speculate. If they had had a problem he would have sent a rider back here. If they had failed Sergeant James would have brought them all back. I think it is safe to assume that no news is good news."

"Unless, sir, they have all been captured or killed."

That thought had been tucked away in the back of my mind. It was a possibility and I did not want to think about that. At the same time, I wondered about Harry, Dago, Jed and Danny. How were they doing?

They were in the same boat as I was. They were hung out behind the enemy lines where everyone and everything was a potential enemy. We had been given a monumental task and a short time to achieve results.

It was almost as though Cecil was reading my mind. "Even if we do nothing else on this patrol we have had success already sir. We hit their artillery hard and, at the very least, their horse herd was driven off."

The Sergeant Major was a dour character but he had the ability to say the right thing at the right time. "You are probably right. Let's get the food on the go."

Chapter 3

We left the camp in the early afternoon. It was still raining although it had stopped briefly the day before. It was now a sort of drizzle which made it difficult to see too far ahead. It was why I had chosen the later afternoon to approach the town. We would have the weather in our favour. I intended to make a bold raid on the town; they would not expect that. If we hit it at dusk then many of the officers would still be at their desks and yet many of the other soldiers would be eating or hiding from the weather.

There was no sentry post in this town and we left the main road before the town to travel through the smaller side streets. Cecil had scouted the town the first day we had arrived and knew where the cavalry were; they were at the northern end of the settlement. We were headed for the livery stable where the officers who worked in the town would have their horses. If there were no horses within then we knew we would be leaving empty handed.

"Detail four men to watch at both ends of the street. You stay with the rest of the men. You two troopers, dismount, draw your weapons and follow me."

It was a well-organised and clean stable. There was just one man and he was sleeping in the small office. I drew my pistol and placed it between his eyes. I tapped him on the shoulder. He awoke with a start. His eyes widened as he stared down the barrel of my gun. "Not a sound my friend and you will live. Understand?" He nodded wildly. "Tie him up and gag him. Make sure he can't move."

I went outside, "Sergeant Major, get the men in here now."

The troop gratefully entered the dry stable. "I want all the horses in here saddling. Hopefully, we will take some Yankee officers back too but these horses will do nicely. I want five men to watch them and another three to guard the door. The rest come with me. Trooper Davis, you are in charge."

There were now just eight of us to cause some mayhem. More would have attracted attention. When we were outside I said, "Act as though you have every right to be here. We are going to ride down Main Street and tie up outside the building with the flags. It is a headquarters of some kind. Have your pistols hidden under your slickers but if we have to fire then we have lost. Is that clear?" They all nodded. "Sergeant Major, stay close to me and follow my lead."

The street had a few riders but they were all looking studiously at the muddy road. They took no notice of eight cavalrymen wearing the ubiquitous slicker. As we rode up I saw that there were two sentries outside the main door and both looked thoroughly miserable. We dismounted and tied out horses up. I saw the two sentries looking curiously at us. "Sergeant Major, bring those despatches and the rest of you wait here. We have to get to Warrenton after this."

We walked up the steps. I have no idea what Cecil held in his hand but it didn't matter. One of the sentries stepped forward. "Sir?"

"We have important despatches here." I leaned forward. "We captured a courier."

His face broadened into a grin and the two of them relaxed. A second later and the looks on their faces turned to ones of horror as two Army Colts were pressed into their middles. Four troopers came with ropes and, as they trussed them up, Cecil and I stepped into the building. The hallway was empty, "Get them in here now. Two of you stay outside; the rest in here."

I held my finger to my lips and I listened. I could hear voices from the first room. There was a second door further down. I pointed to Cecil and the first door and then at Trooper Dawes and the second. I walked down to the second door and slowly opened it. I cranked it open just the slightest amount. I could see that there were two adjoining rooms and there were two doors. I opened the door and stepped inside. Trooper Dawes followed me. We both had drawn pistols. This half of the room was in darkness. The other side had four men. They were illuminated by the light whilst we were in the shadows. I gestured the trooper forwards and I walked into the light.

"Hands up, gentlemen. You are prisoners of the Confederacy!"

The sergeant, the major and the captain all complied but the young lieutenant ran for the door. He opened it and Cecil's fist knocked him out.

"Get in here Sergeant Major and tie their hands behind their backs. Trooper Dawes, get those maps off the wall."

I think up to that point they had been shocked but the major now blustered. "I don't know what you think you are up to but there are armed guards all around here."

I smiled as I grabbed all the papers from the desk and stuffed them in the leather holdall which was on the floor. I looked up and smiled. "It appears so. Sergeant Major, gag the sergeant and the lieutenant and make sure neither can leave."

"Did you hear what I said? This is an armed town. You can't escape."

"Yes I heard and yes we will."

Suddenly he went white. "You aren't Mosby, are you? The Grey Ghost?"

"No, I am afraid I am just a lowly captain in the 1st Virginia Scouts but you two gentlemen are coming with us. Dawes, get their slickers. I wouldn't want them getting wet." I gestured with my Colt as their slickers were draped over their shoulders and their hats placed on their heads. "Let's go outside and, gentlemen, make it nice and quiet. You two will be the first to get shot if any ruckus starts." They began to walk. "Sergeant Major, bring up the rear."

We walked along the street as calmly as men taking an after-dinner stroll. We saw no one, which was just as well as we didn't want to begin a fire fight with so few men. We reached the stables without mishap.

"Get them on their horses. I want a trooper to lead their horses and a second one to ride behind them. We don't want these boys running." When the two men were secured the riders leading the spare horses were ready I took out my gun. "We are going out along Main Street. We will ride slowly but if anyone starts anything then get back to the camp as soon as possible. Sergeant Major Mulrooney, you know the drill by now, bring up the rear."

Cecil laughed, "Sure and it's a grand place to be Captain Hogan."

The rain had eased a little which was disappointing. More people were likely to come out on the street. We made it half way down the soaked thoroughfare before we hit trouble. A gaggle of officers began walking along the street. One of them must have recognised the major and he shouted a greeting. The major could neither reply nor wave back and the men became suspicious. I eased my Colt out of its holster.

Suddenly one of the men saw our uniforms. "They're Rebs! Get ..."

That was as far as he got. My Colt was out and barked in the damp air. He fell backwards. The rest of my troopers who had free hands blazed away. "Ride!"

The troopers leading the captives rode past me as I fired at the officers again. They had taken cover. Other soldiers spilt out from the bars and taverns. Those with handguns began firing. I saw Cecil with two Colts laying down a firestorm. As the captured horses came alongside I yelled, "Sergeant Major, get out of there now!"

I took out a second Colt and emptied both barrels. The officers all remained behind cover. When Cecil came alongside I kicked Copper hard and we leapt into the night. We had almost made it out of the town when the trooper in front of me slumped in his saddle. I rode hard and reached him before he fell. Cecil reached the other side and we both supported him. I could see that he had been hit in the back; how seriously I could not tell.

"When we stop you take two troopers and lay a little ambush."

"Yes sir."

We reached the cut-off into the woods and I halted the patrol there while the horses recovered a little. Cecil and two troopers rode back and I looked at the wounded trooper. He was dead. "Tie him over his horse, Trooper Dawes, and we'll bury him later."

We had lost a man and that was hard. The Sergeant Major came back. "No one is following us, sir."

"Right. Back to camp."

The joy of our success tasted bitter as we buried Trooper McRae. I had not known him well but he was a good soldier and had never let me down. We now had less the nineteen men and, as dawn broke over an empty camp I became worried that Sergeant James and the others had not returned. We were all tired now. With so few men we were all pulling far more duties than was healthy.

"Sergeant Major." Cecil wandered over. "We will head back tomorrow. This place will be like a hornet's nest soon."

"What about the others sir."

"Hopefully we will see them or get some news of them on the way back but…"

He saw my concern, "Don't worry sir. They are good lads. Something has happened but they will get out of it."

His voice told me that he too thought it had ended badly. While he and the others prepared some food I pored over the maps and the papers. It looked to me like the Union was about to launch a major attack. When I reached the third document I froze. They were sending a Cavalry Corps towards Kelly's Ford. Sergeant James could well have fallen foul of them. Regardless of that, this was valuable information. I had to get it to the general.

"Sergeant Major, forget my earlier orders. We have to leave this afternoon. We'll wait until the horses are rested. Have the men take down the spare tents." His look was one of puzzlement. "The Yankees are about to attack Kelly's Ford. It is a major attack. Even now we may be too late."

"But sir, if we travel in daylight we risk being seen or captured."

I shrugged, "We have no choice. If their cavalry gets over the Rappahannock then we could well lose the war. General Lee is the only army between Hooker and Richmond."

Cecil was a simple soldier but even he could understand the ramifications of a Union breakthrough. "Right, sir. Make sure you eat too eh sir? We don't want to lose as well."

The two officers complained, of course, "Sir, this is not the way gentlemen behave. I implore you to untie our hands. I give you my word that we will not try to escape."

The major looked overweight and unfit but the captain was little older than me. "Very well. Dawes, untie them but first take away their belts and their suspenders."

Both looked too shocked to even make a reply but Trooper Dawes grinned. The two men would be going nowhere fast as they tried to hold their pants up. We managed to get the camp down quicker than it was erected.

"Sergeant Major, take the ten most experienced troopers. I want you eleven to guard the horses and the prisoners. Trooper Muldoon can be added to those ten. If we get attacked or if anything happens to me then your orders are to get the plans and the prisoners through to Kelly's Ford." I handed him the papers. "I have made a copy of the important points. They must get through. Is that clear?"

I could see that he was unhappy but he would obey orders. "Yes sir."

"When you have chosen your men, send the rest to me."

The seven men almost ran up to me. I could see that they were the seven youngest men left. "We are going to make sure that the prisoners, the horses and the plans get through to General Lee. If we are attacked then we hold off the attackers." Their grins reassured me.

I saw that there were a couple of reliable scouts amongst them. I had seen them operate before. "Dawson and Lythe, you two will be half a mile ahead of us. We are heading for the river but I want to avoid the roads. Use your noses to sniff out trouble. If you think there is anyone ahead then high tail it back to the Sergeant major. The rest of you will be with me at the rear. Make sure your guns are all reloaded."

As we left the camp, the tents and spare equipment on the spare horses, I remembered when I had been a young trooper and I had been excited when Danny had given me a special task. These boys would acquit themselves well, of that I had no doubt. They might be young but they were the 1st Virginia through and through.

The rain had finally stopped and there was a brighter grey to the afternoon. We had to pass by farms and homesteads but that could not be helped. If they saw us they would still have to send for help. We just pushed on. The uphill parts were not that bad to travel across but as soon as we struck a dip or a hollow then it was as though the ground was sucking our horses down. It was treacherous and we did not make

25

the progress we should have. The two scouts skirted the dangerous town of Warrenton. We all knew that they would be on the alert.

It was getting towards dark when we saw the glow from the Warrenton camp fires. The last town we had glimpsed had been some miles back and it had still been daylight. Suddenly Trooper Lythe galloped into sight. "Sir there is a troop of cavalry ahead and they are combing the woods."

"Sergeant Major, you take the Unionville road. Head for Culpeper. We will lead them towards Fredericksburg. We'll catch up with you as soon as we can lose them."

Even as he saluted and led them off we both knew that it was unlikely that we would be able to do what I had suggested. The best that I could hope for would be to give the men the chance to escape. "Right, Trooper Lythe. Take us towards them. When we see them I want no rebel yells; just three shots from every man and then ride due east as fast as you can."

I took out my Army Colt in preparation. When the action started there would be no time to think. I was relying on the fact that their attention would be on the ground looking for tracks and the last thing they would expect would be to be attacked.

We moved slowly through the woods. They were coming steadily towards us. We would meet eventually. I signalled for the handful of men I had to spread out. I wanted the Yankees to think that there were more of us than there actually were. I placed myself at the right of the line. I would be the most exposed of us all. For some, this would be their first engagement of this type and I knew how frightening it could be.

Suddenly I saw the blue shapes moving towards us. None of them appeared to have a weapon in their hands which gave us the advantage. We kept moving slowly down the gentle slope. I could see my young troopers glancing nervously at me as they waited for the order. When we were just forty yards away and I knew that someone would see us soon, despite the gloom of dusk and the dark of the woods, I raised my pistol and aimed for the middle of the sergeant I could see. As soon as I had fired I cocked and fired twice more. My men all fired three times as ordered. The smoke obscured my vision. Then I shouted, "Ride!"

We wheeled to ride parallel to the Union horsemen. They would have to ride up hill and would make slower progress. Despite what I had told my boys I kept firing until my first gun was empty. I holstered it and, taking out a saddle pistol, kept firing until that one, too was empty. You could mark the line of our escape by the smoke from our guns. By the time they had begun popping away, we were more than sixty yards from them. It was now a chase.

I could hear orders being barked as well as the sound of pistols and the breaking of branches. It was surreal. As we were heading east we were riding into the dark. The only way they would see us was by our muzzle flashes and we had ceased to fire. We crested a rise and then plunged down the other side. I knew that the land to the east was devoid of habitation and we needed to head south soon. I urged Copper on, relying on his sure feet to get us through safely. I began to overtake my troopers.

"Follow me!"

As soon as I had passed the leading rider I wheeled Copper around. I risked cutting across the Yankee line but I hoped that they would still be heading east. I holstered my empty gun and took out my last loaded one. It was a wise move. As I jinked around a tree a Yankee trooper loomed up before me. I just reacted. I lifted the huge Colt and fired in one movement. He fell from his horse which plunged down the slope after us. The single shot must have thrown our pursuers for I heard orders and questions being shouted behind us. The sounds faded as we lost them in the dark.

We did not slow down until we emerged suddenly into a clearing and the road. I had a trooper grab the Yankee horse. "Reload and let your horses rest a while. We are out of the woods but we, sure as shooting, aren't in the clear yet."

The road led to Unionville but that was across the Rappahannock. If they had cavalry patrolling the hills it was a good bet that they would also be on the road. We would have to proceed cautiously.

"Make a column of twos. Keep your eyes and ears open and watch your horses, they can smell a Yankee."

Miraculously we saw nothing. We left the road and headed across country to find the ford. Dawn was breaking and we were exhausted. I had the men walking and leading their horses. It would not do to be forced to walk later if our horses went lame. Suddenly Copper's ears pricked up and I took out my pistol. I held up my hand and we edged forward. Through the gloom of the first light, I saw a shape I raised my gun and then lowered it. It was the rest of my troop. We had found them.

"Captain Hogan coming in!"

The trooper on guard said, "Are we glad to see you, sir. The Sergeant Major was real worried."

I relaxed as I walked towards the other shapes. Irish came up to me. "We heard the shooting. Is everyone alright sir?"

"Yes, Sergeant Major. How come you didn't get over the ford?"

In answer, he led me forwards to the ford itself. There was no ford, it was a raging river. All the recent rains had swollen it and made it impassable. Although we were stuck on the wrong side at least Hooker could not use the fords for his cavalry.

"So sir, what do we do?"

I could see the looks on the faces of all the troopers; they were despondent. Much of it was down to lack of sleep and food but part of it was to have done so much and be stopped by rain! I couldn't just give up; I had to try something. "Sergeant Major, take out the map I gave you earlier." He held the map for me. I could see where we were and how far behind the lines we were. There were bridges that we could use but they were in Union hands. I jabbed a finger at a spot on the map. "Remington. There is a bridge there. We will just have to hope that it is in our hands at the moment."

"And if not sir?"

"Then you had better pray that my luck is still holding."

Remington was a small town with a small bridge. I doubt that the wooden structure would have stood up to an army crossing it but my little group would not trouble it. We reached the outskirts of the tiny burg in the middle of the morning. I could see blue uniforms on the bridge but not many of them. There were few Union flags to be seen which made me think that this town had southern sympathies.

I gathered the men around me. "We are tired and we are hungry. The only thing in our way is that little bridge and those few Yankees. I say we can ride through them and reach our camp at Kelly's Ford. Are you with me?"

"Yes sir!" was their chorus.

"Good. We ride towards the bridge as though we are Yankees. When I give the signal we ride straight through them. In my experience, Yankee soldiers don't like to get in the way of charging horses. Sergeant Major, I'll lead with my group and you follow through afterwards. You bring up the rear."

I heard him mumble, "No change there then!"

As we rode through the town, which didn't take long, I smiled and waved at the civilians. Most just waved back but a couple recognised our uniforms and just stood open-mouthed. The bridge was about a quarter of a mile from the town. I could see the sentries peering down the road at the column which was approaching them. They did not appear anxious and their guns were stacked neatly at the side of the bridge. I waved at them and they waved back. We were within thirty paces when the sergeant became suspicious.

"Ride!" It was a race. We were racing to get across the bridge and the soldiers were racing to get their weapons. We won. Five of the eight soldiers hurled themselves into the river. Two were knocked over by the horses but the sergeant managed to reach his gun. I was in the middle of the bridge and, I was told later, he had a bead on my back until Irish slashed at his back with his sabre. We had managed to cross back into Confederate territory and we had not even fired a shot.

We kept riding. We knew that our camp was a little over five miles away and were anxious to reach home. When we saw the flag still flying we all broke into a canter. I had dreaded finding it captured. As we reined in Sergeant James and Dago came running out to meet us.

Sergeant James was apologetic. "I'm sorry sir we couldn't get back. We reached the camp and then the river rose. I am sorry."

I held up my hand. "Nothing to apologise for. I am just glad you got back. Did you lose any men?"

"Two, sir, but we captured a hundred head of horses." He grinned cheekily, "We took the best and delivered the rest to General Stuart. He was happy."

"Well done. How did it go for you, Dago?"

My old friend's face looked pained. "We were ambushed. We lost ten troopers."

"Dead?"

"I don't know. We were chased by a full troop of cavalry. We got back just after the sergeant and we had to swim the river. The Yanks weren't as stupid as us and they halted."

I then told them my news. "We need to fortify the ford. There could be a whole corps heading this way. Dago, you are fresh. Take the prisoners and the documents to the general. He will need to know what is going on."

As Dago led the prisoners away the major held out his hand. "Sir, you may be an enemy but I have never seen anyone take so many risks as you did. Can I ask how old you are?"

"Let's just say, sir, that I have been fighting for most of my adult life and it is second nature not to give in."

"I admire that sir." He shook his head, "I am just sorry that I will now be a prisoner of war."

"No sir. You and I know that you two will be exchanged. It's the likes of the troopers who get prison."

He nodded, saluted and rode off behind Dago. I had no time to waste. "Sergeant James. Get your boys to rebuild the barricades and trenches at the ford. Dig a couple of ditches too. It will be cavalry who are coming and we need to make life difficult for them."

"Yes sir."

"Irish, make sure our lads get to bed. They will need all their energy when the Yankee cavalry comes. The river will be getting lower sooner rather than later."

"Sir, and Captain Hogan?"

"Yes, Sergeant Major?"

"Take your own orders too and get some rest."

I nodded but I would not. I took Copper to the horse lines and rubbed her down. I found a couple of carrots for her and put a bag of grain over her head. She deserved it. I then went to the quartermaster sergeant. "Winthrop, do we have any artillery left?"

"No sir. The infantry took it to Fredericksburg."

"Any gunpowder?"

"A couple of barrels." He looked intrigued, "Any reason sir?"

"I'd like to make some bombs. Put your mind to it eh?"

I strolled down to the ford. I could see the high water mark and the river's level was falling. "Sergeant put some stakes in the ground to the right and left of the ford. I want to force the cavalry into a killing ground here."I pointed to the forty-foot gap.

"Yes sir. There are plenty of fence posts in the timber yard. We'll get them." He looked at me, concern written all over his face, "Sir, the Sergeant Major is right. You need sleep."

"Don't you worry, sergeant, I will sleep when I am happy that we have plugged this gap." All of us worked until we dropped although I am sad to say that it was me who dropped. I found that I had been put to bed by the Sergeant Major and the guard on my tent given instructions to shoot or cold cock any bastard who disturbed my sleep. I did awake refreshed.

When Dago returned it was with two six-pounder cannon and a hundred Louisiana infantrymen. "The general was delighted with your intelligence and he sent these men because he thinks he might need us. I have been given orders to send riders to find the major and the others. It looks like we are rejoining General Stuart."

Chapter 4

It was a couple of days before the rest of the regiment arrived back at our camp. They too had been knocked about a little. In all the regiment had lost forty men it could ill afford to lose. Danny was as pleased as anyone with my success, especially the horses. "It was a miserable time Jackie Boy. It was like being in Ireland again. It never stopped feckin' raining." He pointed to the sky. "I am just glad the sun has finally come out."

"Yes sir, but that means that the Yanks will probably come as well." In the end, we left before they came.

We left Kelly's Ford for the last time in the last week of April 1863. We had had great success there but it still held the memory of Colonel Beauregard shooting Colonel Boswell. We had camped there for the last time although we passed over the fateful ford more times than I can count.

General Stuart's aide brought us a jug of fine whisky as soon as we had set up our camp amongst the hundreds of other cavalrymen. "The general is pleased with your intelligence and your horses. He thanks the 1st Virginia Scouts."

After he had gone Danny opened it and poured us all a healthy glass. "I have to say boys that we had nothing to do with this; it was all down to Lucky Jack again."

Jed toasted me and then said, "I am beginning to see that it isn't so much luck it's more that he takes more chances than we do."

"Aye, you could be right."

I hated it when they spoke of me. I changed the subject. "We are a little short of corporals, sir. It makes it harder to move in smaller groups. I used responsible troopers to help organise the men but it isn't the same."

"You are right. I'll get Irish to sort some out. The trouble is we need more men. I'll write to the colonel and see what he can do."

"How is he doing?"

"There was a letter waiting when we arrived." He patted his pocket. "He is almost ready to travel." His wound had been life-threatening but we had all expected him back sooner.

If we thought we would have time to recover from our exertions we were wrong. We knew there was something up when one of the 5th Virginia Cavalry came galloping along the road as though the devil himself was after him. He almost threw himself from his horse before it had stopped. He was in the headquarters buildings but a matter of moments before one of the general's aides mounted his horse and rode in the direction of Fredericksburg. As the last camp along the Confederate lines, we knew that whatever was coming would hit us first.

Danny nodded sagely. "Best get ready Jack. Something is up."

General Stuart left soon after the aide and the bugle sounded for senior officers to head for headquarters.

Danny and I had been discussing the new corporals and we stopped to watch the frenetic action. He turned to me, "It looks like something is up Jack, best get the men assembled. It looks like we will be moving soon."

"Yes sir. Sergeant Major, find the other officers and tell them we might be leaving soon. Have the men ready to drop their tents and tell the Quartermaster to get as many supplies as he can."

Danny ran back to us an hour later, "It's the Yankees. You were right Jack. They have attacked but instead of using Kelly's Ford, they have come across at U.S. Ford. Every regiment is riding there now to stop them and we are the eyes and ears of the whole shooting match."

"Sergeant Major, have the bugler sound 'Boots and Saddles'." I smiled at Danny. I assumed the worst."

He clapped me on the back with a huge ham of a fist. "I think we will head to Chancellorsville. The initial reports were a little vague. This may be just a raid although your intelligence would suggest this is a major advance."

Stuart's aide found us just as we were leaving. "It's vital that you find out where the main Union forces are gathered." He lowered his voice, "The general has just returned and there are small units behind us. We are cut off from Fredericksburg."

We headed west with Danny devising a plan as we went. "Harry, you take Jed and scout towards the U.S. Ford. Jack, you take Dago and scout towards Ely's Crossing on the Rapidan. I'll check out Chancellorsville. Be careful."

I turned to Dago and whipping Copper with my hat said, "Come on Lieutenant; we're burning daylight."

We knew the area well and I led us towards Catherine's Furnace. There were few towns in this area and a lot of woods. The area was known as The Wilderness and with good reason. I hoped that we would be able to move without being seen. "Dago, take your troop and ride a mile parallel to us. You take the southern side of this wood." I would not be putting all my eggs in one basket.

It was eerily silent in the woods. We were the only ones making a noise. Suddenly Sergeant James signalled me; there were soldiers to our right. I signalled to keep going. We just had to avoid their scouts and find their main force. We reached the Rapidan River and I halted the column. Dago and his men appear from the woods and he shook his head as he approached me.

"Dago, take your boys west and then north. I'll see what Ely's Ford looks like. I'll meet you back here. If I am not back by nightfall then head back to camp."

He grinned, "It's like the old days with the Wildcats eh Jack?"

"We did not have a whole Union Army against us then."

I led my twenty men along the river bank. We kept within the eaves of the woods. Across the river, I could see columns of infantry and artillery. This was not a raid. I knew that they would have taken Ely's Ford; how else would they have managed to get men across? I wanted to see how it was guarded. Was it possible to dislodge them? As soon as I saw the crossing I realised the impossibility of retaking this without losing many men. They had pontoon bridges which they were throwing over the river.

I was so busy trying to identify units that I failed to see the troop of cavalry heading our way. Cecil shouted a warning, "Yankees!"

Our training took over and we all drew a pistol. I now saw the column heading along the river directly for us. Their bright uniforms and sabres thrusting towards us told me that they were new to the battlefield.

"Right boys! Show these Yankees that a sabre ain't no good against a pistol." We had the advantage that we were in a two-deep line and they were in a column of fours. We blazed away with our pistols. It was a wall of lead into which they rode and the leading riders, officers, guidon and bugler were thrown from their saddles. The infantry battalion across the river saw the dilemma of their comrades and they began to fire at us. When two troopers fell dead I knew that we had to retreat.

"Sergeant Major, take the men into the woods and head back to the lieutenant." I took out my second pistol and emptied that too. I took off hidden by the pall of smoke from our weapons. By the time we reached the rendezvous, Dago was there.

"Dismount the men and form a skirmish line. We have Yank cavalry chasing us. We can ambush them here."

The horseholders took the horses to the rear and we all drew our carbines. I rested mine against a tree but others lay down while some climbed into the lower branches of the many trees. We heard the

33

cavalry as they encouraged each other. They had spread out from the column of fours and a hundred and thirty troopers hurtled through the woods cheering and whooping. The bark of our carbines silenced the cheering and turned them into screams as men and horses were cut down. We all fired until we were empty and then emptied our second Colts. The smoke before us hid the carnage but we could hear the moans and cries from their wounded.

"Mount and let's ride."

Hit and run was the only way we could escape and we left before they could recover. Dago and his men covered the rear while Cecil and I led our little band east towards our camp. When we hit the turnpike I felt a sense of relief for our camp was just four miles away. To my horror, I had to rein in Copper for there was a full Union Corps before us marching resolutely towards Fredericksburg.

I held up my hand and halted the column. If we went north we would hit the enemy force. We had to go south. It was an unknown country. I left the road and entered the stream which flowed north. We galloped down it. The overhanging trees provided some cover but we had no idea what lay ahead. Then I saw a gap to the east. It was the bed of an unfinished railroad. I could see the sleepers stacked to the side. The engineers had made a cutting and it was below the level of the woods. I turned Copper and headed down it. There was no point in saving the horses; we only had a short way to go. It was far more important that we returned with the news.

Hidden by the cutting we made the camp successfully. General Stuart was standing amongst a huddle of officers. I left Dago with the men and galloped over, "Sir!"

My voice silenced the conversation. Stuart recognised me. "Ah, it is my lucky Irishman. What news?"

"The Union are throwing pontoon bridges over the Rapidan River. They have artillery, infantry and cavalry over in large numbers. Chancellorsville and the turnpike are in their control." I pointed west. "They have a full Corps over there already.

"Thank you, captain. That is useful information. Have your troop ready; I may have more work for them."

I walked Copper back to our men. Dago nodded to Irish, "The Sergeant Major has managed to find us some food."

He shrugged, "They had cooked enough for a regiment and it was just for the general and his staff. It seemed a shame to let it go to waste." He thrust a plateful of steaming chicken at me. Hot food was a rare treat and we never looked a gift horse in the mouth. I devoured mine in minutes.

"We will be out again soon. I think we will try to get a prisoner this time. If you see an officer above the rank of lieutenant, grab him."

Dago gave me an indignant look, "And what is wrong with lieutenants?"

I laughed, "Nothing Dago but those above shave tail lieutenant are paid more and so they might know more."

"I suppose." He held up his Colt. "We are running mighty low on ammunition."

We both had the same problem; we had Union guns and we needed to capture more quickly. My last two ventures had not given us any. The two officers we had recently captured had had a gun each and just a handful of ammunition. "We'll keep our eyes peeled then."

Stuart's aide waved me over an hour later. It was dusk and I had thought that we would not be needed until the following day. "Captain, I know it's late but could you take your troop out and find how far down the pike they are." He gave me an apologetic look. "General Lee and General Jackson haven't decided what we are doing yet and I would hate to end up in a Yankee prison."

I smiled, "We wouldn't want that either sir. Ill just take ten men. It will be easier to get close to their lines that way."

"I appreciate this Captain."

"Sergeant Major, I need nine volunteers for a patrol tonight."

"Eight sir, I'm coming."

He was always keen, "Very well. Make sure they are all experienced. This will be no place to learn on the job."

Dago walked with me to the horse lines. "I could go you know, Jack."

"I know but Stuart asked for me and besides I never ask a man to do something I am not willing to do myself. Make sure you are ready to move the troop at a moment's notice. We are the nearest troops to the Yanks right now. If they come through you'll have to get out as fast as you can."

"What about the major and the other boys?"

That thought had been worrying me too. "They might just be trying to get back to our lines. If we hadn't found that railroad we would have still been trying to find a way back here wouldn't we?"

I put on my deer hide jacket. It gave me a little more protection, especially from swords and it made me harder to see at night. "Ready sir."

I took my pistol out and held it in my right hand. We needed to be quicker than any enemy we met. I was the lead rider and so I had to be alert and quick-witted. I did not take the patrol down the road; I rode through the fields and woods to the side. It made us harder to see. I could see the flickering of fires in the distance but I had no idea of distance. They could be a hundred yards away or two miles away. The night was deceitful.

Once again it was Copper who alerted me to the presence of the enemy. I halted the patrol. I signalled for them to dismount and we led our horses forward. None of my men smoked and I could smell the pipe tobacco from their sentries. I tapped Irish on the shoulder and held up five fingers. He tapped five of the others and we left the horses with the other four. We slipped silently through the woods taking advantage of the trees and the undergrowth. I could see the glow of the fire from their camp and it illuminated the sentries. There looked to be about six of them and they each watched a hundred-yard section of the perimeter. I worked out that the men at the end furthest from the road would be our best chance and I led the patrol in that direction.

I took out my cosh and gestured for the others to do the same. Cecil and two men slipped through the woods to reach the man furthest from us. We would, at least, have two prisoners. They might not know much but we might glean some information from them. I nodded to the two troopers and they crept up on the sentry who was peering back at the camp fires. He was knocked cold and trussed up. We tied the two of them together and they were taken back to the horse holders.

The remaining four of us crossed through their picket line and into their camp. We crouched low and headed for their tents. I held up my hand and we halted. I saw four men detach themselves from the fire and head into the woods. We would avoid that direction; that would be where they had their latrines. We turned left towards the large tent. There were a number of officers gathered around a table lit by an oil lamp. We lay down under the bushes which were close to the tent. I had no idea who was speaking but I could hear everything.

"Looks like we caught Lee napping, general."

"I know that wily old bird. I served with him. It doesn't do to underestimate him. Where are General Stonehouse's cavalrymen?"

"They have surrounded Jeb Stuart's cavalry."

"And the bridges?"

"We have pontoons across both rivers. General Sedgwick is ready to cross at Fredericksburg and the other corps will be ready to attack by noon tomorrow."

"Excellent. Make sure those pickets on the pike keep the Rebs at bay until tomorrow. I want our attack to be a complete surprise."

36

We had heard enough and I crawled backwards through the undergrowth. Suddenly I heard a voice above me say, "What have we here?"

I rolled on my back and drew my Colt in one movement. I shot the sergeant who was peering down at me. There was no point in hiding any longer. "Run!" I turned and fired three shots at the general's tent. The others all popped a couple of shots off and then we ran. We ran directly for their pickets. We knew there were just four of them and they would hesitate when they saw us for fear of hitting their own men.

Trooper Harris was a fast runner and he streaked ahead of me. It was he who saw the sentry and he fired as he ran. The sentry was thrown to the ground but a second sentry, less than thirty yards away fired at Harris. Cecil shot his assailant and Trooper Crow and I grabbed Harris and carried him towards out horses. I hoped the others would have our horses ready. We would have to forego the prisoners. We had to escape.

I heard the sounds of pursuit. The worst thing you can do when pursued is to turn around; you waste time and risk tripping. I just ran faster. "Here sir; to your left."

We edged left and saw the horses and our men. "Leave the prisoners where they are. Fire a volley at the Yanks while we get Harris on his horse."

Harris was conscious but in a bad way. We put him on his horse. "Crow, you watch him. Now ride."

I jumped on to Copper and drew one of my saddle pistols. I fired at the sea of white faces which raced towards us. "Come on, let's go!"

We wheeled around and galloped away. Balls buzzed around us like angry bees. We soon overtook Trooper Crow. "Sergeant Major, head for the road, we'll have to risk it." Our pursuers were making almost as much progress through the woods as we were. We needed the road to increase our lead.

We burst on to the road and, mercifully, we were alone. I knew that there would be pickets on the road and they would have heard the noise. I took out a fresh pistol. "Sergeant Major, you ride next to me."

He grinned, "Yes sir. The mad Irish again eh sir?"

I nodded. He knew what I intended. We would just charge the guards. We trotted along the road. We would save our burst of speed for the last few yards. I saw the two braziers up the road. There were just four guards and they peered, through the darkness at the shapes which approached. Our casual gait disarmed them and they looked to be unconcerned. As soon as they saw our uniforms that would change. When we were a hundred yards away I kicked Copper and he leapt forward. Cecil followed a heartbeat later. As soon as we did so they recognised us and their rifle muskets came up. A horse can cover that distance really quickly and the four men were struggling to hold the rifles steady. When Irish and I began firing their aim went altogether and the four shots whistled over our heads. One man was down and the others were knocked out of the way by our horses.

I slowed down, "Keep them going!" I turned and fired at the soldiers who were struggling to their feet. As Trooper Harris galloped past me I followed and we rode down the road. It was with some relief that I heard Cecil shout to our own pickets, "1st Virginia Scouts coming in."

I left the Sergeant Major to see to Trooper Harris and I went directly to Stuart's tent. The sentry saluted. "The general said to wake him when you returned." He put his head around the tent flap and said, "General Stuart. Captain Hogan has returned."

I heard a sleepy voice say, "Send him in and get me some coffee."

As the sentry emerged he said, "You can go in sir."

"Make that two coffees eh trooper?"

"Sir."

The general had slept in his uniform. He lit the oil lamp and got directly down to business. "Well?"

I filled him in on all that I had overheard. "We are surrounded by General Stonehouse's cavalry. There is at least one Corps ready to attack Fredericksburg and the rest will attack from Chancellorsville." I paused, "Sir it is a big army. I think we are outnumbered."

"I think so too." He rubbed his beard, "General Stonehouse eh? Well, I think we can extricate ourselves from this little trap this morning. If there are just cavalry then we can give them a bloody nose eh?" He looked up as the sentry came in with two cups of steaming coffee. "Have this and then get some rest. I think we will soon be in action again." As I sipped it he said, "The major and your comrades arrived last night. We have the 1st Virginia Scouts back together again."

Dawn was just an hour away when I finally crashed into my tent and fell asleep. Despite the coffee, I was so tired that a cannonade would not have kept me awake.

The bugle brought me from my comfortable dream. I had not bothered undressing; I had merely taken off my two jackets. I raced from my tent, donning my shell jacket as I did so. Danny strode over. His hand outstretched, "Glad you made it. That was a little hairy out there."

We shook hands. "Did Harry and Jed make it?"

He nodded, "We all lost a couple of men but it could have been worse. I understand from Irish that we have a couple of Corps facing us?"

"It looks that way but I think we are going to take on the Yank cavalry today."

Sergeant James led our mounts over, "We need more grain for the horses sir. The grass around here is almost done with so many cavalry regiments eating it."

"Well, I guess after this battle we can look for some. Hopefully, it will be Yankee grain."

The courier found us and saluted Danny. "General's compliments and the 1st Virginia are on the left of the field. He says to stop them outflanking us."

After he had ridden off Danny said, "Easier said that done."

"From what I have seen Danny, they still favour the sabre over the pistol."

"I know but we are short of ammunition."

I remembered that I had planned on acquiring some but we had not done so. I hoped that would not come back to haunt us.

Our regiment rode towards the unfinished railroad. We were next to the 5th North Carolina. They were an experienced regiment and it showed in their uniforms and low numbers. The troopers engaged in good-natured banter as we rode to our allotted position.

"I guess us boys from North Carolina will have to save Virginia for you boys."

"That is only because no one wants your piss-poor plantations anyway."

I had no idea what Stuart's plan would be but I guessed that it would be adventurous. That was his way. The bugle sounded for the advance. We could only see the Carolina boys but we moved forwards. It was broken terrain with too many obstacles for a charge and so we all rode with our carbines in our hands. We heard the pop of muskets to our right and the smoke began to drift from the action.

Dago pointed and shouted, "Yankees!" There was a regiment of cavalry ahead of us.

Danny halted the line and ordered, "Fire!"

We all used a different technique when firing our carbines from our horses. I leaned my elbows on the saddle and Copper's neck. It was a stable platform. I aimed my first shot carefully. Once I had fired I would be able to see little. I squeezed the trigger and saw a horse wheel away as I struck its shoulder. That trajectory would work. I began to fire steadily.

The colonel of the 5th North Carolina was obviously in the mood for a little glory and he ordered a charge. Danny cursed and ordered, "Aim further left. Don't hit those boys from North Carolina."

An action like this becomes smaller somehow. All you can see is a wall of smoke. You might be able to see the men next to you but not always. I went to load my carbine and found that I was out of ammunition. I took out my Colt. There was little point in firing, they were too far away.

Suddenly, from the smoke, came the remnants of the 5th North Carolina. From the empty saddles, I could see that they had taken casualties. I turned to my troop. "Watch out boys. There will be Yankees chasing the 5th." It was inevitable. Even if an officer ordered them not to charge, the sight of a retreating enemy was always too much for many men.

Danny yelled, "Echelon right."

There was now a gap next to us and the Union cavalry would be pouring through that soon enough. I slid my sabre in and out of its scabbard. It was some time since I had used it and I did not want it to stick if I had to pull it. The first cavalry burst through on our right. I took a snap shot and saw one of them hit but he carried on. I fired again and again until my gun was empty. The Union Brigadier General must have decided to charge because this was not one or two troopers, this was a brigade.

Most of my men had emptied their guns and we would have no time to reload. "Draw sabres!"

Danny was a few yards from me and I heard him roar. "Charge!"

We both knew that we would not get up to a gallop but we would be hitting them in the flank and that would hurt them. "Come on boys. Give the rebel yell!"

I knew the effect the yell had and my men screamed it as they leaned forward with their sabres held in front of us. We struck the Union cavalry on their right and they found it hard to defend themselves against us. I stabbed a trooper through the shoulder and he fell to the ground clutching the wound. I raised the blade and slashed it downwards as a corporal tried to turn and engage me. He was too slow. My sword cut through his kepi, down his face and across his hand. Blood spurted as he dropped his sword. This kind of savage encounter did not allow you the luxury of ensuring that your opponents were dead; as long as they were incapacitated you moved on to the next man.

Copper was still moving at speed and crashed into the side of a bugler who fell to the ground. I swung my blade at him but he blocked it with his bugle and then rolled away. He was a lucky bugler. A major saw me and wheeled to engage me. Union officers tended to be well-trained in fencing whilst those in the Confederate army were less so. The grim smile on his face told me that he thought I would lack skill.

He was not to know that Colonel Boswell himself had trained me and I was more than competent.

His first blow was intended to disarm me. He gave a flick of his wrist as his blade touched mine. That was easy to parry and I flicked the opposite way. My edge caught his leg and he flinched. I stabbed at him whilst kicking Copper on. My horse was a weapon too. He found himself trying to control his own horse with his left hand. I reached forward and grabbed his reins, pulling them from his hand. I could ride Copper just using my knees and my body weight. As I pulled I turned Copper with my knees and he began to slide forward. I stabbed him in the neck and he fell dead.

I kept hold of the reins and sheathed my sword. I took out a fully loaded Colt and began to aim at the men who were closest to me. As the smoke cleared I could see that we had broken the back of the enemy and they were retreating. I heard the recall being sounded. It was not for us but for the other regiments who were plunging through the smoke after the retreating Yankee cavalry.

I tied the dead major's horse to Copper and searched him. He had a full ammunition pouch which I took as well as his sword. Cecil's sword was little more than a lump of metal. This one would serve better. I found two more dead troopers and I relieved them of their ammunition. Unlike their officers, they also had ammunition for carbines.

"Sergeant Major!" Cecil appeared from behind me. I threw him the sword, "There you go Cecil, have a decent sword."

He beamed, "That's lovely that is. I'll make the other into a knife." Cecil was a master at making and repairing equipment. He was the first one any one went to with a faulty gun and they were normally mended within an hour.

"Did we lose any?"

"Troopers Lowell and Sandy. A few of the lads have wounds but nothing serious."

"It could have been worse."

"That it could."

"Get the boys to take anything of value from their dead. Some have some nice boots. If the dead major's footwear fits you, Cecil…"

"I have tiny feet but Dawesy might be able to wear them."

Trooper Dawes was the tallest man in the regiment. We had learned not to be fussy when it came to the enemy dead; they were well provisioned and well provided for. I knew some infantry regiments where half the soldiers had no shoes at all.

Chapter 5

We had little time to rest on whatever laurels we had won. The Union began their attack. We were not privy to General Lee's plan but we later found out that he intended to hold Fredericksburg with a little over eleven thousand men while Generals Jackson and Stuart marched around the enemy's flank. We did not know that. All we knew was that we had left many dead on the battlefield close to Chancellorsville but the Union had lost more. On that last couple of days in April, we were a thin screen of cavalry in front of General Anderson's men who began to dig trenches and earthworks close to Zion Church.

We were stood down to help us to recover. We had been riding for the best part of four days and we needed rest. The new horses we had acquired were allocated to those whose horses had suffered the most. This would allow the weaker beasts to recover. We now had more ammunition; we would not run out in the middle of the battle but we were still desperately short of men. While we had not lost many men it was like being bled to death slowly. The trickle of casualties made us weaker each time we went into action. Unless we received reinforcements soon we would be back to the numbers we had had when we were Boswell's Wildcats.

The last day in April saw us rise wearily to a sunless dawn and be confronted by a fog so thick that you could barely see your horse from five paces. I wondered if the enemy would choose to attack under cover of the fog but Stuart's aide, Captain George, who was delivering our orders shook his head. "No, Captain Hogan, the enemy has much larger numbers. They don't need the fog. The fog helps us by disguising our inferior numbers. The fog means no attack today."

We took the opportunity of reorganising ourselves into three troops. Dago and some of his men joined the major while Jed and some of his joined Harry's troop. I was reinforced by the rest of their men. I now had a hundred men in my troop. I had no junior officer but I didn't need one. The Sergeant Major and Sergeant James more than made up for a pip on the shoulder.

"What are the general's orders, sir?"

We had waited until Danny had read them twice before asking. "It seems we have to stop the enemy from spotting General Jackson and Second Corps when they sneak around the Yanks and attack in their flank."

"How many brigades do we have then sir?"

"Two."

It was an ominous silence. Two brigades meant five or six regiments at most. We would be facing three divisions. We would be outnumbered by almost five to one. First, however, we had to defend against General Joe Hooker's first attack on May 1st. We were almost spectators on the left flank. I still don't know why General Stonehouse did not send his cavalry to attack us. They could have driven us from the field like a fly from a swatter. Thankfully he didn't and all we did was pop a few balls at each other while the Union tried to attack our trenches and guns. I don't know if he was surprised at the number of men but the attack was half-hearted and Hooker withdrew. We had expected a much harder fight than the one we were given. The field was ours.

General Stuart himself rode up to see me after the wounded had been removed from the field. "Captain Hogan, did you say there was an unfinished railroad running parallel to the river?"

"Yes sir. We escaped the Yankees down it the other day."

"Good. I want to detach your troop. You will advance down the railroad track and screen the Second Corps at Catherine Furnace. You need to leave in the hour. I want you to do everything you can to prevent the Union Army from seeing this column." He must have seen the uncertainty on my face for he smiled, "I know you can do this, son. I have faith in you. General Jackson has to get around their flank without being detected."

I told Danny what my orders were and he shook his head. "Let's hope that famous luck of yours doesn't run out today. I have heard there are sixty thousand Yanks over there."

"I think you and the boys are in more danger. I won't be screening the rest of the army."

We had a cold night ahead of us and I made sure that all of my men had a hot meal before we left. "Sergeant Major, check that every man has at least two pistols as well as his carbine and I want full ammunition pouches."

We just waved our farewells. Prolonged goodbyes were not our way and the sooner we got the job done the sooner we would be back. The unfinished railroad seemed somehow both sinister and threatening as we rode along it. Every moving tree made me jump. I knew that we were beyond our front lines after a mere thousand yards. I kept glancing to the right, expecting to see Yankee rifles firing at us. We made the rendezvous safely.

"I want the horses tied to a line with just two men guarding it. The rest need to make breastworks from dead branches and trees. I want us to be invisible. While you do that I will go and scout out the road that Jackson will be taking."

I knew that the Second Corps would have an easier time in daylight but I needed to see what the terrain was like for myself. There was the skeleton of an uncompleted bridge and a small ford. The road from Catherine Furnace went south. I was glad that I had come to look. We would need to have some men here. A Union patrol could easily come down the road for a variety of reasons. The ford was not deep and even artillery could cross it. I knew, however, that Stonewall Jackson would not be laden with cannon. His foot cavalry moved too fast for lumbering cannon.

By the time I reached the troop, there was some semblance of order. "Carlton, take twenty men and go to the creek. Watch the road from the north."

"Yes sir." He paused. "Any fish in the stream sir?"

I laughed, "Well if you can catch some it will make a nice breakfast."

"I'll keep a couple for you, sir."

The Sergeant Major came up to me. I noticed he was wearing his new sword. I would have to tell him that it would trip him up in the woods. I had left mine on Copper. "The boys are at the line. I sent Troopers Ritchie and Lythe about a hundred yards into the woods, just the other side of the building, to give us warning of any trouble." The building in question looked to be an outbuilding from the main Catherine Furnace. We could not see the Catherine Furnace but we knew it was somewhere to our left on the other side of the stream.

I sat with my back to a tree and Cecil sat next to me. "I would leave the sword on your horse you know. They are a bugger for tripping you up."

"I know sir but it is the finest thing anyone has ever given me."

I shook my head, "It was hardly a gift Sergeant Major. I killed its owner and…"

"And you thought of me. Not many others would have done that. Lieutenant Spinelli, he would have kept it or sold it wouldn't he?"

"I don't know about that."

"I know sir and it's why the lads'll do anything for you. Look at me. I know I was an idiot when I joined but no one else gave me a chance. You saw something in me and look at me now. I'm a Sergeant Major."

"You deserve it."

"Not until you gave me the chance." We sat and watched the sky lighten a little. "Sir, can I ask you something?"

"Ask away."

"Do you think we can win this war?"

Did I answer with my head or my heart? "We have the best soldiers and the best generals so we should."

He nodded sagely, "True, true enough but they have more men and more guns. I'm thinking we will make a good stab at this thing but, unless we get lucky, then we are going to lose."

I said nothing but I knew he was right. I suspected he was still fighting because he did not want to let me down after I had given him his chance. It was the same way with me. I would keep fighting because I had been given a chance when James Boswell came aboard my ship in Charleston Harbour. I had answered myself; it had nothing to do with the head and all to do with the heart.

The Second Corps came through a couple of hours after dawn. The scouts trotted past us with a cheery wave and I wandered down to see them pass. General Jackson halted his horse next to me. "Captain Hogan, I appreciate your efforts, sir. You have done a fine job again. When the end of my Corps has passed if you would be so good as to head towards the Yankee lines and harass them a little."

"Harass them, sir?"

He smiled, which was a rarity. "Make them think your little troop is a brigade. You are good at that sort of thing."

He was a peculiar man; he was quite brilliant as a general and yet he was unlike all of the other generals. I went back to the Sergeant Major. "Another couple of hours and they will have passed. Get some breakfast organised. I'll go and see how Carlton is getting on."

I almost thought that they had disappeared when I went down to the stream but they were just hidden. The sergeant stepped out from cover and handed me a line with six brown trout. "Here you are sir, breakfast. We amused ourselves."

"Good. Make sure you boys eat. We'll be pulling out of here in a couple of hours."

It is amazing the appetite you get when you smell fresh fish cooking. I shared my fish with the Sergeant Major and the troopers who had spent the night close to us. We had just finished them when we heard the unmistakeable sound of gunfire. It was coming from the north. It sounded like the rest of the cavalry was earning its keep.

"Ritchie, go back to the railroad line and let me know when the column has passed."

The firing became more intense and closer. "Trooper Dawes, take some men and bring the horses up." As soon as we were freed I was anxious to get to the aid of Danny and the rest of the regiment.

"The last of the column has passed sir."

"Good, fetch Sergeant James and his men. They are by the stream. Sergeant Major, get the men mounted as soon as the horses arrive."

I moved us out in a column of fours. The trees were thinly spaced enough to allow this and gave us the chance to form two lines far quicker. We rode to the sound of the guns. The drive behind our efforts was that our comrades would be outnumbered and outgunned. We might make a difference. I had no scouts out for I knew that when I reached the pall of smoke I would have reached the battle. Sure enough, a waft of smoke drifted towards us. I could see no grey but there were dark uniforms ahead. The terrain did not suit horses.

"Horse holders!"

The ten designated troopers quickly dismounted and took the reins of the other horses.

"Form skirmish line. Sergeant Major, take the right. Sergeant James, take the left."

I took my carbine and led the line. Miraculously, ahead, I saw a fence line. I was lucky that day. "Quickly men, run to the fence line." All ninety of us were soon behind the wooden fence posts and peering out at the Union infantry who were firing at our cavalry. This was no time for individual action; this was the time for volleys.

"Pick your targets. Ready, aim, fire!"

All ninety carbines bucked at the same time.

"Fire!"

There was now a wall of smoke in front of us but I had seen, before the smoke closed in, that we had cut deeply into their side. I knew that they would now begin to realign. We had to keep up the pressure.

"Fire!" Volley fire would now be impossible and so I shouted, "Independent fire at will!"

My repeater barked until it was empty. I drew my pistol and emptied that. I then began to reload both my weapons. I was surprised that no one had tried to rush us but I suppose our sudden attack had taken them by surprise. I knew it could not last and I peered through the smoke to see the enemy. The muzzle flashes told me that they were now firing back. I ran to the right of the line.

"Sergeant Major, can you see our boys?" I pointed to where the cavalry had been.

"They are regrouping sir."

"When I give the order I want us to fall back in pairs. One man fires and one runs back. Pass the word." I ran down the line and repeated my message to Sergeant James. When I reached my original position I saw that the Union soldiers were now less than fifty paces away. I turned to

Trooper Ritchie, "When I give the word you run back fifty yards and cover me. We are going back to the horses this way."

I stood, risking a shot but I needed my voice to carry. "Fall back!"

As I had expected the enemy heard this and charged. Fifty guns barked. I took out my pistol and emptied it. "Second group, fall back!" I made sure that I watched where I was running. The last thing I needed was to fall flat on my face with a horde of blue coats hot on my heels.

I saw a trooper fall close by me. It was Trooper Carberry. I ran towards him. The ball had struck him in the middle and it was a mortal wound. He looked up at me with a rueful smile on his face. "Didn't run fast enough, sir." He reached into his jacket and pulled out a small leather pouch. "Give these to the boys sir." He winced and his eyes closed briefly. He opened them again. "And my gun its…" and then he died. I took the pouch with his few dollars in and his gun. My men shared in life and in death. I looked up and saw a line of men advancing.

Cecil shouted, "Down sir!"

I dropped to all fours and a volley erupted from my men. I turned over my shoulder and saw three men writhing on the ground, while the others had taken cover. I scrambled to my feet and joined my troop. "Thank you, Sergeant Major."

I could see the horses two hundred yards away. "The same again and we should make the horses."

"Right, sir." He turned to his men. "Fire!" The shots rang out. "Fall back!"

I took out my pistol. "Fire!" I peered through the smoke. Our constant volleys had dented their enthusiasm and I saw an officer trying to organise them into a firing line. I lifted my carbine and took a bead on his back. I saw him thrown forwards and his men dropped to the ground. "Fall back!"

We all turned and ran. The ground was more open here and there were fewer bushes to trip and trap you. I saw that the Sergeant Major had mounted his men and they sat with pistols at the ready. I watched in dismay as Trooper Lythe pitched forward. I ran to help him up. When I reached him I saw that the back of his skull was a bloody mess. He had died quickly. I grabbed his carbine and his pistol. They were both good ones. The trooper had been with us for a long time. I threw the guns I had gathered from the two dead troopers to Sergeant James. "There will be spare horses, take charge of them." I wheeled Copper around and saw that the Yankee infantry was a hundred yards away and had formed a skirmish line. There appeared to be half a regiment.

"One more volley from every gun and then we fall back to the railroad line!"

Our guns roared and we escaped under the cover of the smoke. I heard the cheer from the Yankees as they chased after us. We now had open ground and rested horses. They would not catch us. When we reached the railroad line we set sentries. "Water the horses, Sergeant James. Sergeant Major, make sure they eat."

"Sir. Where will you be?"

"Trooper Ritchie and I will see how close the infantry is. Trooper Ritchie, with me."

"Sir!"

We rode slowly back until we could see, in the distance, the infantry building a defensive line. They were expecting another attack. I had an idea. "Tie your horse to that tree and bring your carbine."

We crawled along the ground until we were a hundred and fifty yards from the enemy. They had half of their men watching and the other half building.

"Go a hundred yards to the right. I want you to fire then move ten yards closer and fire again. Keep doing that until you are back here. I want them to think that we are dug in here."

Ritchie was young and full of life. He was a quiet trooper but he was utterly reliable. "Yes sir."

I crouched and ran in the opposite direction. I made sure I had my ammunition handy and then I knelt, aimed and fired at their lines. I knew it was unlikely that I would hit anyone but it would ginger them up. I heard Ritchie's rifle as I ran and fired again. There was a ripple of fire as they shot at where I had been. By the time I met with Trooper Ritchie again, the fire was all along the line and they were wasting ammunition firing at nothing.

"Back to the horses."

We reached the others who were looking anxious as they waited for our return. The Sergeant Major was like a mother hen and he wagged an admonishing finger at me. "Sir, I thought you were just going to have a look."

I grinned, "I just wanted them to know we were still around." I glanced around and the grin left my face. "How many?"

"We lost ten men sir and there are twelve wounded. None serious."

It was a hard blow to take. Some of these men had fought alongside me for years. I did not have much time to mope for we heard the sound of battle from the north. Jackson had begun his attack. My problem was that I no longer had any orders. I had done my duty but I could not desert the field. I tried to put myself in the shoes of the colonel of the regiment we had just drawn south. How long would he wait while he heard the sound of battle to his rear? It was now noon. I decided to give the men an hour's rest and then we would return and see if they were still there.

We distributed the ammunition from those too wounded to carry on the fight and they were assigned as horse holders if we should need them. Both the Sergeant Major and the sergeant were happy with the men and horses and we rode back towards the Union lines. They had not left! In fact, they looked to be reinforced and were marching towards Catherine Furnace. This was more than a regiment and looked to be a division.

"Trooper Smith, ride to General Jackson. He should be closer to Wilderness tavern but any of his officers will do. Tell him that the enemy looks to be moving towards him. He may be being outflanked"

"Sir!"

"Right boys, we are going to hit and run and try to slow down these Yankee soldiers. We do not want to die here so do not do anything dumb! Remember you ain't Yankees!"

They all gave me a rousing cheer which made the blue-coated enemy look up.

The Sergeant Major said, "How do we harass them, sir?"

I looked around and saw that we had about fifty men who were fit enough to fight. "Divide the men into five groups of ten. We take it in turns to ride at their flanks and empty our pistols. Every time we ride at them they will have to slow down."

"We won't be able to hit much with our pistols."

"All we have to do is fire at a large body of men. More will hit than you think but we just need to slow them down. Look yonder." I pointed to the northwest where we could see the smoke from musket fire rising against the sun which was beginning to sink in the late afternoon. "That is General Jackson and his attack. We don't want these to reach him before he has had time to rout his enemy."

"Right, sir."

I was the first to ride in and fire. It was scary and exhilarating at the same time. The infantry had to stop and be dressed. By the time they had levelled their rifles, we had fired and wheeled away. We reined in out of range while the next group charged in. We slowed them down to a crawl. They spent longer each time in line; anticipating our charges. I was wondering when they would send for cavalry when they did just that. I heard the cavalry call and yelled, "Fall back, cavalry!"

Just in time, we managed to wheel into a column of twos before the troop of cavalry burst through their infantry and hurtled after us. Our horses were not the freshest and I had to hope that they were in the same position. My other worry was the ammunition. We had already used more than I would have liked. I led the troop towards the unfinished railroad. We knew it and they did not. As we rode I shouted, "All wounded and the spare horses go with Sergeant James back to camp." I saw the shake of the head from Carlton. "That is an order sergeant." He saluted.

When we reached the railroad the sergeant took off with the wounded. "Wheel and give them a volley then head west. Sergeant Major, lead them off. Trooper Ritchie, with me." We had more ammunition than the others and I intended to irritate the Yankees.

I glanced over my shoulder. They had closed to within two hundred yards. I had to make sure that they followed us and not the wounded that were disappearing east into the gloom of the railroad cutting. "We are going to ride towards them, fire and then retreat after the Sergeant Major."

"I only have two rounds in my pistol, sir."

"That will be enough. Aim for the officer and the sergeant. That should annoy them and let's give a rebel yell. That always seems to make them mad."

"Yes sir."

They were a hundred yards away. "Charge!" We both gave the rebel yell.

I saw the look of shock on the faces of the leading group. "Now!" As we jerked on the reins to both stop and turn our mounts we fired. I was more fortunate than Trooper Ritchie and I had a full gun which I emptied."

As we wheeled I felt something tug at my arm and it felt as though I had been stung by a bee. "Come on Copper; let's show these Yankees a clean pair of heels." I pressed myself low over my saddle as the lead buzzed around my head.

Ritchie risked a look under his arm. "They are coming, sir!"

I could hear the thundering of their hooves. It was with some relief that I saw the horses of the rest of the troop ahead. I could also see and hear firing from ahead. Had we run into the rear of the battle for Chancellorsville? Suddenly my men veered left and I followed them. I saw the flags ahead of the 23rd Georgia. As I passed their front ranks their major shouted, "Fire!" and the pursuing cavalry were stopped in their tracks. My men all whooped and cheered. I looked at their horses. They could run no more.

I turned and took off my hat, sweeping it before me. "My compliments sir. Your intervention was timely."

50

The major bowed back. "It is our pleasure, sir. My men love to kick Yankee ass. Your horses look a little weary might I suggest you rest them awhile."

It was now dusk and I could see the flashes to the north where Jackson's attack was proceeding. "I will sir, but first I will make sure the Yank cavalry have withdrawn."

I left the brave Georgians and led my men back the way we had come. I was sorry to hear that they were all captured later that night. I worried that we might have caused their incarceration.

As we rode down the railroad track we passed the bodies of the dead cavalry. Feeling like a vulture I had the men take as much ammunition and equipment as they could from the dead men. By the time we reached the stream we had all filled our pouches and we began the weary journey back to camp. Had we met any Union soldiers I doubt that we could have resisted them. We had been on duty since the previous night. We reached a camp devoid of soldiers save the wounded and Sergeant James and his charges.

As the exhausted horses were led away I stood with the Sergeant Major and watched as the remnants of my troop crawled into their tents.

"Well, Cecil we did what the general asked but what a cost eh?"

"You're right sir and that's without the losses the major might have suffered."

As we waited for the rest of the regiment I hoped that it had all been worth it. Suddenly Cecil looked at my bloody sleeve. "Sir, you have been wounded."

I looked at my left arm as though it was a stranger's. I had been wounded? I tried to think back; the bee sting. "It doesn't hurt."

"Never mind let's go and see the lieutenant."

Lieutenant Dinsdale had seen to the other wounded and was cleaning up his operating table. He saw me and shook his head, "I might have known that you would be the last one in sir. Sergeant Major, get his jacket off." He washed his hands as Cecil took the jacket off as carefully as possible. I had not been lying; I felt no pain. It was sort of numb.

He cut the sleeve from my shirt, "Hey that is a good shirt."

"And now it is good for a bandage or cleaning your gun." He frowned and jabbed a sharp needle into my lower arm. "Did you feel that?"

"No." I looked at the needle, almost expecting it to be blunt. "It is probably the shock."

I could see that he wasn't convinced. He repeated the action with my left hand. "Anything?"

"No."

"Let me just tend to the wound and then we'll try some more tests. "He swabbed the wound down and then quickly stitched it. "The ball looks to have struck your elbow and then spent itself." He cleaned his hands. "Wiggle your fingers." I did so. "Good. Now raise your hand above your head." I did that too. "Well, the good news is that you can use your hand and your arm."

"And the bad news?"

"You will have no feeling in your left hand and arm below the elbow. The ball damaged the nerve endings. I'm sorry."

I shrugged, "So I can't feel anything. That won't be a problem."

He looked serious. "I am afraid there is a problem. You could put your hand in a fire and not feel it but your hand would still burn. Boiling water... the list is endless. You will have to be careful."

"I told you, sir. You have to look after yourself. You are lucky, not immortal."

As I went to my tent I reflected that he was right.

Chapter 6

The regiment arrived with the rest of Stuart's Cavalry Corps. They were weary and their numbers depleted but they had been successful. We met in the mess tent and Irish cooked us up some ham and eggs he had somehow acquired. We didn't ask where he had got them from but they tasted mighty good.

"We spent all day putting ourselves between the Yankees and the line of Jackson's march. Their cavalry kept trying to shift us but they can't fight worth a damn." Dago had a low opinion of Union cavalry.

Danny was less bullish, "Things slackened off in the early afternoon. They began to shift men to the south."

I smiled and Harry said, "Don't tell me, Jack, that was you."

"After Jackson had gone he said to harass them. I guess we did."

Danny pointed at my arm, "That where you got hit?"

"Yeah. Didn't seem much at the time but David reckons I have lost all feeling in my left hand." I shrugged. "I'm alive anyway." I drank some more of the coffee. "Did we win?"

"We are still here and the Yankees aren't so I guess we did."

Just then a rider galloped in to the camp shouting, "Stonewall Jackson's been wounded!"

All of us ran from the tent. The courier was in the middle of the field. "How bad?"

"It is touch and go if he will live but he will lose an arm at the very least."

The fact that he still lived was some consolation. We all knew that he was the best general we had apart from General Lee. Many held the view that he was better. It was a moot point. He could still lead even with one arm. I looked at my bandage. I could have lost my arm too.

The news then spread around the camp that the Northern Army had retired back across the rivers they had crossed and all of the fords were back in our hands. We truly had won. This was a major victory and all down to General Jackson. That night, men drank toasts to him. When we discovered that it was our own side that had shot him there was disbelief and then anger. Lee had wisely sent the erring unit to the western theatre. This was seen as far-sighted, later, when General Jackson contracted pneumonia.

We only heard the news sporadically for General Stuart sent us to Brandy Station. The Union army had left the whole of the country south of the Rappahannock and we were to establish the cavalry camp there. The good news was that Colonel Boswell was returning and he had forty volunteers from Richmond and Virginia with him. We left in high spirits. We had done all that was asked of us and more. We were still undefeated both as an army and as a regiment.

It felt strange to be travelling openly through the same country we had recently attacked and raided. We found discarded Union equipment littering the roads as we headed north. Most of it was unusable but some we took. The damaged guns and harnesses would be repaired or used as spares. We were very resourceful. It took just four hours to reach the small town. It was three miles from the river and three miles from Culpepper.

As we rode in we saw Confederate flags hurriedly raised. I was cynical enough to realise that the Union ones would have been raised just as swiftly. Riding down Main Street Danny sent Harry off to find a suitable camp site and me and Dago to see if there was any Union equipment which had been left behind. We left Danny organising Jed and the rest of the regiment.

Dago pointed to the south east. "You know that Kelly's Ford is just over there." He shook his head. "All this fighting and we have barely moved."

I pointed north. "And Leesburg isn't that far away either."

Just then we heard the Sergeant Major shout, "Sir! Warehouses."

We were close to the Orange and Alexandria Railroad and there were four warehouses close to the line. Their doors were wide open as though they had been emptied in a hurry. "Dago you take that one. Sergeant Major you take the one on the end and Sergeant James the one on the right."

I led my ten troopers to the warehouse with the gaping door. Inside there were scattered boxes and packing crates. Some still had their contents undisturbed. They were breeches and trousers. The fact that they were blue didn't matter. Some of the troopers had worn theirs through and these would come in handy. For once we were in a favourable position. We also found some shirts and a real find, socks!

We emptied the warehouse properly and joined the others. There were no weapons but they too had found some food as well as other items of uniform. We headed back to the major in even higher spirits. The camp was established on the north eastern side of the town. We knew that our job would be to protect the army which would be at Culpeper while scouting and harassing the Union forces towards Washington. We straddled the river called, Flat Run, and were close to the railroad. If we ever managed to get some trains then we might just be able to get supplied.

We chose socks, breeches and shirts. We looked like a rag-tag army but at least some of our clothes looked new. I knew that the dark blue would soon fade in the bright Virginia summer. Our jackets and hats were still grey. We were still Rebs.

The rest of the cavalry arrived the next day and I have never seen so many before or since. Someone told me that Stuart had gathered over nine thousand cavalrymen. The smell from the horses soon made it obvious who we were and where our camp was. Colonel Boswell and the new men rode in from Front Royal the next day. The major had issued all the new uniforms we had found and we formed two lines as the smartly dressed recruits rode along the Main Street and into the camp. I could see the colonel was quite touched by the gesture. Being the first ones in the town meant that we had managed to acquire the limited supplies that were available. We had a fine meal to welcome our leader. He did look a little thinner but then his wound had been life threatening.

As we smoked the cigars he had brought he gave us the grim news from Charleston. "The Yankees have begun to shell it I'm afraid." He looked directly at me. "It looks like we might both lose our homes."

I shrugged, "It isn't as though I ever lived there."

"Yes, but you had invested in that for your future and that of your sister. I was the one who advised you."

"You weren't to know; besides they might leave them alone. They are both run by our negro overseers, aren't they? Aaron and Jarvis are both good men."

"I wouldn't hold your breath. Most of my slaves ran off and there is precious little trade coming in and out of Charleston these days."

This was not the Captain Boswell who had led us behind enemy lines. It was not even the resourceful Colonel Boswell who had been Fitzhugh-Lee Stuart's right-hand man. This was a shell of the leader we had known and followed. He sounded depressed. "Are we losing then sir?"

"I don't know Jed. Chancellorsville was a great victory but with Jackson so ill I just don't know. Most troops and recruits don't even have a uniform." He waved his cigar in the direction of the camp. "I used the last of my money to buy the horses and the equipment for the recruits. I figured the Yankees were going to take it anyway. At least this way we can hurt them a little."

The joyful mood at the start of the meal had evaporated and we were all thoroughly depressed when we returned to our tents. We did not have the luxury of staying depressed for General Stuart himself came to our mess tent the next morning. He beamed when he saw the colonel. "I am delighted to see you recovered and with your new recruits. Things are going to get better from now on." He lowered his voice although there were only the officers present. "I believe that we will soon be in a position to take the fight to northern soil. Let the civilians there suffer what our people have had to endure for the past two years. However, before we can do that we need the army building up and we are mighty short of resources." He waved an expansive hand around the camp. "We are all here because we will be close to the northern warehouses. We want you to take as much as you can from the Yankees."

The colonel had been out of the war for a while and he looked puzzled. "What sort of materials are we talking about? Guns? Ammunition? Powder?"

Stuart said bluntly, "Anything! If it is in a northern store or a warehouse then we want it. We are short of food, clothes, shoes, and feed for our animals. The Yankee blockade means that there is little coming in and nothing going out. If we are going to win this war we have to do it before our people starve to death."

This was not the death or glory Stuart we knew so well. He had become more pragmatic and practical.

"We will do that sir."

"You have until the end of May to gather as much as you can."

"And then?"

General Stuart tapped his nose meaningfully, "And then we shall see."

After he had gone the colonel said, "That means we invade the north in June or July. Danny, how many men do we have?"

"With the troopers you brought our strength is up to two hundred and twenty but eighteen of them are like Jack here, wounded."

I took off the bandage. "Seventeen!"

The colonel laughed and slapped me on the back. "Good fellow. Still as spunky as ever. Four columns then. I will lead one, the major and the two captains will lead the others. Dago you go with me and Jed with Danny. David, we will leave you in charge of the camp. Try to get as many wounded fit as possible."

"Sir."

This time, as we set off, we were not trying to avoid the Union forces; we were seeking them. I was given the task of raiding the railroad at Manassas. It was a busy crossroads and the tracks led north, south, east and west. The problem was it was thirty miles away. We would have to allow plenty of time to get there and back. Nor could we use our normal tactic of using the night. We suspected that the trains would be running largely during the day.

We risked the road and left before dawn. We could make better time on the road. Troopers Grant and White were on point. They were both good men. I had the new recruits, all ten of them in the middle of the column. Sergeant James rode with them along with Corporal Cartwright. No matter how well prepared they thought they were it would not be enough when the action started. I needed a steady head leading them.

Cecil rode next to me. "We'll need wagons you know sir."

"Not necessarily. They will slow us down. We would do better with mules and horses."

He nodded, "And we could eat the mules when we had finished with them." We had never been fussy eaters but the war had made us appreciate every mouthful and morsel of food. The only inhabited place we passed through was Bristow Station which was a small stop on the Orange and Alexandria Railroad. We halted a mile from the station. I decided to leave Sergeant James and the new men there.

"Tie up the station employees and hide until a train comes. If none come then we have not lost anything and when we return we know we will have reinforcements here." I lowered my voice, "Watch out for these new boys, Carlton. We need to bring them on slowly."

"I understand sir." He looked beyond me. "And I spy some horses in that field. We'll see if these new boys are any good as horsemen eh sir?"

The sergeant and his men galloped off to the station. They would make sure that no one sent a telegraph message but they would not cut the lines. The last thing we needed was to have a cavalry patrol riding to investigate the silence of the wires.

We rode on, knowing that Manassas was quite close. There had been two battles here already and I knew that there would be a military presence of some kind here. We halted in a small wood half a mile from the station. We left the men improvising a tangle of bushes to hide us while Cecil and I moved closer for a better look.

We crept along a drainage ditch which afforded us a good position to spy out the land. There were soldiers there but only a handful. It looked to be less than a dozen. There was a train in the station and what looked like a warehouse nearby. The train had steam but the engineers were not in the cab. It did not look as though it would be moving any time soon. The soldiers did not look to be particularly alert and the rest of the area appeared to be deserted.

When we reached the men I gathered them around me. "Four of you will stay here with the horses. Half of you will follow the Sergeant Major. Your job is to make sure that the train does not leave. Try to keep the engineers alive; we may need to move the train. When we have captured the guards then we bring over the horses."

They needed no more instruction than that. These were all my most experienced men. I could trust them to use their heads. I did not take my carbine nor did I take my sabre. Both of them would only get in the way. I preferred just to have the pistols. I had a spare one in my belt, one in my hand and one in my holster. We ran from cover and headed towards the station. I was counting on surprise and we had it. The guards' rifles were neatly stacked and we reached them before they had the chance to grab them.

"Corporal Jones, secure the prisoners. Troopers Dawes and Ritchie, come with me."

We ran into the telegraph office. The dispatcher was looking up at the door in surprise. I sighed with relief; no message had been sent. "Take him outside and tie him up." I looked at the papers and books on the desk. Most appeared innocent but I saw one with the Union flag emblazoned on the outside. It was a code book. I grabbed it and stuck it in my jacket.

By the time I returned, the prisoners were securely trussed. "Corporal Jones, take five men and see what is in the warehouse. You two stay with the prisoners and the rest come with me."

We had to work quickly. So far it had all gone better than we could have expected. Not a shot had been fired. The engineer and the train crew were all tied up and looking less than happy. I decided that the train could be disabled. It would effectively block the line and was quicker than taking up rails. "Get some water and put the fire out. This engine is going nowhere. Release the steam valves. Sergeant Major, detach two men to take these prisoners inside with the others and then come with me."

I was like a child with a wrapped present as I opened the first of the doors on the railroad cars. To my disappointment it was empty. The second contained boxes and when we examined them we found that they contained tins of beef. It was better than gold. Now we just needed some horses to transport them. "Get these boxes unloaded. See if you can find any horses."

"Sir!" Cecil raced off. The last two cars also had tinned food. These were intended for the Union soldiers.

A trooper ran up to me, "Sir Corporal Jones says could you come to the warehouse."

"Trooper Dawes, take charge here." As I ran with the trooper I asked, "What has he found?"

"Ammunition sir!"

The day was getting better and better. When I reached the corporal he had a huge grin on his face. "There are just ten boxes sir but they are all full."

"Well done corporal. Get them taken to the others." I was just about to order the warehouses to be fired when I heard the wail of an engine. A train was coming into the station. "Better hurry boys. It looks like we have company."

I ran into the open and looked around. The train was heading from Washington and was about a mile away. Hopefully, it would pass through the station without stopping. There were two lines and I hoped that the points were set for the other train to pass. The train we had disabled was on the track the furthest from the platform. I now regretted my order to disable the train. We could have travelled on the train to Brandy Station. Now we might have to fight.

I saw Cecil leading six horses. "Sergeant Major, get those horses under cover and then get all the men into the station; there is a train coming."

As the men scurried for cover I looked at the station. It looked normal except... there were no guards. I ran into the building. There were four Union jackets hung up. It was a hot day and the men had obviously decided to discard them. I pointed to the nearest three troopers. "Put these on jackets, grab a Yankee hat and then come outside."

I took a wide-brimmed hat from one of the prisoners as I threw a jacket over mine. "Grab a rifle and smile. We are Yankees for the next few minutes." Over my shoulder, I shouted, "Sergeant Major, keep us covered. We do nothing unless we are discovered. If that happens then unleash hell!"

I heard a reassuring, "Yes sir."

The train began to slow as it approached the station. They sometimes did that when passing through but I had the feeling that this one was stopping. "You three make sure your gun is loaded but do it quietly. We don't want to arouse suspicion." I just prayed that this wasn't a troop train or our war could end very suddenly.

My heart sank as I saw a face wearing a blue uniform peer from one of the cars. There were soldiers on board. The train hissed to a halt. A wall of white steam rose as it shuddered to a stop. The blue uniform I had seen turned out to be a lieutenant. He stepped from the train and strode towards me.

"Where is your officer?"

"He is out the back taking a leak sir."

He looked me up and down. The jacket looked right but everything else looked wrong. "You boys are a little messy. What unit are you?"

I had to lie. "The fifth Michigan sir."

He frowned, "I thought they were in the Shenandoah Valley."

"On detachment sir." I glanced down the platform. About twelve soldiers had stepped from the train. It was unlikely to be a troop train then.

Perhaps my nervousness and my lie gave me away for he suddenly reached for his gun. I shouted, "Let them have it!" as I swung the butt of the rifle to smash into his jaw. I threw the rifle to the ground and grabbed by Colt. A sergeant was aiming at me with his pistol. I fired as I brought my gun up and he spun around as my ball caught him in the shoulder. There was a cacophony of noise as rifles and pistols blazed away. It was frenetic. More men poured from the train.

I emptied one gun and drew a second. I was firing as fast as I could at anything in a blue uniform. I suddenly remembered that I was wearing blue and, when I emptied my next gun, I discarded the jacket. I hurriedly reloaded one of my guns and looked for another target. As far as I could see and hear the only shots were coming from our men.

"Cease fire!" I checked the troopers who had been with me on the platform. One was dead and Trooper Reed was slightly wounded. It could have been worse. "Trooper Dunn, tie up this lieutenant and put him with the other prisoners."

Sergeant Major Mulrooney emerged grinning from the station. "Sergeant Major, secure the engine. I have an idea." As the smoke cleared and the surviving Northerners were rounded up I began to formulate a plan. "Trooper Dawes cut the telegraph wire, you four start loading the boxes on the new train."

I walked through the carnage of the dead and the dying to the railroad cars. There was one flatbed car with four horses tied to the rail running along its sides. Their white eyes showed their fear. I stroked one as I passed. They would soon calm down. Two of the other cars were empty and the last one held uniforms. My plan might just work.

"Trooper Dunn, bring the prisoners and put them in this car." I pointed to another trooper. "Go and fetch the horses and put them on the flat car." I virtually ran down the platform to the engine.

The engineer and his crew were cowering under Cecil's baleful stare. "Now you boys are now prisoners of the Confederacy. We are going to drive this train to Bristow and pick up some of my men and then on to Brandy Station."

Cecil's eyes widened, "You're going to steal a train?"

"Can you think of another way to get the prisoners and the contraband back to the general?"

He grinned. "No sir."

"You stay with them until we are ready to leave and then I will ride the footplate." I ran back to organise the men. The boxes were all loaded as were the prisoners. The horses were being led on to the flatcar. It would be a tight fit as we had the horses stolen by Cecil but we would just manage it. I grabbed half a dozen troopers. "I want every building burning. Use the coal oil. As soon as they are blazing, jump on the train. We are riding home in style."

They whooped their pleasure. There is nothing more exciting than being told to set fire to something that doesn't belong to you. Once back at the engine, I said, "Sergeant Major, go back and take charge. When the troopers who are setting the fire are on board then wave and we will leave."

I looked at the engineer, "When I give the order I want this train to fly. You understand?"

"Yes sir."

As Cecil waved and the train started to move I heard the crack of gunfire. A troop of cavalry had seen the flames and ridden to the train."Full speed now!" I stuck my head out of the cab. "Open fire!"

Every trooper fired and we had such a wall of lead that the cavalry was stopped, literally in their tracks. The problem was they knew where we were going and they could ride down the road. Would the train beat them to the station and our men? I just hoped that Sergeant James had his wits about him,

We covered the few miles really quickly. I leaned out and waved my cap so that my men would know it was our train. It was with some relief that I saw my men emerge from the station.

"Get the horses on board and your men too. There will be some Yank cavalry on our tail. Get the flag out and hang it from the side. We don't want our boys shooting at us too."

"Sir." He paused, "A train?"

I shrugged, "I thought you would be happy sergeant, it gives the horses a rest!"

As we pulled out we saw the blue coats of the cavalry thundering down the road. The Sergeant Major had put the best shots in the caboose and they deterred any further pursuit. The engineer and his crew were no trouble. I suspect that they were just doing what they always had done and I kept my pistol holstered whilst I smiled at them. I glanced back along the train and saw that the flag was flying from one of the cars. It would have been better from the engine but it meant that the guards at the station would, at least, pause before they opened fire.

The engineer brought the train to a stately halt at Brandy Station. The steam hissed and the infantry came out with guns levelled. I stepped from the train. "You can lower your guns boys. This is the 1st Virginia Express from Manassas Junction."

They cheered as my men stepped from the cars. A major rode up. "Well, captain. You have done well. What is the cargo?"

"Twenty prisoners, guns, ammunition, food and uniforms sir."

"Goddam, but you are a sight for sore eyes. What is your name sir?"

"Captain Jack Hogan of the 1st Virginia Scouts."

He slapped his leg. "So you are Lucky Jack! You live up to your name and reputation. I'll inform the general of your success."

"Can I leave everything in your hands, sir? My men and I would like to get our horses off the train. They prefer solid ground beneath their hooves."

He waved an expansive hand. "By all means."

"Sergeant Major, get the horses unloaded; all of them!" I would keep the stolen horses for us. Our need was greater.

We rode in high spirits towards our camp. Night was falling but we had achieved far more than I had thought possible. Danny stepped from the mess tent as we rode in. "I was getting worried about you. Did you get much?"

As I dismounted I flashed a superior smile. "Just a train, twenty prisoners, guns, ammunition food and," I waved a hand at the horses Sergeant James was leading in, "horses. And you?"

Danny slapped me on the back as Jed laughed. "We captured ten horses and five Yankees and we thought we had done well."

"It all counts sir. Where is the colonel?"

"He is not back yet. I will now worry about him. Get Copper seen to while I get you some food."

After we had eaten and washed it down with some fine whiskey sent by General Stuart we waited for the colonel. Danny was impressed by my success. "You did really well and you only lost one man."

"Yes sir, I did well but I should have destroyed the other train. Even the Union will struggle to replace two trains quickly."

"Well we have the engineers and the telegraph is down. I think that is enough."

Just then we heard the sound of cavalry arriving. We went out of the tent and the colonel and his troop began to dismount. The numbers did not add up and I could tell there was a problem. "What happened, sir?"

"We ran into an ambush. Lieutenant Spinelli and five men were captured. It was a disaster."

The joy we had felt at our success evaporated. Dago was now a prisoner of the Yankees.

Chapter 7

We sat in stunned silence as the colonel told us what had happened. "We headed for Leesburg. I figured that we knew it well. Dago took ten men to scout it out but they must have seen us as we approached it and were waiting for us. There was a fire fight and they were surrounded. I saw at lest four men fall and then they had to surrender. We couldn't reach them and had to escape the troop of cavalry who followed us. It took us until now to escape."

"But Dago is alive?"

"Yes, he is alive. I saw him hand over his sword."

I stood, ready to leave immediately. "Then let's get after him. We can be there by dawn."

The colonel shook his head."He is a prisoner and we have to accept it. They will have a close guard on him. it will be impossible. I am not going to send more good men to their deaths."

I began to leave the tent. I was angry and I was not going to let my friend rot in a prison camp. The colonel had been away too long and forgotten our code. "I am going."

The colonel stood and faced me. "You are not and that is an order."

Danny stood. He could see how angry we both were. The colonel was not used to us speaking back to him. "Now then boys we are all a little tired. Let's sleep on it until the morning." Colonel Boswell's expression told me that he would not be changing his mind.

I turned and left. If I said anything I would regret it. I was going, no matter what Colonel James Boswell said. Copper would be well rested. I would wait until they were all asleep and slip out. I spent the next hour checking my equipment. I slipped a spare knife into my boot. I loaded my guns and made sure that I had spare ammunition. I left my sword. Finally, I donned my deer hide jacket and black slouch hat. I crept to the horse lines and saddled Copper. I was walking away when Copper snorted. Sergeant James and Trooper Ritchie stepped from the shadows. They both had their horses and were armed.

"What are you two doing?" For a moment I wondered if they had been sent to stop me.

"We figured you would want to rescue the lieutenant and thought you might need some help."

I shook my head, "This might be seen as desertion."

They both adopted an innocent look. "Not if you order us it won't be."

I wavered for a moment. Could I embroil them in my adventure? I knew that, if I went alone, I might not succeed. I would take them and then take the blame if we managed to return. I would not leave any man in Union hands. I had suffered that briefly, and I had not enjoyed the experience. I nodded my thanks, "I appreciate this."

We left the camp unseen and headed north to the land around Leesburg; the land we had known so well the previous year. As we rode north I wondered what would have changed.

We passed Gainsville in the middle of the night and rested for an hour or so in some woods where we ate a frugal meal of jerky and water. Carlton made sure that the horses were well cared for. We had already given thought to the problem of acquiring horses for our comrades should we succeed in rescuing them. Sergeant James was certain that we could steal some. "There's bound to be a livery stable or something and they will be good horses too. Those northern boys like fine horses." He was right the Union supplied their men with the best horses that they could. We had to buy our own.

The late afternoon saw us looking at the outskirts of Leesburg. We found a deserted barn to await darkness. We could sneak around the town in the evening but we would stand out during the hours of daylight.

When we left the barn we took the smaller roads which led into the less busy parts of the town. We knew where the barracks where, we had raided them before and we knew they would be guarded. We had to rely on surprise and ingenuity to get us in. We halted and dismounted about two hundred yards from the main gate. We could see that there was a guard house with at least ten men within. After watching for half an hour we saw that four of them would be on patrol the whole time; they marched in pairs around the perimeter.

We retraced our steps and walked our horses to the other side of the barracks where there was a headquarters building adorned with flags. A half hour observation showed us that there were just two guards outside. While we were watching Trooper Ritchie suddenly pointed to another building just down from the headquarters. There were another two guards but the windows were barred, "Sir, that might be the jailhouse. Do you think?"

"It could be. The problem is that they are within shouting distance of those men in the headquarters building. We will have to do this quietly. Do you two have your coshes?" In answer they both took them out. "Right then here is the plan. You two go around the back streets with the horses. Tie them up on the far side of the jail and then walk slowly back along towards the jail. I will go to the headquarters building and then the jail. I will engage the two guards in conversation and you two knock them out."

It was a rough and ready plan but I trusted my two men. The question was could I pull it off? I hoped that my Union slouch hat and deer hide jacket would fool them. I wore a pair of the Yankee pants we had liberated but beneath my jacket I was dressed in grey. They led Copper around the back streets and I crossed the street to the headquarters building. I had learned, when serving as a Ranger, that confidence often succeeded when dealing with sentries. I strode confidently up to them.

"Is Captain Hargreaves of the 5th Maryland Cavalry inside? I have a message for him from our colonel."

They looked at each other blankly. The older looking soldier said, "There are no Maryland Cavalry officers inside and certainly no captains."

The younger one nodded. "Yup, Major Blake and Sergeant Davis will be finishing soon anyway."

I shook my head wearily. "Ain't that the way though. I hoped he would be here and now I will have to go through every bar in Leesburg looking for him." I leaned in and spoke confidentially, "He likes a drink. Between the three of us I didn't really think he would be in here but he is a nice guy and I was hoping."

They nodded sympathetically. "Sorry we couldn't help you."

"Thank you anyway. I'll try down the next street." I walked slowly the one hundred yards to the jailhouse. Half way down I leaned against the wooden building and lifted my boot as though I had something stuck on it. I looked under my arm and saw that the two men had gone back to their conversation and had forgotten me. I strode on.

The two guards at the jail looked at me curiously. Behind them I saw Sergeant James and Trooper Ritchie striding towards us. "The two sentries at headquarters asked me to ask you two if you have seen Major Blake. There is a message for him."

They shook their heads. "No, he isn't here. I thought he was in the headquarters building."

"So did they. He must have slipped out. He isn't inside there is he?" I gestured towards the jail.

"No, there's just Sergeant McNeil and two guards with those Rebs we caught the other day."

I nodded and smiled, "Yeah I heard about that. How many were there again?"

The corporal seemed happy to chat and I could see that my two men were almost upon them. "Six of them. They will be taken away tomorrow."

The private said, "What a sorry bunch they were too. They had no uniform to speak of. They looked like scarecrows."

I laughed and it distracted them long enough for Trooper Ritchie and Sergeant James to hit them on the back of their heads. I caught the two rifles and they caught the men. They laid them on the floor. While Sergeant James tied them up Trooper Ritchie and I picked up their guns and stood where they had stood. If the other two guards looked down they would just see two sentries in the gloom of dusk. I tried the door; it was open. We had to move quickly. We dragged the two unconscious sentries inside and then went to the next door. I tried the handle and it was locked. I rapped on the door.

"Who is it?"

"I have a message for Sergeant McNeil from Major Blake. It is about the Rebs." We all had our pistols out ready. I held up three fingers and the other two nodded. I heard the key turning. As the door began to open I hit it with my shoulder and heard the thud as someone hit the ground. I saw a sergeant struggling to reach his pistol. I stamped on his hand and he yelped. The private who was with him was cold cocked by Trooper Ritchie. I held my Colt to the sergeant's head and said, "Ssh."

I pointed at the other door and Sergeant James nodded. He and Trooper Ritchie slipped through. I gestured for the sergeant to rise, I waved for him to turn around and as he did so I struck him on the back of his head with my gun. I heard the sound of noise and shouting down the corridor. I looked at the wall behind the sergeant's desk and saw some keys. I grabbed them and hurried down the corridor. Time was of the essence. Eventually someone would notice the lack of guards on the door and investigate.

Ritchie and James had overcome the guard and were disarming him. I shouted, "Dago! You here?"

I heard Dago's voice shout. "The cell on the end."

I ran down and tried the keys until one worked and it swung open. "Where are the others?"

"They should be in the other cells."

I threw the keys to the sergeant and grabbed Dago's hand. "Good to see you. Tie this one up and grab his gun."

We stripped the bodies of their guns and their hats. It wasn't much of a disguise but it was all we had. "As we stood in the guardroom Dago asked, "Where is the rest of the troop?"

"Back in camp. There are just the three of us and we aren't supposed to be here."

Dago shook his head. "That is dumb, Jack. But thank you."

"And we have no horses for you yet either. This could be the shortest jailbreak in history unless we find some soon."

I peered out of the door to make sure that the coast was clear and then strode casually towards our three horses. We had guns for all six of them. We could fight if we had to but if we did then the odds were we would all die. Sergeant James pointed towards the end of the street. "I think that is a livery stable. Let's just walk down there and see if it is. If not then we might just as well head out of town and see if we can find some horses on a farm."

The smell soon told us that it was a livery stable. The sergeant held up his hand to halt us and then he led his horse into the stable. There was silence. I peered down the street. It was still quiet but every minute increased the chances that someone would spot the lack of sentries outside the jail. I heard a muted cry and then Sergeant James appeared and waved us in. The stable boy was lying unconscious on the floor. "There are just four horses so two of you will have to ride double."

Dago grinned, "Just so long as we get out of this town then I don't care."

We put the four smallest men on the two biggest horses. Trooper Ritchie waved us out and we rode slowly out and into the street. Dago and I led with Sergeant James and Trooper Ritchie at the rear. When we passed the last house I breathed a sigh of relief. We had cleared one hurdle. Now we just had fifty miles of hostile territory to navigate and we would be home free.

We were less than a mile out of the town when we heard the bugles. It was our signal that we had been spotted. I pointed to the empty barn we had used before, "Let's hide in there."

Thankfully they obeyed my orders. They must have seemed stupid orders but I wanted them scouring the country further ahead and not look so close to home. We half closed the doors and kept watch on the road. It seemed an age but eventually I heard the thunder of hooves as a troop of cavalry thundered down the road. They galloped on without even pausing at the barn. We just had to be patient and wait. We spent the time filling each other in on what had happened on our patrols.

Dago shook his head, "I knew I should have been with you. The colonel just isn't as lucky as you." He lowered his voice. "He didn't scout out the town enough. He thought we could just charge in like the old days and the Yankees would give up. They are getting better. We were surrounded. I lost some good boys back there."

I nodded, "I reckon that is one reason why he didn't want me to come looking for you. I suspect he felt guilty."

Just then we heard the sound of hooves as another group rode along the turnpike. "Sir, I reckon if we leave in the next ten minutes or so we might be able to lose them."

Sergeant James was correct. They would soon turn around and begin to look for where we might have turned off the road. "Mount up then and let's go."

It was now pitch black outside and we had our best chance to escape. My plan was simple; we would follow the riders until we came to a side road. Even if we had to head west to the Blue Ridge we would have a better chance of escaping. Sergeant James led the way; he knew the country around here better than any and he had an uncanny knack of finding the easiest route for horses.

He suddenly waved his hand right and we wheeled through a gap in the fence. It looked to be a track leading to a farm of some description. We could see the lights in the farm and smell the smoke from the wood fire as we trotted through the farm's outbuildings. Even if they saw us they would not be able to get word to the Union soldiers quickly.

I wondered where he was leading us as we left the track and crossed a field of corn. Our horses made a trail which would be easy to follow. We traversed a small stream and then Copper whinnied. There were horses nearby. I drew my gun in anticipation of a fire fight but Sergeant James restrained me, "It's just a couple of horses I spied. The boys will have to ride bareback but it will mean we can travel faster."

I had no idea how he had seen them but I was grateful. He and a couple of the boys roped them and we made rough reins from rope. It felt better to be mounted and able to flee at will. We carried on across the field and we came to a road. "This leads to Upperville sir. We can then head south."

"That seems a good idea. It will take longer and there are Union soldiers there but we might lose these cavalry boys."

We halted south of Upperville on the road to Marshall. We needed to rest. The only place we could find was a small copse a mile or so from the road. We posted guards and then lay down for a sleep. Dago and I were too much on edge to sleep.

"You know you will be in trouble Jack."

"I know. When we were Rangers we might have got away with it but we are now part of the army. This is desertion in the face of the enemy."

"You mean you know you could be shot for this?"

I shrugged, "I knew it was a possibility but I couldn't stand by while you and the others were carted off to a Union prison. Most of them are death camps." I pointed to Trooper Ritchie who was sleeping. "I told them I would say I ordered them to come with me. They might get away with it."

"I would have said that you would have been let off if it wasn't for the fact that Colonel Boswell appears to have come back a changed man."

"I don't know about that. It might be that he has been brought up to live by the rules. His disgrace was not his fault and I think he has been trying to become accepted again ever since we met him. He wouldn't want to jeopardise that by overlooking something as serious as this."

"You seem very calm about the prospect of a firing squad."

"I am not. Inside I am wound tighter than a clock spring but if I have learned one thing in life it is that you never know what is around the corner. Take each minute as it comes."

We waited until late afternoon to begin the last part of the journey. We were still wary. We had to pass through Marshall and Warrenton and both were in Union hands still. Marshall looked to be a one horse town as we spied it from the small hill overlooking the Virginian town. We decided to avoid the road and travel cross country.

As we dropped down on to the road we heard the sound we had been dreading; it was the sound of a bugle. I looked behind us and saw a patrol of Union cavalry a mile away.

"Right boys, head for the road. It looks like it will be a race to Brandy Station." In the back of my mind was the worry that there would be more soldiers waiting for us at Warrenton. That bridge would have to be crossed eventually.

Dago and I dropped to the back while Trooper Ritchie rode at the front with the sergeant. We were the best armed. I had given one of my spare Colts to Dago and it would be up to us to slow down the pursuit. The Northern cavalry appeared to be gaining. Sergeant James was conserving our horses while the blue coated horsemen were thrashing their mounts. It was a test of nerve.

We heard the crack as they fired from their horses. It was a waste of lead. Their horses were moving too quickly and they had no control over their aim. When we eventually fired it would be from a stationery position. I risked a glance and saw that they had closed to within a couple of hundred yards but I could see the sweat on their horses and the wild eyes of their mounts. We were still riding within our horse's comfort zone.

I saw Warrenton in the distance. If the Union soldiers kept on firing it would alert the citizens of the town. We were clearly Rebs and they would fire on us as soon as they realised we were being pursued. It couldn't be helped. We had to pass through the town to reach our destination. Once we had passed Warrenton we would be just fifteen miles from our camp. Sergeant James was obviously of the same mind as I was and he headed for the road through Warrenton. When we hit the road we kicked on. We reached half way down Main Street before they realised who we were. Suddenly guns began to pop at us. I was not sure they would hit anything for we were moving quickly but it was nerve wracking to have to endure the heated fire from both sides of the street.

We erupted out of the town and flooded down the road. We had begun to leave the Union cavalry behind. I glanced over my shoulder and saw that their horses were now labouring. I heard a volley ahead. To my horror, as I turned I saw ten Union soldiers with rifles levelled and the smoke clearing. Two of Dago's men lay cut to pieces. This was no place for the faint hearted.

"Fire!"

Unlike the soldiers who had fired we had fought almost every day for the past two years and when we fired we shot to kill. They were busy reloading as our pistols barked. Four of us poured over twenty shots at them and the troopers with the rifles added their fire. The blue coated men soon lay on the ground or cowered behind whatever shelter they could but our delay had given our pursuers heart.

"Ride."

It hurt me to leave the two bodies on the ground but if we stayed we would have died or been made prisoner. I knew that we had to do something dramatic or they would catch us. Away to the east there were fields beyond the stone wall. The fields were divided by wooden fences.

"Sergeant James, let's see if these Yankees can ride." He turned in his saddle and I said as I mimed with my hand, "Jump the wall!"

He nodded his understanding and suddenly wheeled Apples, his horse, towards the wall. The Appaloosa soared over. The rest all followed. Dago and I jumped together. Copper cleared it easily. "Keep a steady pace."

The sergeant headed south east and we had lost our column formation. We rode now more like an arrow. I risked a glance over my shoulder. Half a dozen had cleared the wall but some of the others had to retry and coax their horses. I saw that some of them had ridden down to a gate. They would not have to jump but they would have a longer journey. We were all able to clear the first wooden fence easily as we were in a line. Behind us the northern cavalry were still trying to retain a column formation. It was a mistake.

By the time we had cleared five of the fences the Union cavalry were strung out in a long ragged line almost half a mile in length. There were gaps of between twenty and thirty yards between some whilst the last twenty were a few hundred yards behind the leaders. Ahead of us I saw some trees next to a gap in the wall. I galloped Copper and overtook the sergeant.

"Follow me and have your guns ready!"

As we thundered through the gap I wheeled Copper to the left so that we were hidden by the trees. I took out two pistols.

"I want us in a line here. When they come through I want the leaders blasting. When we ride we ride along the road."

A few moments later the leading ten riders rode through the gap. We opened fire as soon as we saw them. Every gun blazed. They had no chance to fire back as they had not drawn their weapons. The last four wheeled around and rode back through the gap.

"Let's ride!" It hurt me to leave those weapons lying with their dead and wounded riders but we had given ourselves a chance. I could see that the rest had slowed up to draw their guns. They were also impeded by their casualties. Our gap lengthened. We were bone tired but home was less than five miles away. We slowed to a trot. Our horses needed a rest. I kept looking behind us and saw that they had not given up the pursuit. We had hurt their pride and I had noticed that the Union cavalry were getting better; they had toughened up.

I breathed a sigh of relief when I saw the Rappahannock ahead and the Confederate flags flying. We were almost home. We crossed our own lines with little fuss other than a salute from the sentry but when we rode into our camp we were cheered and acclaimed as heroes. Troopers ran from their tents and their food to slap us on the back. I couldn't help grinning. After I had dismounted I threw my arms around Dago. "We made it!"

"Thanks Jack. I owe you for this."

"You would have done the same."

When the colonel and the major strode over I knew that we were in trouble. The colonel's face was as black as thunder. He shook Dago by the hand. "Welcome back Lieutenant Spinelli. Major Murphy arrest Captain Hogan, Sergeant James and Trooper Ritchie. Confine them to their tents until I can arrange a court martial for Captain Hogan."

"Sir the sergeant and the trooper were obeying orders. My orders."

His eyes narrowed. "I think you are lying. Major, carry out my orders and disarm them too!" He stormed off.

Danny looked apologetic, "You are a mad bugger, Jack and I admire what you did but you have really annoyed him. Your guns if you please."

"I did order them, Danny. Tell him."

He nodded, "When he has had a chance to calm down I will."

I lay down in my tent feeling remarkably relaxed. The trooper sent to guard me, Trooper Smith, was embarrassed about the whole thing. "Sorry about this, Captain Hogan. The boys all think it was a fine thing that you did. You should get a medal and not be treated like a criminal."

"Kind of you to say so, Trooper Smith, but I knew what the consequences would be when I lit out."

I took off my boots and uniform for what seemed the first time in months. I lay on my bed and within minutes was asleep. I was awoken by Trooper Smith. "Captain Hogan, the major is here to see you."

It was dark and Danny brought in an oil lamp when he entered. He had a bottle of whiskey and Smith handed him a plate with some food on it. "You have been asleep for four hours. We thought you might like some food."

"Won't you get in trouble for this Danny?"

He shrugged, "He's changed, has the colonel, but he will soon be his old self again and he will realise what a mistake he has made." He poured some whiskey into my mug. "Dago told me how you managed to rescue them." He shook his head. "I am certain that no one else could have managed that." He laughed, "You even got some fine remounts and weapons."

"How about James and Ritchie?"

"I think he will let them go in the morning. He will probably reduce the sergeant to corporal."

I felt awful about that. I should have gone alone but then I wouldn't have been able to rescue my friend. I was learning that you needed your friends around you.

"Of course the one you really annoyed was Irish."

I was puzzled, "Why?"

"He wanted to go with you."

"But he is Sergeant Major."

"I think he sees you as being more important than the rank. He has been begging the colonel to reconsider. We had to send him back to his tent. He was in danger of being reduced to the ranks himself."

"And the court martial?"

"He has asked for a panel of officers in the morning. I will be defending you."

"Thanks Danny."

73

"You might lose your rank you know? I don't think he will go for a firing squad. That is a little extreme even for the colonel."

"Tell me Danny, if it was me and you had rescued me would you mind being reduced to the ranks?"

He laughed, "Of course not. What has annoyed the boys is that you have done so much; the trains, the intelligence, and the prisoners. Even if this was what the colonel says they think that he should have taken the other things into consideration."

"He is old school remember."

As he rose to leave Danny shook his head, "Colonel Cartwright would not have done this and we both know it."

As the light was taken away and I was left in the dark I reflected that he was right. Colonel Cartwright had been old school but he was old school with a heart.

Chapter 8

After breakfast I was escorted by my new guard, Trooper McKay and Sergeant Major Mulrooney to the latrine.

"You could have taken me sir."

Cecil sounded indignant. "I didn't plan on taking anyone. Those two were waiting for me. What else could I do? Come and wake you?"

"That wouldn't have been a bad idea sir."

"Anyway this will soon be over one way or another."

"By this afternoon sir. The general himself is coming with some senior officers to sit on the court martial himself."

"Stuart or Jackson?"

He looked sad, "Didn't you know sir? General Jackson died of pneumonia. He never recovered. It will be General Stuart."

That news saddened me more than anything else. Stonewall Jackson had been more than Lee's right hand man; he had been the reason for all our victories. He had always taken on superior numbers and won. Every soldier who fought for him would have gladly died for him and yet he was the sternest disciplinarian. It was a shame and made even worse by the fact that it had been our own side which had shot him.

When I returned to my tent Cecil insisted on cleaning my best uniform and polishing my sword. "Those officers need to see how smart you are sir. It might help your case." Poor Sergeant Major Mulrooney was almost in tears.

He fussed over me like an old woman and polished my boots until they shone. He waited with me until Danny arrived just after noon. "The general is here Jack. Let's go."

As we walked over he said, "It's as I thought, he just demoted Sergeant James to corporal. He'll soon get his stripe back." I felt relieved at that. I could face whatever they threw at me now.

I was marched into the tent and saw General Stuart, Colonel Boswell and a major I didn't recognise. General Stuart frowned when he saw me and turned to say something to Colonel Boswell. The colonel stood. "Lieutenant Smith, will you read the charges."

Jed looked uncomfortable as he stood in his best uniform and read from the sheet. "Captain Jack Hogan is charged with desertion and disobeying an order from his commanding officer. He recklessly endangered the lives of two other soldiers when he went to Leesburg to rescue Lieutenant Spinelli and his men from a Union prison."

Jed sat down and looked assiduously at the ground. Colonel Boswell stood, "How do you plead?"

I had never experienced anything like this before and I just answered honestly. "I suppose I must be guilty because I did go to Leesburg and I did rescue Lieutenant Spinelli."

He beamed, "There you have it members of this court martial. The accused admits his guilt. Now we will decide your...."

General Stuart stood, "Now before we get to that can we just sit down and think about this." Colonel Boswell reluctantly sat down. "Now I did not know that the officer in question was Captain Hogan. This puts a different complexion on things. Nor did I know the charges. When you said desertion it sounded more serious than it is."

"But it was desertion!"

"No colonel, at worst it was being absent without leave but his motives were laudable. Besides which he has had two Union regiments searching for him for the past two days." He beckoned me over, "Captain Hogan, tell me why you went to Leesburg."

"Lieutenant Spinelli is a good officer and I did not want him or the others to rot in a Yankee prison. I have done this before sir." I was reminding the general of the time that Dago and I had rescued his nephew from the prison at Gettysburg.

"I know and I will always be grateful for that but why did you sneak away? You should have known it would put you in a bad light."

"I asked the colonel's permission and he refused." I shrugged. "I would do it again sir."

Colonel Boswell's face was as black as thunder but General Stuart smiled. "As the senior officer here I have decided to squash the charges. Captain Hogan's motives were of the highest order. You are returned to duty." Colonel Boswell began to rise and General Stuart said, sternly, "If you gentlemen would leave us I think I need to have a word with the colonel here."

As we left I was slapped on the back by Jed and Danny, "Lucky Jack again. Sure and someone is looking after you, Jackie boy."

"I want Carlton making up to sergeant again."

"You don't want much do you?"

"Come on Danny, you can do it and you know it. Is it fair that I get off and he gets punished?"

"No." He shook his head. "You had better keep out of the colonel's way for the next day or so."

Dago was waiting for me outside. "Well I guess we aren't in the colonel's good books."

I shrugged, "There was a time when that would have upset me but I am no longer one of Boswell's Wildcats. I am part of the 1st Virginia Scouts. I think Colonel Cartwright would have approved."

"Let's go and celebrate."

"No, I had better change. I have a feeling that I am going to be given some fairly unpleasant duties soon."

"The colonel? Sure he is mad now but he'll get over it. You watch, within a week or so, it will be the same as it always was."

"You said it yourself; Dago, he has changed since he was wounded and went home. He has lost so much already in Charleston. I never had anything before so I am not worried about losing my house but the colonel was brought up a gentleman with a good life. He has lost far more than I ever had. That is bound to change a man; even the colonel."

I was, sadly, proved right. I had just finished changing when Sergeant Major Mulrooney arrived at my tent. He did not look happy. "We have been sent on patrol sir."

I gave a rueful smile, "I take it the colonel chewed you out?"

"He told me to watch my step or I could lose my stripes."

I shook my head, the colonel was becoming vindictive; the Sergeant Major had only shown sympathy and yet he was being punished too.

"Where to?"

"The major will meet us at the horse lines and tell us there."

Sergeant James was there although he had only two stripes. "Sorry about that, Carlton."

"It doesn't matter sir. I'm still the same man with or without the extra stripe."

It was a small patrol. There were just fifteen of us. Trooper Ritchie was also amongst them. Danny strode over, looking unhappy. "You are to check out Warrenton and Upperville. The colonel wants to know what activity there is in that area."

I bit my tongue. We had escaped through that region and he knew that there were at least two regiments of cavalry there. Instead I just smiled, "Right major. Sergeant James, bring a spare horse and some supplies." Danny looked puzzled, "We can't do both in one day sir. We will be out at least one night."

"Of course." He leaned in to me. "You take care, Jack. The colonel will soon be back to his old ways soon enough."

"I hope so Danny because this new one is a little too much like Colonel Beauregard for my liking."

He nodded, "It's the wound I think."

There was no way I would risk the road once we had crossed the Rappahannock. The Union cavalry would be swarming all over it. The colonel had done us a favour by giving me so few men. It was easier to hide and to move swiftly. We headed for Warrenton using tracks and woods whenever possible. When we did have to ride across open fields we kept a watch on the farms to see if we were being observed. We managed to reach our destination just before noon and we hid in the woods which were closest to the town.

There was now a camp just south of the town. From the number of horses it looked to be cavalry. I took out my pencil and paper and drew a map and marked the camp. We moved north of the town and there was a second camp there. "They can't be there just to look for us sir, can they?"

"A flattering thought, Sergeant James," I continued to use his defunct title. I would make sure he got his stripe back. "No, I think they are up to something. Look at the uniforms; they are bright blue. These are new boys. Let's head to Marshall."

Marshall was a one-horse town between Upperville and Warrenton. I did not expect anything to be there; in fact, I was contemplating trying to buy some food. We had learned that civilians appreciated money and could turn a blind eye to the colour of the uniform. We were not proud of it but we all had Yankee dollars relieved from dead soldiers. We halted halfway between the two settlements and ate some of our rations. Thanks to the raid on the train we still ate well.

One of the younger and newer troopers, Brock, plucked up the courage to speak with me as we ate. "Sir, is it true that you met the colonel when you were a sailor?"

"Yes, trooper. He rescued me from a life at sea. I owe my life to the colonel. If he hadn't taken me from the Rose then I would be at the bottom of the sea."

He looked puzzled, "Then why did he have you court-martialled sir?"

"That's enough!" snapped Sergeant James. The boy recoiled at his tone. Carlton rarely shouted.

"No that's alright sergeant. I daresay the rest are all wondering that and he had the courage to ask." I turned to the young man. "The colonel believes in rules. I broke a rule and I accepted the consequences. That is what life is about son. If you do something then see it through and accept the consequences. There is no point moaning about life being unfair. A one armed sailor taught me that. Anyway let's get on now and see what the Yankees have done to Marshall."

Marshall told us the same story; Union camps and many horses. Sergeant James rubbed his chin thoughtfully. "Now why do you think the Yankees have so many cavalry so close to Brandy Station and Culpeper?"

"I think they are planning something. Remember when they attacked at Chancellorsville? We saw them gathering the soldiers for days and weeks before they actually did attack. I reckon the northerners are building up and they will hit us again."

"And we haven't replaced those men we lost in the last battle yet."

"There is no point moping. Let's get up to Upperville and then head on back."

The track to Upperville was difficult. The rains the previous month had made the ground sodden and, in some places, it was still impassable. The road would have been quicker but we needed to remain hidden and so we took many detours. One such detour saved us from an ambush.

We had to trek up a shallow valley and over a small ridge to drop down the other side. As we emerged from the trees we saw a gun emplacement and infantry guarding the road below. Had we not detoured we would have stumbled upon the men. They would not have missed. I led the patrol back into the shelter of the trees.

We rode along the ridge and dropped down a mile or so further on and then headed for Upperville. It was the same story but here there were infantry as well as artillery. I could see that they had learned their lessons and the artillery park was both protected and watched closely. We were not here to raid but to observe. My notes now covered a couple of pages and would provide valuable information.

"I think we can head on back now although I fear we will have a night in the open again." I shielded my eyes to look at the sun. It was the middle of the afternoon and we were far from home.

Perhaps we had tarried in the open too long or maybe our luck had run out. Whatever the reason, we heard the bugle and saw the cavalry galloping from the town. We turned back into the cover of the trees. "Trooper Ritchie, keep an eye on the cavalry." We rode steadily without any pursuit coming close.

When I halted the trooper said, "Sir, they headed down the road."

That was it. They were planning an ambush. We also had the problem that they could alert the men at the gun emplacement and they would be watching for us. It would be difficult to escape this particular trap. We would have to use our superior skills of horsemanship and our knowledge of the terrain.

"Check your weapons."

After I was satisfied that we were prepared we rode on and skirted the artillery position. We rode back along the ridge towards the impassable ground and there we saw the Yankees waiting for us. There were forty men in the patrol and they were halted on the other side of the shallow valley a hundred and eighty yards away. I halted my men and the Yankees watched us.

One of the troopers asked, nervously, "Aren't we going to run sir?"

"Not yet, Morgan. Take out your carbines and wait for my order to fire." I knew that we could not go forward and I also knew that we could not cross that ground. It was like a swamp, we had discovered that earlier. I was waiting to see what the young lieutenant in charge of the smartly dressed troops would do. I smiled when he made his mistake. All that he saw was a shallow valley and a handful of Rebs waiting for him. I watched as he drew his sword and ordered the charge.

"Open fire when I give the orders but don't hit the officer he is worth more to us alive and making dumb decisions. Go for the corporals and sergeants. Fire!"

We had stationary horses and the Yankee cavalry were going nowhere. Their progress halted when their mounts sank up to their saddles in mud. They were like sitting ducks and we picked our targets carefully. My first shot hit a sergeant in the arm, throwing him from his horse. When the trooper next to him dismounted to help the sergeant, Trooper Ritchie hit him too. The young officer gallantly tried to rally his men but it was in vain. Some of them tried to use their carbines to return fire but their struggling horses did not afford them a solid platform. The hillside was filled with our barking carbines. There were so many that we could not fail to hit them. They had had enough and began to fall back out of the range of our handful of carbines. The six horses from the fallen horsemen stood forlornly in the mud as the survivors regrouped.

Our forward progress had been halted which left us but one alternative. "We will have to go back and take on that artillery emplacement and use the road."

I had expected an argument for there were at least fifty men in the emplacement but they merely sheathed their carbines and prepared to return. They were the best of men to lead. We returned to the shelter of the woods as the lieutenant tried to organise his men. They would find the route we had taken and pursue us eventually but I knew that we should be able to lose them in the dark.

Knowing where the emplacement was allowed us to approach quietly using the cover of the trees. I used hand signals to order the men to draw their Colts. The infantry and artillerymen would have heard the gunfire and would be on the alert but I counted on the fact that they would be looking to the sound of the gunfire and the road rather than behind them.

We would hit the Yankees in a column of twos. It meant we should be able to carve a path through them. I halted just within the eaves of the trees. The sun was setting in the west and we were almost invisible in the gloom of the east. The Parrot gun had a crew of twelve around it. The thirty or so infantrymen were behind earthworks. They were all looking down at the road. The engineers had left a path, wide enough for three horses, to go down to the road which lay a hundred yards beyond the gun. It was a well-placed site for nothing could approach Upperville without having to run the gauntlet of their guns.

It was now or never. I pumped my right arm three times and we erupted from the trees. We were less than fifty yards from them as we gave our rebel yell and they looked around in terror as we appeared from nowhere. I aimed at the gun crew. They were unarmed but they could fire at us with their cannon if I didn't. Three of them fell to our guns as Copper thundered at them. I heard the fire from my men behind me. I switched my gun to aim at my left where I saw that some of the infantry had lifted their guns and were preparing to fire. My gun barked three times and I holstered and drew a second.

I was almost through their lines when I fired two shots at point-blank range. I glanced behind me and saw a pall of smoke surrounding my grey troopers as they carved a path of death down the slope. To my horror, Trooper Morgan was struck by a bayonet and fell screaming from his horses and then there was a huge flash as a spark ignited the powder which was behind the gun. The smoke wreathed the emplacement and then the roar of the explosion and the concussion of the air hit us. I could hear little but I saw the blue-coated infantry thrown to the ground. I dug my heels into Copper and suddenly struck the road. I wheeled left as I turned to watch the survivors of my patrol follow me. We could not stop until we were clear of the gun but I desperately needed to see how we had fared.

A quarter of a mile down the road I halted. I did not want winded horses. It looked like Trooper Morgan was our only loss but many of the men sported wounds and injuries. Sergeant James had been at the back. "What happened, Carlton?"

He shook his head to clear his ears. "I think they hit their powder themselves. I was at the back and I saw them aiming at me; I put my head low and kicked on. They fired and must have all hit the powder and not me."

"Well, it saved our bacon. We will ride steadily for a while and then try to hide for the night. They will be combing this neck of the woods for us soon. Well done boys. Those Yankees will be talking of your charge for some time to come."

As we road back towards Brandy Station I began to evaluate our options. I had no doubt that they would have alerted both Marshal and Warrenton. Those cavalry regiments based there would be out the next day and looking for us. How would we evade them? When we camped I would have to look at the map closely and see if I could plot a way back which avoided detection.

I spied a track leading up into the Blue Ridge and I led us up it. It twisted and turned. I knew that we were not far from one of our earlier camps and an idea struck me. Once we had reached the top of the ridge I headed south until we came to a clearing.

"Take off your saddles and let the horses graze. The grass isn't the best but it will have to do. Eat while I work out how to get back home."

"Sir, I brought some grain for the horses. You guys come and get it. Ritchie, bring Copper while the captain reads the map."

I nodded to Ritchie as he led Copper away. The light was going fast but I could still see. If we headed due south we would only have to cross the turnpike to Front Royal and then we could use the small country road to avoid both Marshall and Warrenton. We would not reach Brandy Station but we would reach General Lee's headquarters at Culpeper. It was a circuitous route but it would be a safe route.

I waved the sergeant over and explained what I intended. "Good plan sir."

"Now what about the horses? Will they get us there?"

"MacKay's took a thrust from a bayonet. We need to mount him on the spare. The supplies we brought will be gone by the time we leave. Yes, they should do it but we will have to look after them."

I stabbed a finger at the pike. "That is our only worry. I want to hit that before morning. I reckon it will be busy during the day. If Hooker is building up his army then that will be his key road."

In answer, he handed me some jerky. "Then make sure you eat, sir. These boys would like to get home and you are their only chance."

"You could do just as well Carlton."

He shook his head. "I know horses and I reckon I know men but when it comes to making decisions like you do then I am useless."

We rested for two hours. I knew we ran a risk of allowing the Union cavalry to tighten their noose but I relied on the fact that it was a large area to cover and they had no idea where we actually were. This time Trooper Ritchie took the rear. He had proved to me that he had the ability to think and react quickly under pressure and he had sharp ears.

We wound our way down the slope towards the road. We knew this part of the Blue Ridge well. It had been one of our escape routes in the past. As the sergeant and I led the way I reflected that the sergeant and I were the only ones on this patrol who had been here back then. We halted just above the road and listened. Sound travels a long way at night time. We heard nothing. I looked at Sergeant James and nodded. We rode slowly towards the road. We were looking for the small road which wound its way through the hills towards the Warrenton pike. We would have to cross that road too but I hoped that we would have out run our pursuers by then. We had to risk the road for a short way. The moon came out from behind a cloud, briefly, and showed us the turning. We gratefully took it and entered the shelter of the hills which ran southeastwards.

We had achieved our first goal and crossed the road in the dark. Would our luck hold on the second road? We could see small homes and farms dotted along our route but they were mercifully dark. There were no early risers. When we reached the small crossroads we halted. There was a cluster of buildings. The road east led to Marshall. If we disturbed whoever lived here then they could send a rider to Marshall and we would be trapped. We had almost made it when a door opened and, from the glow of the light from within I saw a man with a shotgun.

"Who are you boys?"

The man was on my left and as I spoke with him I began to ease my pistol from its holster. It was unlikely that I survive an exchange of fire for the shotgun was aimed at my middle. I had learned never to give up, even when things looked to be impossible.

"The 1st Virginia Scouts sir."

There was a heart-stopping pause and then he lowered the hammers on the gun. He smiled, "You must be the boys them Yankees are looking for." He turned into the house, "Betsy, bring that pot of coffee here." He pointed down the road. "A troop of cavalry came down the road just before midnight looking for you. Seems you stirred up a hornet's nest up north eh boys?"

His wife was pouring coffee into our mugs and smiling at us. They looked to be a middle-aged couple which explained why he was not in the army. "Yes sir. We come down from Upperville."

"You boys ain't with Mosby are you?"

"No sir. We're regulars but we were with the Wildcats."

He nodded, "Seems I heard of you boys."

"Thank you for the coffee. We had better be off."

"You boys take care now."

As the door was closed and the crossroads plunged into darkness once more I breathed a sigh of relief. Our luck was holding. If that had been a Yankee sympathiser then I would now be dead. There were many people who supported the Confederacy in the Blue Ridge. It was one of the reasons Mosby and his men survived. It was dawn when we reached the Warrenton Road. East lay Union cavalry and we rode west until we reached the road to Rixeyville. I consulted my map again. We could fork left down this road and ride directly to Brandy Station. We would not need to detour to Culpepper. Things had worked out well.

We had just crossed the Hazel River when the Yankees found us. I have no idea how they picked up our trail but the troop of blue coated horsemen were spotted by Trooper Ritchie as he let his horse drink from the river.

"Yankees! A quarter of a mile away!"

We whipped our horses to race down the road. We could neither slow down nor fight the cavalry who were pursuing us. They could see us and therefore avoid anything we could do. The handful of people in Rixeyville looked in amazement as we thundered through their tiny town, hotly pursued by the cavalry eager to finally capture us.

"Sergeant James!" The sergeant brought Apples next to Copper.

"Sir?" He glanced over his shoulder.

"Keep going to Culpeper. I'll drop back with Ritchie."

He nodded a reluctant, "Sir." He might not like me putting myself in harm's way again but he knew that I might see a solution to our dilemma. I just hoped that their horses were as tired as ours were.

I let the others overtake me and settled next to Trooper Ritchie. They were closing but not rapidly. They were now three hundred yards from us. Although Culpeper was nine miles away we would be safe if we could cover the next five miles before capture. I figured that Lee and Stuart would have scouts on this road too.

I heard the pop of pistols, as the Union pursuers chanced shots. We were not in much danger but I was acutely aware that they just needed one lucky ball to strike man or beast and we would be in trouble. Trooper Ritchie grinned at me. He was young enough to still enjoy this. "They must want us real bad, sir."

"I think we have upset them and their pride." I glanced over my shoulder again and they were inexorably closing with us. Dare I risk us going faster? The horses were tired. Copper could run all day but even my mount was labouring a little. We were half a mile closer and I could feel their shots coming alarmingly near to us.

I raised my voice to shout to the men in the front. "Sergeant James, let's try to go a little faster."

"Sir!" I had placed the sergeant at the front for he could judge the pace better than anyone.

I saw the men in front of me go faster and I turned to Trooper Ritchie. "We will keep the same pace for a while. I want the boys ahead to get a lead."

"Yes sir."

When the gap was fifty yards I turned and saw that the Union cavalry were just two hundred paces away. I drew my Colt and, holding it as steadily as I could, I fired six shots at the blue-coated horsemen. "Now Ritchie, ride like the wind." As soon as I kicked Copper the game horse leapt forwards. The shots had caused the Yankees to slow and the gap rose to three hundred yards by the time we reached the rest of my men. We had bought a little time and that was all.

The gap stayed the same and I began to believe that we would escape when Trooper Ritchie's horse suddenly began to slow. "Sir! My horse, she's been hit." I glanced at the flanks and saw that the chestnut had been struck sometime during our pursuit. "Leave me, sir. You get to the general with the information."

"No, we'll get you out of this." I could see that the Union cavalry were now more strung out than they had been. We had a spare horse and all we needed was a few minutes. "Troop halt!" They obeyed instantly. "Turn and fire. Ritchie get on the spare horse."

I had my two loaded Colts out in an instant and blazed away. The leading riders must have emptied their guns firing at us and had not had the opportunity to reload. They looked in horror as we poured lead into them.

"Done sir!"

"Then let's go!"

We turned and galloped away. We had hurt them but they were now less than a hundred and fifty yards away. The riders at the front had loaded guns and it was a matter of time before they managed to hit one of us. I had ridden my luck one time too many. As I glanced over my shoulder expecting to see them close with us I heard the joyful sound of a bugle, a Confederate bugle. As the troop of Carolina Cavalry thundered past me firing and whooping I saluted with a beaming smile on my face. I was still Lucky Jack.

Chapter 9

While the cavalry from South Carolina chased the Yankees back to the Blue Ridge we rode directly to General Lee's Headquarters. General Stuart was just leaving as we rode in.

"Captain Hogan. Good to see you, sir." He frowned. "I take it this is not a social visit sir?"

"No sir. We have just patrolled as far as Upperville. There are Union camps at Warrenton, Marshall and Upperville. We counted at least seven regiments, four of them cavalry." I handed him my notes.

"Well done captain. I shall take these to General Lee. You may rejoin your regiment."

Riding back to Brandy Station I reflected that was all we would ever get; a pat on the back and well done. It had cost a trooper his life to get that information and he would not even be remembered, save by his comrades.

I did not have to face Colonel Boswell when I arrived back at the camp. He and the major had been invited to a meeting with the other commanders to plan a war game General Lee had ordered. I was relieved. Harry, Dago and Jed were all glad to see me and we were able to talk freely in the mess.

"Major Murphy was like a bear with a sore head these past couple of days."

"Yeah, Harry is right. He worried that this might be a patrol too far for you. He knew you and the others were tired. I heard him and the colonel having words about it. I sure hope things get back to normal soon. I don't like what it is doing to the regiment."

I shook my head, "You know, Dago, I yearn for the days of Boswell's Wildcats when there were neither politics nor rules. It made far more sense than now."

Harry poured me a large whiskey. "It will all make sense once we invade Pennsylvania and we can get back to whipping the Yankees."

"I am not so sure about an invasion Harry. We found a lot of new regiments just north of us. I think we may be fighting them sooner rather than later but it will be on their terms."

All thoughts of an invasion were dismissed when we were briefed by Colonel Boswell the next day. "The general has decided that we will need to have some war games to allow us to learn how to fight together as one Cavalry Corps. The day after tomorrow we will be setting up a battle between the different regiments."

I saw Harry scratch his head, "I am sorry sir but how does fighting each other help us to learn how to fight together? That doesn't make sense."

For once the colonel looked as confused as we were. "I know but General Lee himself wants to watch us fight so we do it as ordered." He looked at me; his eyes still cold and unforgiving. "Captain Hogan and his men will have to patrol north of the Rappahannock to make sure that we are not surprised by the Union cavalry."

I saw Danny begin to rise. I think he was going to defend me but I didn't need any further rifts between my friends. I gave him a slight shake of the head and he sat down.

"If that is all then I suggest that you prepare your men for the coming games."

If Colonel Boswell thought he was punishing me by sending me on patrol he was wrong. I was more than happy to be on patrol with my men. The task he had given me was an easy one anyway. We would not have far to ride. By crossing Beverley Ford we could ensure that no one could approach the camp without us seeing them. It would be a pleasant day; unless the Yankees came. They didn't and it was a good day. Trooper Ashcroft managed to bag a couple of rabbits which would make a welcome change from the rations. There were shortages of food which meant that we augmented our diet whenever we could.

General Lee had, apparently, missed the review, which meant it would have to be repeated when he could see it. General Stuart had been pleased with the way everyone had performed. Of course, the men and horses were exhausted from the constant charging and countercharging.

When we sat outside the mess tent that night Dago was very pessimistic about the prospects. "Everyone knows that you can't keep charging horses. You have to rest them. If this had been a real battle today then we would have all been killed. You had the best duty, Jack."

I nodded, "It was very peaceful.

We drew the same duty when the review was repeated. This time it was not so peaceful. We had discovered a pleasant stand of trees by the ford and we had a couple of fishing lines out. Trooper Ritchie and I took our carbines to see if we, too, could bag some food for the pot. It was our stalking of animals which hid us from the Northern patrol which approached from the north. We were hiding in the undergrowth when we saw them. "Trooper Ritchie, go and bring the men up with their carbines."

As he slipped silently away I stared at the approaching riders. There were just two scouts but I knew that there would be more following. These cavalrymen had seen action. Their uniforms were faded and they rode with their pistols drawn. It would not do to underestimate them.

By the time my men arrived, I could see that there were twenty men in the patrol. They were scouting the ford. Sergeant James spread the men out and he took the right end of the line. We let them ride towards us. The road was slightly below us and dropped down to the ford; we would have the advantage of height when we opened fire.

I waited until they were within pistol range and then swung my arm down. Our carbines bucked as we opened fire. They were briefly confused, but they showed their quality when they dismounted and drew their own weapons. The advantage was with us for, although they outnumbered us, we had height and surprise on our side. Their officer and sergeant had been knocked from their saddles in the first volley and they were taking more casualties. They were firing blindly at our smoke and they were not harming us in the least.

There was so much smoke it was hard to see where they were. When their fire slackened I held up my hand and we waited for the smoke to clear. The survivors were heading back along the road towards their own lines. They had loaded their dead and wounded on to their horses and were heading north.

"Give them another volley."

We fired again and managed to hit one of the troopers who fell from his horse. We ran to him as his comrades fled. He was a Maryland cavalryman. We found no papers on him but he had a fine pair of boots, which we took as well as an Army Colt and a full ammunition pouch. Disappointingly he only had five dollars on him. We returned to camp with the news that the enemy soldiers were scouting the ford.

The colonel looked tired when we reported to him. I don't think he enjoyed the review. He even forgot to scowl at me as he rode off to give the news directly to General Stuart. When the colonel returned he told us that our task the next day, as a regiment, was to scout out the land to the north of Beverley Ford. We would be up before dawn.

We had just paraded before the colonel when we heard the sound of gunfire coming from the ford. There was no time for a parade and Colonel Boswell became his old self as he led the regiment towards the firing at the river. As we passed the artillery camp close to St. James' Church the colonel ordered the bugler to sound the alarm. The artillerymen erupted from their tents as we charged by.

Ahead we could see, highlighted by the dawn, the Pennsylvania cavalry streaming across the ford. The pickets were fleeing in our direction. This was not the time to pause and reflect; if the cavalry got amongst the camp then our men, already exhausted from war games, would be slaughtered in their beds. The charge was sounded. We were too disorganised to hit them as a solid line but the colonel's intention was obvious, to put us between them and the artillery. This would give the troops at the camp time to organise. We were like the boys in the Alamo; we were buying the army time to prepare. I spurned my sword and drew my Colt. I could be more effective with that at this close range.

We hit their line at a bend on the Beverly Ford Road. I suspect that they thought they had done the hard part in chasing away our vedettes. We had the advantage of slightly higher ground and had momentum. They were a blue sea washing up from the river. I saw a colonel appear before me, his sabre in his hand and I fired. He was thrown from his saddle. I shot his bugler too. The lieutenant who was on the other side of the bugler swung his sword at my head. I ducked and fired blindly at the same time. I saw him clutch his stomach as he wheeled from the battle. They had been briefly halted and the horses milled around in confusion. The front ranks were being pressed forward by more men who were streaming across the ford. It was a furious battle.

As I emptied my gun I was forced to draw my sword. I managed to parry the blow aimed at my head from the enormous grinning trooper. He was no swordsman and, as he raised his sabre for a second attempt I stabbed him in the chest. I saw three troopers galloping at me and I drew my saddle Colt and emptied it in their direction. The one trooper who reached me had his arm thrust forward to spear me. I leaned to one side to evade it and slashed at his middle with my own.

It was with some relief that I heard the bugle sound the order to withdraw. We headed up the road. I saw that the artillery had managed to position a gun on either side of the road. I heard Danny roar, "Dismount and form a skirmish line between the guns."

I slipped from my horse and drew my carbine as the trooper designated as horse holder led Copper away. "Good to be back with you sir!"

I grinned as I saw Sergeant Major Mulrooney behind me. He turned to shout at the troopers. "Find as much cover as you can and wait for the order to fire."

I looked down the line of my troopers. I could not see any familiar face that was missing. We had been lucky. We now had to wait to see what the enemy would do. If their commander had any sense he would form a skirmish line and his superior numbers would soon whittle us down. I saw at least one brigade do that.

"Ready boys. Choose your target- there are enough of them!"

The men laughed at my weak joke. They were not intimidated by numbers. It was the quality of the mettle which would determine this battle. Danny roared, "Fire!" We began to pick off the visible targets.

"Watch your ammunition. Don't waste any!" This was going to be a long day and I was grateful that all of my men had full ammunition pouches as well as a spare. There were advantages to being given the dirty jobs.

Suddenly we heard the charge sound. A line of Union cavalry galloped at us. I later heard it was the 6th Pennsylvania. They were brave boys, but they were doomed from the start. The two cannons blasted out a wall of death and we fired into the smoke. Once the cannons had fired we could see nothing but we knew that there was a brigade of cavalry coming at us. The artillery men were firing as rapidly as they could. Each time they fired they had to realign the gun. The 1st Virginia Scouts stopped the Yankees from closing with them as they reloaded and fired. Had they dismounted and made it a fire fight then they might have succeeded but horse and man were scythed down by the murderous hail of lead, ball and grapeshot. None even came close and I was glad when the bugle sounded retreat. Those brave boys had suffered enough.

I stood and went around my troopers. One or two had slight wounds, which David had tended to but there was nothing serious. I had time to look at the scene. This was the major attack I had feared. I looked behind me to Fleetwood Hill. General Stuart had had his camp there the previous night. Of him, there was no sign. Oddly there was just one howitzer and its crew occupying the top. The thought flitted across my mind that they would have a good view.

A courier rode up. He saluted the major in charge of the guns. "General Stuart's compliments, major. Would you pull your guns back and have them face south."

The major and Colonel Boswell, who had wandered over, both looked perplexed. "The south?"

"Yes sir. Another division has crossed Kelly's Ford. We are about to be flanked. "

As the artillery limbered up the colonel said, "Sergeant Major, get the horses." He turned to us, "We need to see what is going on here."

I pointed up the hill. "Sir, what about going up the hill? We can see the whole field from there and the slope will help us to attack quicker."

He smiled at me, "Good idea. To your troops, gentlemen."

"Sergeant James, take ten men and get to the hill as quickly as you can."

As I mounted Copper and turned to look at my men I heard the pop of pistols from the hill. I looked up and saw that Sergeant James and my men were under fire. "Follow me!"

There was no time to wait for support and we galloped up the slope. I saw that the howitzer crew were firing at the approaching cavalry and my men had dismounted to form a skirmish line. We hurtled over the crest of the ridge and saw horsemen streaming up the other side. This was no time for caution. I drew my sabre and yelled, "Charge!"

We thundered down and struck the leading troopers of the enemy brigade. Our horses were still relatively fresh and we had the hill on our side. The enemy soldiers were bowled over and they crashed into the ranks behind. I slashed left and right with my sabre. There was no finesse and no subtlety; I could have been using an axe to chop down trees but it was an effective technique in such a pell-mell battle. The blade seemed to whirl in my hand. It was when I found that there was no one before me that I halted. I had outrun my men. Copper was lathered and the blue-coated cavalrymen suddenly saw that I was alone. I drew my Colt and fired at the nearest men before turning Copper to gallop up the slope to the security of the howitzer.

The gun was still firing and its vertical trajectory meant that I was safe from its balls but not so the cavalry pursuing me. Major McClellan, General Stuart's adjutant shook my hand as I reined in. "Well done captain. I have sent word to the general but you gave us time to organise. Dismount your men please and form a skirmish line."

As my horse was led away I saw Cecil shaking his head. Trooper Ritchie joined me. "We tried to get to you sir but you flew down that hill."

"I think Copper was keen to get into this war."

"Sergeant James has been wounded, sir."

"Badly?"

"Hard to say. The lieutenant is with him."

He was in good hands then, David Dinsdale was a good doctor. I drew my carbine and crouched behind the wall. We had a good view of the battle from our lofty elevation. We were like a rock surrounded by the sea; the sea in this case was the Union Cavalry Corps and I had never seen so many cavalry in one place before. The respite was brief as they charged up the hill to get at us. Some were on horses and some were afoot. The one advantage we had was that we all had similar weapons with a similar range and our howitzer was slaughtering the men in the rear of their lines.

"Aim for the leaders if you can. Fire!"

I carefully aimed at an officer, sabre held aloft, who was rallying his men. He fell clutching his shoulder. I saw Cecil hit the trooper with the guidon and the regimental flag fell. It was only one man but the effect on the others was dramatic. They slowed as the dismay spread through their ranks. "Keep firing! Push them back!"

We fired even faster at the stationary men who began to stream down the hill. We had beaten off another attack. "Corporal Jones, go and check the dead Yankees for ammunition." There were dead soldiers less than twenty yards away and they had full pouches. He had just returned with the black gold when they charged for a third time. This time they had dismounted and used the dead horses and men on the slope for cover. The howitzer crew reacted by cutting their fuses shorter so that they exploded in the air over their heads. The effect was devastating; it indiscriminately cut a swathe through the whole brigade and they fell back once more.

There was a short lull. "Make sure you all drink something."

Danny appeared at my shoulder. "You have done well Jack. That was a mad charge before. Even 'himself' was impressed."

Just then we saw a battery of guns appear at the foot of the hill. They were going to neutralise the effect of our howitzer. "Well Danny, it looks like we are going to have to take some of this medicine."

"You take charge of this side. I'll go and see the colonel."

The howitzer tried to fire at the artillery but it was hard to hit such spread-out targets. Trooper Ritchie appeared at my shoulder. "Sir, if I take a couple of lads closer then we can pick off the gunners."

"Not a bad idea. Pick the best ten." As he ran off I shouted, "Lieutenant Spinelli!"

Dago appeared next to me. "Sir?"

I grinned, "Well this is fun eh Dago?"

"I am just thinking about all the pockets we can pick after this is over."

I laughed, he was incorrigible. "I am going to take ten men to pick off the gunners. You take charge here."

"Yes sir, but Jack... be careful!"

"I always am. Come on Ritchie."

We ran in pairs down the hill. The Yankee cavalry tried to hit us but we were moving down and towards them. We were hard to hit. When we were a hundred and fifty yards away I shouted, "Down!" I looked and saw that we had lost two troopers.

"Aim for the gunners." My first shot pinged off a wheel and the ricochet spun off to strike a sergeant on the arm. I saw a gunner with a linstock fall and the man with the swab drop. One of the guns began to slow its rate of fire. We now had the range and soon we had hit enough of the gunners to make the rest take cover.

The cavalry commander had had enough and he ordered his own men up the slope to dislodge us. I was about to order a retreat when I saw them begin to fall from shots emanating from our rear. I glanced over my shoulder and saw Dago leading the rest of my troop.

I shook my head, "I thought I ordered you to stay there on the ridge."

"Jed came over so Irish and me thought we would give you a hand sir."

I saw the Union cavalry mounting. "Well we had better get back up the hill or we will be staying here permanently. Withdraw in pairs!"

We turned and ran. One man fired while the other raced up the hill a few yards and then covered the other. In this way, we made the safety of our own lines but I could see that we had left comrades behind.

Major McClellan came over. "Well done boys. We have steadied the line." He pointed at the gunners and the cavalry at the bottom of the hill. "Those boys down there are Irish. They aren't the Irish Brigade but they are tough fighters. You boys did well."

The Union cavalry charged up the hill again. They were tired but there were plenty of them. We barely had time to aim our carbines before they were upon us. I soon eschewed my carbine in favour of my Colts. Suddenly a trooper threw himself from his horse and he landed upon me, knocking the wind from me. He raised his hand to punch me and I put my empty Colt up to catch the blow. He shouted as his hand hit the metal. I brought my knee up between his legs and he rolled off screaming. I whipped my knife from my boot and stabbed him in the throat.

The Sergeant Major looked at me with concern written all over his face. "You all right sir?"

I grinned. "I am now. Aim for the horses!" It went against the grain to shoot horses but it would stop them closing and provide an obstacle to any more charges. I took in the scene as, with shaking hands, I reloaded my gun. The tide inexorably slowed as they took more and more casualties.

Colonel Boswell came over. "How are we for ammunition?"

I looked at the Sergeant Major who said, "The boys have about ten more volleys, sir."

"It's as I thought. Right, get your horses. We'll clear the hill the old-fashioned way."

We mounted and formed up behind the howitzer. Its short fuses were still causing havoc on the lower slopes. I could see little beyond the hill as the musket and cannon fire had created a pungent cloud of smoke. I had no idea if we were winning or losing. When we were formed up, the colonel ordered the charge sounded. Our horses were rested and we hurtled down the slope with sabres held before us. I knew that we had to save our supply of ammunition in case the charge failed. It didn't. The gunners had had enough and they jumped on their horses to flee the field. The cavalry horses were blown but they gallantly turned to face us. The only way to counter a charge is by charging yourself and they lacked the horses to do that. We hit a static line and horses and men were knocked aside as the wall of horseflesh and steel hit them.

I was not aware of even raising or lowering my arm. The blue coats just seemed to disappear as we swept down. Colonel Boswell had learned discretion and, as the cavalry fled he sounded the recall. One or two of the younger troopers failed to heed the call but the rest halted. I sheathed my sword and drew my Colt.

"Corporal Jones, check for casualties."

I saw that Harry, Dago, Jed and Irish had survived. I looked at the sun and saw that it was beginning to set. We had fought for almost ten hours. Danny's voice boomed out, "Check for prisoners and ammunition. Lieutenant Spinelli, form a skirmish line."

I dismounted and handed the reins of Copper to the horse holder. I holstered my gun. I could hear the Yankee bugles sounding retreat. They were leaving. We had won. It had been a near-run thing. My troopers were taking the boots and guns from the dead while the prisoners were being lined up.

I heard my name being called from further up the slope and saw Danny and the colonel waving to me. I ran over to them. They were standing over the bodies of four of our troopers who had fallen in my attack. They had had their throats cut and a crude M burned into their chests. Around the neck of Trooper Lowe was a crudely written message. 'This is what we will do to Boswell, Murphy, Hogan and any other of the murdering bastards from Boswell's Horse who killed our brothers. Mick O'Callaghan.'

I looked at Danny whose face was white with anger, "Who the hell is Mick O'Callaghan and what is this about?"

He looked blankly at the colonel who looked dumbly at the bodies of his men. Then Danny slapped his head, "I know what this is. This is revenge and a feud. Remember those Irish spies who infiltrated us and we hung one of them? I think one was called Callaghan."

"But that was war, sir."

"It makes no difference to an Irishman Jack, you should know that. Out there," he pointed to the north, "are Irishmen who won't rest until either we or they are dead."

My war had just changed. I now had a hidden enemy who knew my name. I knew that there were many Irish who fought for the Union; any one of them could hunt for me. Part of me was grateful that they did not know the names of the other troopers. Although, as I looked at the mutilated bodies of my troopers I reflected that it had not done those men much good. We were a marked regiment. General Stuart was saddened by the whole thing. I think he had an old-fashioned view of the cavalryman. To him, we were like the knights of old. We weren't; this was a hard cruel war with brother fighting brother. Our Irish brothers would discover that. We would fight fire with fire.

We had little time to reflect on the battle itself. General Lee had decided that, having routed the Union cavalry it was time to take advantage and strike at the heart of the Union. We were heading for Pennsylvania.

Part 2

The Road to Gettysburg

Chapter 10

The whole of the regiment shared our anger. The fact that we had been named was bad enough but to do what they had done to dead and dying men went beyond the pale. The feud was on and no Irishman was going to be safe from our vengeance.

We found that our role had now changed. We did not serve with General Stuart. The bulk of the cavalrymen were sent with him while the five depleted regiments were to accompany General Lee. We headed back to the Shenandoah Valley and there would be no more death or glory charges for us. The General's nephew, General Fitzhugh-Lee came to brief us on our role. We knew the general from the Fredericksburg campaign and we all liked him; he was a good leader.

"Gentleman we are going to cross the Potomac at Harper's Ferry. You have two tasks; firstly you have to make sure we aren't surprised but your second task is even more important. We want you to tell us where the Yankees have their supplies. We need to hit them and hit them hard. This will be more like the job you did as Boswell's Rangers. The General does not want the northern civilians to suffer. You will buy food when you can."

Jed put his hand up, "Sir, does the general have any objection to us taking from the blue coats?"

The general laughed, "I think that would be just perfect lieutenant." He pointed to the map. "The Army will have to eliminate the garrisons at Winchester and Martinsburg. That will take a few days. It means you can slip over the Potomac and be there well ahead of us. I need to be kept informed about what you find. I will regard no news as good news, so don't let me down." He leaned back in his chair. "Any questions?

Colonel Boswell looked at us. We all shook our heads. He smiled, "I think my boys will do just fine sir."

After he had gone the colonel handed out some cigars and opened a bottle of French brandy. "I have been saving this for a special occasion. I think this is one such." As we lit up and held our mugs he said,

"Here's to Boswell's Wildcats. I think our orders and the Irishmen's message have just caused it to be reformed!"

"Boswell's Wildcats!" We were like children again and we all cheered wildly.

He stood and went to the map. "I want four columns. I will lead one, Danny, Harry and Jack the others. We will spread out like a fan and we will screen the army. I am not worried about the garrisons in the towns so we will get straight across the Potomac. Our first task is to disrupt the railroad. We are good at that. Then we resupply ourselves. I want that done early and not late. Find yourself a base. I will be in the hills north of the Potomac close to Brunswick." He smiled, "We did well there last time. The rest of you will be to the west of me. You heard the general; keep sending reports back when you find something. We are the eyes and ears of the army. There may be less than two hundred of us but we are going to make the Yankees remember Boswell's Wildcats and the 1st Virginia Scouts."

We left the next morning. I was sad not to have Irish riding alongside me but he was Sergeant Major and his place was next to the colonel. Sergeant James had to remain with the wounded. I was just as unhappy to be without him; he was always reliable. Corporal Jones was promoted to First Sergeant and Trooper Ritchie to sergeant. I liked to reward my men when I could. I only had forty men but I knew them all well. I left Brandy Station tinged with sadness that I had left so many of my comrades there; it almost felt like desertion.

We left the army as General Lee prepared to assault Winchester. We headed up the valley and the Potomac. I intended to cross the river west of the ferry. If this had been spring then the river would have been impassable but in summer, by using the islands, it was possible to get across without too much difficulty. We crossed under the noses of the Union troops at Harper's Ferry. They might have seen us but there as little they could do about it. Once we reached the northern shore I made the men strip and clean their guns. We were now in enemy territory and I wanted us to be able to fight as soon as we saw a blue uniform.

The troop mounted and looked expectantly at me. I had been making my plan as we had ridden north." We are going to ride around the bluffs over the river and see if we can destroy a railroad track." Their grins told me what they thought of that plan. As we rode through the hills I explained to my two sergeants what my thinking was. They needed to understand what we would be doing.

"Colonel Boswell will be destroying the railroad closer to Brunswick. By destroying it here as well we make it much harder for them to repair the damage we will inflict upon them. Then we will swing up past Boonsboro and then to Hagerstown. The hills to the west of South Mountain are perfect for a base. Even if the Yankees know we are there it will be the devil's own job to winkle us out."

We kept a close eye on the sentries at the ferry. It was unlikely that they would risk crossing the river to chase down a bunch of Rebs but it paid to be careful. The railroad was a single track running close to the river. It has been the scene of our first successful raid in the north. I felt someone walking over my grave as we passed the place we had hanged the spy. It was strange the way things came back to haunt you. I had forgotten those two infiltrators. I didn't regret what we did to them; they had been responsible for good men dying and they had nearly cost the colonel and the major their lives. I just wished that the colonel had handled it more discreetly but he had been angry and keen for vengeance. It was not a good combination.

Having done this more than once, we knew what to look for. We found the tool box next to the track and took out the spanner and crowbar. Sergeant Jones assigned a new boy with one of the older troopers so that they too could learn how to wreck a train. Sergeant Ritchie kept watch for the train. We removed four lengths of rail and threw them in the river. Had we had time we would have lit a fire and bent them to make them unusable but we just needed to disrupt the line until Lee had crossed the border. We had finished and there was still no train. It was disappointing to derail a train and not be able to watch it but we had more work to do.

We headed north through the Maryland hills. The forests were thick here and we felt comfortable and safe. We rode towards the battlefield of Antietam and Boonsboro. We found a deserted farmhouse a couple of miles from town. There were many such farms. Men went off to war and got killed; their wives struggled to make a living and they either died or left. It was sad and was something else that the south and the north had in common. We could see no traces of recent habitation. We wondered about the owners until sad faced Sergeant Ritchie came into the farmhouse where we had just got a fire going.

"I found the last owner sir."

I left the warm room and followed him. When we reached the barn there were two skeletons, a cow and, from the remains of the dress, an old woman. She must have come to milk the cow and died. The cow had died later. The rats and foxes had left little for us to bury but we did so anyway. She had been someone's wife and mother. We laid her in the ground and bowed our heads. This war didn't just kill soldiers.

The burial was sobering for all of us. I mounted guards at the edge of the wood but I could see why no one had visited; it was on the slopes of South Mountain and the entrance was little wider than that needed to get a small cart up. As a base it would serve.

The next day I went with Ritchie and three troopers to scout out Boonsboro. It was a small town and I could see nothing military there. Although disappointing it was also reassuring as it meant that we were unlikely to bump into any Yankee patrols. The pike led to Hagerstown and we followed that road. We left a mile before the outskirts of the busy town. We saw the railroad line which ran north of the city and made our way there. The shiny rails showed that it was in constant use and, even as we watched, a train came from the north. We dismounted and left our horses in a stand of trees. We made our way to the station.

The station was a small version of Manassas Junction. My eyes soon lit upon the warehouses. There were not as many as Manassas but I was certain that they would yield a healthy harvest for us. I had seen enough and we crept back to our horses. When we reached our horses, to my horror, there was a young woman feeding carrots to Copper. One of the younger troopers went for his pistol but I restrained him.

She turned around at the movement. "Good morning ma'am. A fine horse eh?"

She nodded, "I can see the spirit in the animal. What beautiful eyes and a gorgeous colour."

I put my hand on Copper's mane as I gestured for the others to mount, "Copper this is…?"

"Mary Malone, Miss Mary Malone."

"Miss Mary Malone. Copper appreciates carrots. They are much better than some of the poor grass we have around these parts."

She suddenly looked me in the eye. "Except you aren't from these parts are you? You are Rebs from south of the river."

My heart sank. I had taken her for a simpleton. "Yes ma'am." I swung myself in the saddle. I could see the nervous expressions on my men's faces.

She gave a smile. "Don't worry. I am a Stephen's City girl. I was brought here as a servant when the war started I work in a large house over yonder. But be careful. There is a company of Maryland Infantry stationed in the town." She stepped back, "Nice to have met you Captain…?"

"Hogan, John Hogan. And I am pleased to have met you." We turned and headed back towards the turnpike.

Ritchie said, nervously, "She might go to the authorities you know sir."

"If she was going to do that she wouldn't have warned us about the infantry. I have a gut feeling that she will not betray us but, just to be sure, we'll double the guards tonight. Tomorrow we raid the railroad."

For some reason I was not worried about the woman. She had seemed genuine but Sergeant Ritchie looked relieved to be woken by the sentry and not a blue coated northerner.

I gathered the men around me in the barn. "I know that we could attack at night but I want to make sure that we get a train this time. We were told to get supplies and we will. Half of us will be dealing with the train." I pointed to Sergeant Jones and his company, "That will be you men with the sergeant. The rest will be with me and Sergeant Ritchie. We will make sure that we are not surprised by any Yankees. We know there is a company of infantry in the town. Our job will be to slow them down. When we have whatever is on the first train then we high tail it back here." I paused, "If anything happens to me then Sergeant Jones is in charge and he continues to follow the colonel's orders."

I could see the looks of surprise on the men but Dago's incarceration had been a warning that things could go wrong.

"Let's go."

I led the column towards the railroad. We had chosen a cutting two miles from the town. There was a bend which would cause the train to slow anyway. While Sergeant Jones and his men located a trackside tool box I ordered Sergeant Ritchie to head a mile down the track towards the town. "I'll join you once we have begun the demolition."

When we had first done this we had had the luxury of watching for trains for a whole day before derailing one. General Lee's accelerated timetable meant that we had to take more chances.

When Jones and his men appeared with the tools I watched to make sure that they would be able to take up the rails. Even though many of the troopers were new to this they soon picked up the hang of it. "Carry on sergeant, and good luck! I hope it is something that we can use eh?"

"Yes sir and you take care now."

"I will."

I found Sergeant Ritchie. We were close to the spot where we had seen the girl the previous day. We dismounted and tied our horses to a tree. Hopefully it would be an easy duty and we would not be needed but we improvised a barrier from some of the undergrowth. If it was infantry who came to investigate then we merely had to slow them down, our horses would give us a quick escape route.

The men hunkered down with carbines at the ready. This was the hard time when you just waited. I hoped that Jones and his men would have finished their work. However, as just one rail had been removed whilst I watched, I knew that the train would not reach Hagerstown. We heard the wail of the engine's whistle in the distance.

I turned to Ritchie, "They will hear that in the town. I reckon they will expect it to reach them in twenty minutes or so. I think that gives us an hour. Make sure the boys eat and drink something. In one hour all hell will break loose."

"Sir. If I might suggest sir? Why don't we lay one of those fallen trees across the railroad line in case they send a hand car down?"

"No, I don't think so. We could capture the hand car and it would allow Jones more time. Make sure we have a couple of the boys on the other side of the track. We will use a rope to stop it should they send one."

He smiled, "Will do sir. Now I see why you are an officer and I am just a sergeant."

"Don't knock yourself son; I was a sergeant once myself. That shows initiative and that you are thinking."

We waited nervously. When we heard the unmistakeable sound of the squeaking wheels of a railroad trolley every gun was cocked. I knew that I could leave Ritchie to deal with the trolley. I went to the troopers at the barrier.

"Don't fire until I tell you."

They nodded their understanding. The squeaking drew closer and I glimpsed it through the trees. There were two railroad men and a single soldier. I kept watching ahead knowing that the three men would soon be captured. The trolley passed us and we remained hidden. I heard the sound of something falling into the bushes and a scuffle. A few moments later Trooper White appeared. "We have a handcart now sir and three prisoners."

"Tie them up and then take the handcart with them on board down to Sergeant Jones. Get back here as soon as you can."

I was ensuring that all the prisoners were in one place and, this way, I could discover our progress. "Right boys, I reckon some time in the next half hour we will find some Yankees coming down this track. Keep an eye open."

It was sooner than half an hour when we heard the crunch of feet on the stones beneath the sleepers. They were marching down the track. Trooper White appeared next to me. He whispered when I put my hands to my lips. "Sergeant Jones has the train. It is tinned food and ammunition. He is loading it on the horses now. He said he would blow up the train too."

I nodded. I should have ordered him to do that anyway. I focussed my attention on the track. I saw the officer leading the fifty or so men and he was about a hundred yards away. I wanted to have the maximum firepower and I waited until they were but fifty yards away.

"Fire!"

The column was caught cold and the leading soldiers all fell in a heap. The Maryland men quickly left the track and began firing back. They could not see us and would be firing at the smoke. Their dark uniforms made them hard to see in the undergrowth and I was not sure that we were hitting anyone. Suddenly there was an explosion from behind us. Sergeant Jones had destroyed the train.

"Sergeant Ritchie, fall back to the horses. I'll be with the rearguard." I turned to the four men with me. "Stay behind me and walk back slowly." I slung my carbine over my shoulder and drew my Colt.

The northerners were still firing but they would soon realise that we had gone. Sure enough, I heard the order, "Cease fire and move forward." There was still someone in command.

"Pick your targets. We will see them soon enough."

Our improvised barrier meant that they could not fire as they struggled to cut through it with their bayonets. We began to pick them off and that slowed them down even further. "Fall back to the horses."

Ritchie and the rest of the troopers were already mounted.

"Lead them off, sergeant. We will keep an eye on these boys until we are clear."

It had been a successful raid. We had captured valuable booty, destroyed a train and bloodied the Yankees' noses. We waited until we saw the blue uniforms filtering through the undergrowth and then we fired. They answered with some wild shots which scattered leaves and branches above our heads.

"That's enough. Back to the farm!"

The troopers turned and galloped off with me in hot pursuit. I allowed the troopers ahead of me to open a gap. Copper could outrun anything else in the troop. I turned to watch the blue coats and was relieved to see that they had stopped. As I turned back I suddenly saw a log on the trail; I wheeled Copper to one side and we leapt into the air. I did not see the branch in front of my face until it was too late. All went black.

I awoke and it was dark. I opened my eyes in panic. Was I in a Yankee prison? My hands were not tied, which was a good thing. I tried to sit up but my head hurt. I put a hand to my forehead and it came away bloody. I remembered now, I had hit a branch. My eyes had become accustomed to the dark and I saw that I was in a small wooden outbuilding of some description. There were some tools and broken pieces of wood and metal. It was a workshop. I stood, a little gingerly, but I managed to stand upright. I went to the tools to find one which might be used as a weapon. As I did so I put my hand to my holster and found my Colt. I was still armed. I was thoroughly perplexed. How had I got here? Where was here? I was about to open the door and run out when I stopped. Whoever had brought me here had left me armed and, I assumed would return at some point. I could see, through the cracks at the edge of the poorly made door, that it was still daylight. When I moved it would have to be at night. I had no doubt that we had stirred up a hornet's nest with our attack on the railroad.

I turned to examine the workshop again and saw that, on the other side of where I had lain, was a tin mug with a liquid in it. I sipped it. It was lemonade. This was becoming stranger by the minute. Someone had left me there and provided a drink. I went to the door and peered through the crack. The building was in the woods but there appeared to be a path leading up to it. I would have to wait for my benefactor to find me. In the dark I would have no idea which direction I should take. I sat down in the corner to wait for the dark or my rescuer, whichever came first.

I must have dozed off for I was suddenly alert. I had heard a noise. I slipped my Colt from its holster and then cursed myself; I had not checked to see if it was loaded. The footsteps on the path were faint, but they were heading for the door. I slipped behind it. The door swung open and I held my pistol before me. I contemplated clubbing whoever came through the door and then I got the faint smell of flowers. This was not a man.

Mary Malone peered into the darkness. "Are you there Captain Hogan?"

I stepped from behind the door and she gave a little squeak like a mouse. "Sorry if I made you start. Where am I? How did I get here?"

I saw that she had a bowl of water in her hand. "First let me tend to your wound and I will tell you as I dress it." She gently began to wipe my head. "I heard the shooting for it is close to the house where I work. When the soldiers had gone I was curious and I came to see if there were any of your men wounded. I found none and I was about to go home again when I saw your boot sticking out from beneath a bush. I dragged you here to this workshop. It is a little way from the main house and I knew that you would be safe. I went back to where you fell and covered our tracks. They will not know you are here." She finished dabbing it. "I do not think it needs a bandage. You are done."

"Thank you for you ministrations and for your rescue. It was brave of you and you risked your life for me. I am grateful."

"I told you before captain, I am a Virginia girl. My father and brother both died at Antietam. I have no love for the north."

"And yet here you are in Maryland."

She shrugged, "I am well thought of here and I earn a decent wage. I save it and when the war is over I will have saved enough to return home and begin my life anew."

She was an eminently sensible girl. "I thank you again."

"And what of you captain? From your accent you are not American born."

"No, I am an Irishman but I have fought for the south since the start of the war." As much as I enjoyed talking to this pretty young woman I had to get back to my men. "Are they still hunting us?"

She nodded. "They have brought some cavalry from Frederick. You and your men annoyed them by blowing up the train and killing their soldiers. They had felt safe here."

I bit my tongue as I almost said that soon they would have an army to face and not a handful of raiders. "I will leave when it is dark." I glanced at the door. "That will be soon I feel. Am I far from where I fell?"

"I dragged you about half a mile. I am sorry; we lost your hat along the way."

I smiled, "A hat for a life is a fair exchange. Which way is the railroad?"

"We are about half a mile south of it."

I began to work out where the farm we were using as a base was. By my reckoning it was about three or four miles south east of my present position. My time at sea had helped me to understand the stars and I could steer a course back to my men.

She took my hand in hers. "You should stay here captain. I can bring you food. They will stop searching in a day or so."

I shook my head. They use the phrase, 'the kindness of strangers', and it was true from Stumpy and James Boswell through to Mary, people had been kind to me. I did not know why. "It is good of you to think of me but each minute I stay here increases the danger to you and I would not have you hurt for the world."

She smiled at me and gripped my hands a little tighter. "I just want to help you." She looked at the ground. "I like you. I know that I should not be so open and forward but this war has shown me that you need to hang on to that which you desire and love for it can be taken away in an instant."

I was taken aback, "And I like you Mary Malone. It is unexpected to find such beauty and kindness in the middle of a war. I promise you this; I shall return and find you when this war is over. I would have you know that I have a property." I did not know why I blurted that out but her honesty and openness had disarmed me. I shrugged, "Or I did but I have money and I can provide but this is not the time for such things. I have men to lead and battles to fight. You may find someone else. But I promise you that I will return and if you feel the same way, whenever that day dawns, then we can then begin to plan for a future away from this war."

I saw tears in her eyes and she buried her face in my chest. "There was a boy and he died along with my brother and my father. Until I saw you I thought that he would be the only man in my life and I will wait but please do not rush off yet. I would not have you captured."

I laughed, "Do not worry. I will evade capture but I must get back. My men will worry about me and I meant what I said about returning." I could see that it was dark. "And now I will leave."

I felt embarrassed. What should I do? I felt I ought to do something. She did it for me. She leaned up and kissed me full on the lips. "And I shall be here when you return. Now come. Follow me and I will take you close to the road."

I took out my gun as we walked. I stayed a couple of yards behind her in case we met anyone. She moved well through the woods as though she was familiar with the trail. Suddenly two horses appeared before us and there were two Yankee troopers. I pointed my gun at them. I had to think quickly.

"You two will do better than this woman. Get off your horses and keep your hands in the air."

"You'll not get away with this Reb."

"Up to now I have. Now get off those horses and keep your hands where I can see them."

"Typical Reb; taking a woman prisoner."

"Shut your mouth Yank. Now step over there. I kept my gun pointing at them. Had I been in their place I would have gone for the gun as I would have only been able to get one shot off but I think they worried about Mary.

With my spare hand I grabbed both sets of reins. "I nodded to Mary. "I am sorry for frightening you ma'am. But you have to know I would never have harmed you."

She hid her smile and said, "I was not frightened sir but I am glad that you are going. " Her back was to the men and she pursed her lips in a kiss.

I mounted the horse and backed it up, keeping my Colt pointed at them. "Do not try to follow me boys for if you do I shall kill you." I managed to put venom in my voice.

I wheeled the horses around and galloped off down the trail. I hoped that I would not meet any other troopers. The troopers fired their Colts at me. They missed but they would alert any other soldiers hunting me. I saw it becoming lighter and knew that the road would be ahead. I burst out on to the pike and found myself next to a road block. Luckily I was on the open side. I fired my gun three times at the soldiers who guarded it. I wanted to keep their heads down rather than try to kill them. I turned and galloped off down the road. By the time they had recovered enough to aim their rifles I was far enough away to make a hit extremely unlikely. I was just lucky that it had been infantry and not cavalry who had been there. I knew that there would be other troopers searching for us but I hoped that they were closer to the railroad.

I was not sure which road I was on and I looked up at the skies for help. It was cloudy. I took comfort from the fact that I seemed to be going up hill. If I could find South Mountain then I could find the farm. I came to a cross roads and saw the huge mountain ahead of me. I took that road. As soon as I could I left the road and found the shelter of the trees. I changed horses. I had no sooner done that than I heard the hooves of a cavalry patrol. I had left the road none too soon. I made my way up through the trees until I found a path of sorts. It wound its way up the mountain. I took heart from the fact that it widened as it climbed. Eventually I reached an open knoll a little way below the summit. I dismounted to make me less obvious and I led the two horses.

I did not think that we could be seen from the road but I was taking no chances. When I smelled wood smoke I knew that I was near habitation and I took out my gun. This time I reloaded. If I met another patrol I would be ready this time. I edged forwards and noticed that the trail began to drop. I re-entered the woods and went even more slowly. Suddenly I spied a light in a building and saw a man smoking a pipe. I tied the horses to a tree and crept up on him. He did not see me and I pointed my gun at his head.

His head flicked around and he looked at me in shock. "Captain Hogan! We thought you was dead or captured. The sergeant will be sure glad to see you!"

Chapter 11

To say they were glad to see me would have been an understatement. Sergeant Ritchie, in particular, appeared overjoyed. "Captain Hogan sir, I am so sorry for leaving you there."

"I wasn't left there. You were obeying orders and I would have had your stripes if you had come back for me." I shook my head, which was a mistake as it still hurt, "I was knocked off Copper by a tree." I suddenly remembered my horse, "Copper?"

Sergeant Jones gestured with his thumb, "In the stables. Followed the other horses home."

That was a relief, "Did we lose any men?"

"No sir, just Lucky Jack."

They all laughed at that. "But you managed to get back with the booty."

"Most of it sir but we needed more horses."

I gestured behind me to the forest. "If you go back in there you will find two fine Yankee horses with saddles and carbines." As Trooper White went for them I added, "There are some Yankee cavalry in the area so we had better go a little more carefully next time. They nearly had me and they know there is Reb cavalry in the area."

"How did you escape sir? We are not surprised but we are mighty interested. When Lieutenant Spinelli got separated he had to be rescued. How did you do it all by your lonesome?"

I told them although I left out my conversation with Mary Malone. Sergeant Jones slapped his leg and said, "And that is why he is Lucky Jack. Not only does he escape but he is helped by a pretty young Virginia girl."

"How do you know that she is pretty?"

Trooper Ritchie looked shamefaced, "That's me sir. It sort of slipped out."

"Well I think I am ready for my sleep now but we need to be up early tomorrow sergeant. We need to strike while the iron is hot."

"You mean up early today sir." He pointed to the sun rising in the east. I would get little sleep this night.

The next day I sent two troopers back. One was to find Colonel Boswell and report on our findings whilst the other would report to General Lee. We kept the food and the ammunition at the farm. Leaving four men on guard I took the remaining troopers on a patrol. We headed for Gettysburg.

I had not been there since Dago and I had rescued General Stuart's nephew. There had been a strong military presence there then. We approached the town cautiously but I saw little evidence of soldiers this visit. It looked like the administrative units had moved on. I was aware of General Lee's instructions in terms of the civilian population and so we headed for the railroad.

We surrounded the station and entered the telegraph office. We quickly overpowered the employees of the railroad and tied them. I sent Sergeant Jones to investigate the warehouses while Sergeant Ritchie and his men lifted a couple of rails. The warehouses were empty but we cut the telegraph wires and destroyed the equipment. Looking back now it seems petty but at the time I knew what effect that would have on the Union. We were deep inside Pennsylvania and we were destroying their railroad without being worried by their army. They would have to move forces here and that meant that General Lee and his army of Northern Virginia could cross without having to fight a battle.

We took the small quantity of food, weapons and ammunition which we discovered in the railroad station and we headed back to the farm. We ate well again that night.

We awoke the next morning to the sound of guns from the south of us. I sent a patrol to look but they reported that they had seen nothing. It had to be General Lee's forward units. They had made good time. "Sergeant Jones, I want six men leaving here to guard the food and the ammunition. The rest need to be mounted. We will ride towards the guns."

I knew that the army would be advancing from Harper's Ferry towards Hagerstown. I also knew that there were some Union forces in the area. The last thing the general would need would be to be ambushed. We headed south. I sent out four troopers to find the enemy. My men were past masters at blending into the background. They could see without being seen.

They soon returned with the news that we needed. "Sir, we found the Yankees. They are a mile yonder. They have a barricade across the road and they are dug in."

"How many?"

"It looks like that company from Hagerstown and the cavalry with them."

That meant that we were outnumbered. "Follow me." We rode along the road towards the ambush. I decided on a different approach this time. "Sergeant Ritchie, I want you with me. Sergeant Jones, when I give the word I want you to bring the men forward. Hide them. We are going to try to bluff these soldier boys into surrendering. Follow my lead; pretend you are a brigade"

"Are you sure sir?" Sergeant Jones' worries clearly showed on his face.

"Copper can move like lightning and Sergeant Ritchie here is no slouch. I think we can get away if they turn nasty. If they do then you will have to cover us."

I took a piece of white cloth from my saddlebags and tied it to my sabre. We rode forwards. "You watch for any sign of treachery." I hoped that they would respect the white flag as a flag of truce but I had never used one before.

We trotted around the bend in the road and the sound of our hooves made the officer and the sergeant turn. Their hands went to their guns.

"Flag of truce, gentlemen."

They kept their guns in their hands but at least they did not point them at us. "What do you want Reb?"

"I want you to save unnecessary bloodshed and the lives of your men."

The sergeant laughed, "What, from the two of you? You Rebs sure have a high opinion of yourselves."

I pointed to the south where the popping of guns still sounded. "That is not a raiding party. That is the army of General Lee. Those guns you hear will be the guns of General Jubal Early's men. Do you think your one hundred men are going to hold up a whole Corps?"

"Why should we to surrender to you two?"

In answer I shouted, "Sergeant Jones, bring the first troop forward! Keep the rest of the regiment hidden!" I kept my eyes on the young captain. His eyes widened as my men appeared. Although we had less than thirty five men the fact that they were spread out and on horses must have made them seem like more for his shoulders drooped in resignation.

"There is no dishonour in saving your men's lives captain." Just then there was a particularly large explosion from the cannon which made the captain jump. I could see him looking at the horses in front of him. He looked at the sergeant who shrugged.

The young captain nodded and took off his sabre. "We surrender."

I nodded, "That was wise captain." I risked a lie. "The rest of my brigade is already at Hagerstown. You would have all been slaughtered." I could see that it made him feel better. "Sergeant Jones, collect the weapons. Captain, if you would like to begin to have your men march south."

As they began to organise themselves I turned to Sergeant Ritchie. "Take two men and head down the road. I wouldn't want the general to begin firing on these men because of their blue uniform."

I dismounted and led Copper so that I could talk to the captain. His look told me that he appreciated not having to look up at me. He gave a rueful smile. "Are you the one who escaped the other day? The one who held that girl hostage?"

I nodded, "I am not proud of that but I did not relish the prospect of a prison. I have seen what they look like and it does not appeal."

"And yet you would send me there."

"As an officer you may be exchanged."

"There is no honour in that sir. These boys are from my home town. I will share what they endure."

"They are noble sentiments and I applaud you for them."

He looked at my badges. "I do not recognise your regiment sir."

"We are the 1st Virginia Scouts. I am Captain Jack Hogan."

He suddenly looked around at the sergeant who shook his head. "You boys are worth money." I must have looked puzzled. "You know there is a price on your head sir."

I looked at the grizzled veteran. "No sergeant, I did not."

"Yup. Some Irish boys have put a bounty on you and a couple of other officers; Murphy and Bosworth."

I said absent mindedly, "Boswell."

"Yes sir, that is the fellow; seems you hung his cousin or brother or some such." He paused, "Did you?"

"Yes, after a court martial. He was one of a couple of spies. They had betrayed us and many fine men were killed."

"It doesn't seem to make much difference. They are looking for you."

The captain nodded. "I would avoid the area around York sir; it is where they are based. I have heard that they are almost savages. My men are all Pennsylvanian men but these Irishmen are from New York and Boston. They are different to the rest of us."

"I thank you for your concern but as I am Irish myself I think I know what to expect."

The colonel leading the 13th Virginia was delighted to see us. "We thought we were the first ones to liberate Pennsylvania. It is good to see you boys here. If you escort these prisoners back to Williamsport you will find the rest of your regiment."

"Sir we have some ammunition and food. We captured a farm. Corporal MacKay, show the colonel where it is."

He doffed his hat, "Thank you sir. My men will be grateful for that. Rations have been mighty short."

"You are welcome." I turned to the corporal and said quietly. "Show the colonel the food first and then load all the Colt and carbine ammunition on the horses. I think our troop earned that."

He grinned. "Yes sir!"

A little louder I said, for the colonel's benefit, "Bring the boys and the horses back to Williamsport when you have done that."

It was only four miles or so and I was looking forward to seeing Dago and the others. We found ourselves swimming against the tide that was General Early's Corps. Many of the regiments made disparaging remarks about the blue coated soldiers. I began to feel sorry for the captain and his men. I knew that in his position I would not have surrendered. My men and I would have fought on and sought an escape. Perhaps it was the way we hade evolved. The provost marshal at the bridge gratefully took charge of the prisoners.

"Good luck, captain."

"And to you, Captain Hogan. Now that I know who you are I am grateful that I will just be a prisoner and will not have the mad Irish hunting me."

After ensuring that we had taken the best of the weapons and the ammunition we handed the rest over to the quartermaster and sought our comrades. We were directed to a large barn on the edge of town. I was pleased to see Danny and Harry were there already. They greeted me warmly. Sergeant James came over to take Copper and I was pleased to see the stripe had been returned.

"How is the wound, Carlton?"

"All healed sir. I am a little slower at the moment but that will change. I'll look after Copper for you."

Harry gave me a glass of whiskey. "It seems the garrison here ran away and left their booze. Cheers."

"Cheers." I swallowed a healthy mouthful of fiery liquid. "Had much success?"

"Captured some horses and some powder. And you?"

I told them of the train and the capture of the soldiers. "You have done well." Danny nodded his approval. "As the colonel wasn't here I gave Sergeant Ritchie his stripe back. I think the colonel will have forgotten that now."

"Have we any orders yet sir?

"No. I think they are waiting for the colonel to return."

"The captain I captured told me that there is a price on our heads from those Irish boys who killed our troopers."

He nodded as though it was not news, "We'll have to do something about that. The lads are upset and they might not have their minds on the job."

I shook my head, "We can't go off hunting them sir. That would be madness."

"No but if we know where they are then who knows what can happen in a battle?"

Danny was an Irishman through and through. He could forgive and forget but not when there was a feud. "Anyway it is unlikely that we will see them. They are based at York and that is over sixty miles away."

"You never know, Jack."

When the colonel arrived with the rest of his troop they had been knocked about a little. "We ran into a regiment of Pennsylvania cavalry and they chased us every which way. We lost some good men."

We told him of our achievements and he seemed genuinely pleased. "I don't think we will be here too long. The whole army is heading north. General Lee wants to give the northerners a taste of war. I had better get to headquarters and find out what our next role will be."

After he had gone, along with Danny, I turned to Dago. "It seems he is a little more like his old self."

"You know how it is; you forget what war is like. We have never stopped since we joined up. I am not sure that we could stop being soldiers, even if we wanted to."

"I know what you mean." It worried me that we took stealing and killing as normal. What would we do when the war ended? If General Lee succeeded and forced a peace on the north then we would go back to being ordinary citizens again. Could I go back to the house in Charleston? I had barely spent a night there. What would I do? Then I remembered Caitlin. I still had that promise to keep. I would find my sister and then work out what to do when peace broke out.

When the colonel returned we found that would not happen too soon. "Well it seems we have to do another job for General Lee. He wants us to find Stuart and give him some orders. We are heading back to Leesburg."

The depleted regiment left before dawn the next day. It was almost a repeat of the ride to Williamsport. We passed every Corps in the army as they headed north and we wondered if we would even see any Yankees.

Colonel Boswell told us that Stuart and his Corps was heading for Frederick. I had looked at the map and saw that we would have the army and the cavalry converging. It was a good plan. Unfortunately the northerners were not cooperating. When we reached Leesburg there were Union infantry there. They too were marching north. We were grateful that they had no cavalry or it would have made life difficult. We kept away from the roads and used the trails through the woods and fields.

We headed for Manassas Junction. We could then swing back around the Union forces and join up with General Stuart there. Once again we ran into an immovable object; a Union division heading north. We had crossed the Potomac over one of the islands. We knew the area well; or at least the veterans did. It had been close to here that I had had to cut a man's throat for the first time. That seemed a lifetime ago now.

We hid in the woods overlooking Middleburg where the Union forces were gathering. Colonel Boswell held an officer's conference. "I do not think that General Stuart can be north of Middleburg. We will have to cross the pike and continue south to find him."

Danny looked down at the map held in the colonel's hand. "How do we get almost two hundred men through the Union lines sir? There must be five thousand men down there."

No one had an answer. I was idly turning my black slouch hat in my hands. My kepi was still somewhere in the woods near to Hagerstown. I suddenly smiled. Harry looked at me, "What the hell is the smile for?"

"Let's just do it like we did when we were the Wildcats." They looked at me as though I was mad. "If we were still Rangers we would slip through at night. If we were questioned then we would pretend to be Yankees. Why can't we do that?"

"Because Jackie Boy , there are five thousand men we have to pass."

"No major, not at night. They would have a few cavalry vedettes out and this far from the front they won't expect a regiment to be passing through."

The colonel smiled, "I like the idea but I don't think that we could slip all the regiment through without becoming suspicious."

He was probably right. I had another inspiration . "Then why don't we use a sucker punch, sir. Make them notice a small group of men . They will chase them and then the larger group could go through."

Harry nodded, "That would work. They would send the cavalry after those and leave great gaps. It would be possible sir."

"It sounds like a suicide mission to me, Jack."

"No sir. Give me ten good men and we can do it." I pointed at the map. If you and the regiment are to the east of the town I will cause a ruckus to the west. When they ride to find out what is happening then you slip through. We know the roads around here like the back of our hands. We would meet you at Manassas Junction."

I could see the colonel's dilemma. He did not want to risk losing us and yet there was no other way without losing the whole regiment. Eventually he nodded. "Pick your men. When will you do it?"

The sun was setting in the west and I said, "Now! It seems as good a time as any."

I chose Sergeant Ritchie, Sergeant Jones and eight men who had just been with me. I would have taken Irish but I knew that the colonel needed him. There were no goodbyes. If we didn't see each other again then they would remember me and what I had done. It was the way we were. They would raise their glasses to toast me and share out the belongings I had left. We headed out just a short time before the colonel. He and the rest of the regiment had a shorter journey. As we waited in the undergrowth just half a mile from the town I explained my plan.

"We will ride slowly towards the Main Street. I intend to erupt in the middle of the town. I want them to look everywhere for us. We will head south once we are through." I paused so that they would all hear my words. "We cannot stop for wounded. Keep going and keep firing once we start. We know the effect that has on the enemy."

They grinned back at me. They were all ready for the excitement of another madcap run. None of us thought we would die. I had learned that they thought I was so lucky that they, too, might be invincible. I never felt invincible. I just knew that if you pushed it to the limit you had a better chance of surviving.

We waited until the cavalry patrol had moved west and then rode directly towards the town.

"Follow me then and keep your pistols ready."

I knew just how good they were on a horse; all of us could ride with just our knees if needs be. We rode through the poorer houses which led to Main Street. Once we reached Main Street, I halted us next to a large store and peered down the street. There were only a few people taking the night air. I took a deep breath and led them across the street. The main Union camp was to the south of the town. So far we had been lucky and had remained unseen. Our luck ran out as two soldiers came from a building to our right. I suspect they were going for a call of nature. They could not miss our uniforms; my Union slouch hat would not fool them. One reached in his belt for his gun as the other shouted a warning. My two sergeants shot them both.

"Right boys! Let's give them hell!" Giving the rebel yell, we launched our horses forwards. My plan had always been to ride through their camp causing as much confusion as possible and that had not changed.

The camp was well laid out and there was a wide avenue between the tents. We rode straight down it in two lines. Soldiers appeared from the tents in a confused state. We kept firing as we rode through their camp. I heard their bugle sound and hoped that the colonel would hear it. That was his chance to cross their lines unopposed. Any firing would be confused with our charge. One of my guns emptied and I drew a second. A soldier, dressed in just his pants rushed from his tent screaming at me. He had his rifle with a bayonet on the end. I fired when the end of the bayonet was less than a hand span from my gun. His face disappeared.

I could hear my men yelling and firing behind me. I knew from experience that we appeared to be more men than we actually were. I saw the end of the line of tents ahead. There was a wooden fence. I yelled, "Fence coming up! Be ready to jump."

Copper sailed over it and landed in the field on the other side. I slowed my horse down and watched as the others leapt to safety. Only six men followed me. The two sergeants were safe but we had lost s trooper. They had made the sacrifice to save the rest of the regiment. It was our way. This was no time to rest on our laurels. We were not out of the woods yet.

"Keep heading south!"

We galloped across the field. I could hear the bugle calls behind me and recognised the cavalry one. They were sending horsemen after us. I spied a road to the south and we headed for it. Once we made the metalled surface I led us east. I kept scanning ahead of me. I was looking for a good place to ambush our pursuers. I saw, just ahead, some bushes next to the stone wall. I held my hand left and we wheeled behind it.

"Stay on your horses and reload. When they come down the road give them everything we have got."

I heard the hooves as the cavalry thundered after us. We barely had time to reload. As they galloped before us we opened fire. It was point blank range the first eight riders were thrown from their horses. Some were shot others fell as their horses reared in panic at the sudden fusillade.

"Ride!"

Sergeant Jones led the men as they rode parallel to the pike. One braver horseman leapt the wall and landed close to me. He had his sabre out and slashed at me. I blocked his sword with my pistol and leaned Copper into his horse. The wall was quite close and the horse stumbled. I fired blindly and the ball struck his leg and went into the horse's side. Horse and rider crashed in a heap. Our pursuers had the better surface and were now gaining on us. We needed to move away from the road. The problem was that turning too far left meant heading towards Middleburg. I saw the hills rising ahead.

"Sergeant Jones, head for the hills."

Almost as one man we wheeled left towards the distant shadow that was the safety of the mountains. It took our pursuers a few yards to realise what we had done and then they had to waste time clearing the stone wall. We had our lead again but they were on fresher horses. It was a race. We had to reach the safety of the forest and the hills before they caught us.

The shadows and the poor light aided us as we headed away from the northerners. None of us risked turning to fire; we just lay low over our horses' manes and we trusted to their endurance. The trees seemed to be further away than they had ever been. Copper faltered a little on a piece of uneven ground and I slowed down a little. I did not want to be afoot. I was relieved to see the first of the scrubby trees appear before me. As I turned around one I glanced to my right. Our pursuers were a good half a mile away. We now had a chance.

Sergeant Jones had an old head on his able shoulders and he took us diagonally across the slope. Although it enabled the enemy to close with us it meant that we conserved our horses whilst tiring out those chasing us. There were now just twenty men pursuing us and we would soon be in a position to turn and fight. If they thought that we were afraid of a fight then they were wrong. We just needed better odds.

Sergeant Jones found a trail which headed to our left. It was perfect. We were now closing with the cavalry even though we were still moving up the slope. Two of the troopers decided to try the slope with their horses. They slowed almost to a walk and Sergeant Ritchie and Trooper White fired at them. They hit one and the other fell off his horse as he tried to take out his gun. The rest followed our tail and we began to lengthen our lead again. I knew that Copper was struggling and I hoped that Sergeant Jones would find somewhere soon.

We were almost at the top and we found a spot where they had been logging. The sergeant didn't need orders to choose this as our last stand. We threw ourselves from our horses and knelt behind the logs. The column hurtled to their doom as they crashed into our ambush. We only had six guns but they were Colts. The first riders fell without even seeing us and then they too dismounted and lay down behind the trees below us.

"Secure the horses and bring our carbines Trooper White."

We kept popping away with our pistols although the range was extreme. It would take a brave man to cross that killing ground. When we had our carbines firing then the tide turned in our favour. They were below us and their cover was not as good as ours. We did not kill any more men but I knew we were hitting them from their cries. Their balls thudded into the thick logs behind which we sheltered. Pieces of wood splintered and flew at them. A splinter travelling at speed can give a nasty wound. I saw the first light of dawn peeping over the ridge to the east of us. It would soon be possible to count our enemies.

"How are we for ammunition?"

They all shouted their answers.

"Ten."

Twelve."

"Nine."

"Fifteen."

"Eight."

"Ten."

I had fifteen left for my carbine and eight for my Colts although two of my Colts were still in my saddle holsters.

"Conserve your ammo. Only shoot when you are guaranteed a kill."

I wondered if any other troopers would follow this handful. I was merely waiting until our horses were rested before continuing our escape.

"How many can you see down there, sergeant?"

"I make it twelve, sir. But I might be wrong. They may have left some holding their horses."

With more light I could see that there was cover to their left and their right. White and Carberry were next to me. "I want you two to crawl, one there and one there. Work your way around their flank and when I yell 'Troop A', charge, then just let loose with your carbines. Don't worry about ammunition. If this doesn't work we will high tail it out of here."

"Yes sir."

They both slithered away like snakes. I turned to the other four. "When I yell then aim at the ones in the middle."

I saw that both men were in position. I yelled, "Troop A, charge!"

We rose as one and began to fire at anything blue. We heard the two troopers yelling like banshees and suddenly the remaining Yankees leapt to their feet and ran for their horses.

"After them!"

I had emptied my carbine and so I shot at the departing troopers with my Colt. We saw the last eight racing down the trail.

"Check for ammunition and guns. Sergeant Ritchie, secure those four horses. Then its time to head for Manassas."

Chapter 12

When we reached Manassas Junction the colonel and the regiment were there and they had secured the rail head but of General Stuart there was no sign. Danny threw his arms around me, "You did it again Jackie Boy."

The colonel nodded and said, "Well done Captain Hogan you have redeemed yourself this night."

I saw the flash of anger cross Dago and Cecil's faces but I just smiled. "Just doing my duty, colonel."

"You and your boys better get some sleep captain. We had an easy ride. We arrived hours ago."

If that was meant to make me feel better then it failed. I had bought that precious time with the lives of four good men. I think Danny saw the anger in my face for he put his arm around my shoulder so that I could not move towards Colonel Boswell and he led me away.

"We have some beds made up for you boys." He put his head next to my ear. "The boys know what you have done, Jack. Just be happy with that. The colonel is getting better but it will take time for him to be his old self again."

"And how many dead men will it take to heal him?" I added bitterly. Every time I left on patrol my men and I achieved all that we were supposed to achieve and more; yet each time I left men on the battlefield.

The men who had not accompanied me greeted us warmly when we headed for our beds. Corporal MacKay pulled me to one side. "Sir, I have the extra ammunition you asked me to keep. What shall I do with it?"

At one time I would have said to give it to the colonel but I was becoming more concerned with my own men. "Distribute it to the troop. Thanks MacKay."

He gave me a lopsided grin, "We look after our own sir."

I was woken by the sound of hooves outside and the hubbub of Stuart and his men arriving. I hurriedly dressed. I had appreciated the sleep but I had no idea how long I had slept. I reached General Stuart when he and the rest of the officers were discussing what had gone on.

"Damn Yankees kept blocking our way with cannon slowed us to hell and back, colonel."

"Well sir, we have more bad news. It looks like General Meade and his army are to the north of us and between us and General Lee."

"Damn! How did you boys get through?"

"Captain Hogan caused some commotion and he rode through their camp. We slipped through their lines while they chased him to hell and back."

The general spied me and applauded me. "You are a true cavalryman, captain." He took off his gauntlets. "So colonel what would you suggest? You know the area north of us as well as any man."

Colonel Boswell rubbed his chin. "Well sir if we head due north there are a couple of fords which are low enough at this time of year to let us cross. They would not be any use to artillery or even infantry but we could cross. We could then head across country and rejoin the general."

"That's a good idea." He turned to an aide. "Send a rider to General Lee and tell him what we intend. Colonel Boswell, if your regiment would act as the vanguard I would appreciate it. Your men seem to have a nose for smelling out the enemy."

The colonel almost grew a foot at the apparent honour. "Yes sir, we would be delighted." As the busy little general strode off, Colonel Boswell turned to Major Murphy. "Have the regiment ready to ride in thirty minutes, Major Murphy."

Danny glanced at Dago and me. "But sir, some of the men have barely had two hours sleep."

"The Yankees are not sleeping Major Murphy. Just do it. This is war and not a Sunday School picnic."

I knew that Danny was thinking about my troop in particular. I shrugged. "We can always sleep when we are dead sir."

Sergeant James had ensured that our horses had been both well fed and cared for when we had arrived back. Copper looked fresh but I knew that I would have to be careful for a broken horse could never be used in war again. Copper was as much a part of me as my name.

We were lined up less than twenty five minutes after the orders were given. Colonel Boswell nodded his approval. "Captain Hogan and Lieutenant Spinelli take us north and find a ford without Yankees."

We galloped off northwards. Dago turned to me, "You got the short straw again Jack."

"I don't mind. I quite enjoy the freedom." I grinned. "It means I give myself the orders and I quite like that. What the colonel doesn't see won't hurt me." I swept an expansive hand at the forty men who followed us. "They are very loyal and protective. I feel safer with these men around me than when we are with the army."

The ford we chose was not a ford in the accepted sense of the term. There was a slope down which was very steep and then the water of the Potomac was quite deep in parts but the mighty river had small islands which acted as giant stepping stones. We had discovered that the knack was to swim upstream in the deeper parts and allow the current to take you to land.

"Lieutenant Spinelli and Sergeant Jones, you stay here with half the men. I'll head to the other side and see if it is clear. When I signal then bring the rest across."

Copper and I plunged into the chilled waters. We were able to walk the first twenty yards and then we had to swim for the next ten. The water poured from Copper's flanks as we stood on the first island. We had two swims and that was all. It was summer and we had had little rain lately. When we were all ashore I ordered the men to draw weapons.

"Trooper White, you stay here and when I yell then wave the lieutenant across." The bluffs on the northern shore were steep and covered in pine but there was a trail of sorts which zig zagged up to the top. If I had been the Yankees I would have had some sort of sentry post on the bluffs but, when we reached the top it was empty.

"Send them across, Trooper."

We now had to secure this beachhead. We were less than twenty miles from Washington and I could not believe that they would not have patrols out. We soon came to the Chesapeake and Ohio Canal. I had not heard of boats using it since the war had started but I was taking no chances. We found a lock and an abandoned lock keeper's house not far from where we had landed.

"Trooper Lowe, bring Lieutenant Spinelli and his men here. We can use this until the rest of the cavalry come." I led the fifteen men who remained with me and we headed north towards Rockville. This was good Maryland earth and prosperous looking farms littered the land as we crossed. We used whatever cover we could. I checked my map; Rockville would provide a quick passage to Pennsylvania and General Lee. I was aware that we were still in Union territory.

"Sergeant Ritchie, take two men and see if Rockville is safe."

The three men trotted off and then tied their horses to some trees. They disappeared into a small stand of trees. The town looked, from the smoke of chimneys, to be on the other side of the wood.

As we waited my thoughts went back to Mary Malone. Would I ever see her again? It seemed unlikely that we would be in Hagerstown soon. General Lee was intent on driving towards Philadelphia and Washington. Perhaps she had been a dream, a tantalising picture of a good life for me. Events had transpired to put barriers in the way of my happiness since the day I was born. My men called me Lucky Jack but that name tasted bitter to me when I thought of my murdered mother and father and my sister forced to whore to earn a living. I had luck, but not in my own life. I just did not expect to be happy. I was just grateful to be alive.

The sergeant and his men led their horses back to us. "Sir, there are Union troops dug in around the town. It looks to be artillery and infantry. They are all just the other side of the trees and they are facing west. It appears like this is one of the places they are using to guard Washington sir. There is also a wagon train with over a hundred brand-new, fully loaded wagons and mule teams. They are a little further west."

"Thank you, sergeant. Let's get back and give the bad news to the colonel."

The colonel and the rest of the regiment were at the lock when we arrived. "Sir, the road west is blocked at Rockville. There is a wagon train and a company of infantry as well as artillery."

"We will have to see if the general has an alternative plan then."

General Stuart was not depressed when we gave him the news. "Brand new wagons you say? General Lee impressed upon me the need to gather supplies. This would be perfect."

General Hampton did not look so sure. "Are you sure General Stuart? If would slow us down. I think that General Lee would prefer us to arrive there sooner rather than later."

"If we knew where there was general." One of the advantages of being a scout for the general was that you tended to hear more than other officers. This was giving me an insight into how the general thought. "For all we know General Lee is heading in this direction already." He looked wistfully to the east. "Washington is just over there boys. Why we could ride right up Pennsylvania Avenue, capture old Abe and end this right now if we had a few more men and fresher horses."

Somehow I thought that our general was deluding himself. There would be more than a few guns defending the President of the United States of America.

"No, my mind is made up. Colonel Boswell if your regiment would lead off we will see about capturing this wagon train."

The colonel rode next to me with the Sergeant Major just behind. "Well Jack, how do we do this?"

"The guns are facing west as is the infantry and there is a stand of trees. If we dismount then we can surprise the gunners. I can't see the wagons being able to be hitched up quickly sir. We just have to neutralise the soldiers."

"Good plan." He turned to Major Murphy, "Send a rider back to the general and tell him that we will dismount and engage the guns. It will allow the general the opportunity to surround the town and capture the wagons."

We left the horses by the stand of trees we had used earlier and, taking our carbines, made our way through the spindly trunks. Sergeant Ritchie had been correct. This was a barricade to General Lee's advance. The men would not hold an army up for long but they would enable other troops to close. That worried me, for it meant there would be other soldiers nearby. We had to capture the town first.

Colonel Boswell led the line of troopers with Cecil on his shoulder. Despite his loyalty to me the Sergeant Major would protect the colonel with his life. Once we reached the edge of town we halted. We had four hundred yards to run to reach the guns and the infantry. It would be a hard run for men in boots and spurs.

Colonel Boswell drew his sabre and said, "Sound the charge!"

I frowned as I ran forward. I would have remained silent to gain surprise but the cat was now out of the bag and we screamed our rebel yell and raced up the road. The infantry all ran to their stacked rifles while the gunners tried to man handle their cannon to face us. It was a race that they would lose. I had spurned my carbine and I pointed my Colt at the blue coated infantry who were rapidly deploying into line. We were less than a hundred yards from them when I saw the officer raise his sword. I fired and he stumbled. It bought us a few more seconds. All of our troopers were now firing as the ragged volley erupted. These were green troops and the rifles made more smoke than anything. We crashed into them.

When Colonel Boswell cut down the major who commanded them he yelled, "Surrender!"

They were green for they all obeyed. The gunners were less obedient and I watched them, too late, as they spiked the cannon. They would be no use to us now. Our men quickly disarmed the prisoners. Our troopers took everything from them that could be of use to us. It was sad to see the corpses being robbed of boots but it was necessary in such an impoverished army as ours. General Stuart and General Hampton arrived as we had herded the prisoners together.

"Well done Colonel Boswell! Once again your men have performed wonders." He frowned as he saw the spiked cannon, "A pity about the cannon but still a great haul."

General Hampton pointed to the prisoners. "And what do we do with those general. The wagons and mules will slow us up somewhat but they will make it impossible to reach the general in time."

"You are right Wade. Send the commander to me."

The most senior officer was the artillery major. "Major, thank you for your surrender, it saved your men from unnecessary slaughter. If you give me your parole I will allow you and your men to return to Washington."

The major looked sceptically at General Stuart, "My parole sir?"

"Yes sir. If you promise not to fight until you have reached Washington then I am satisfied."

"In that case I will give you my word." I think the major was anticipating a fast walk back to Washington and then a rapid return to recapture the wagons. We were only fourteen miles from the capital.

After they had left I was still looking to our wounded men along with David. General Hampton strode up. "Do you think that was wise general? They could be after us before we have got very far."

General Stuart smiled, "When they reach Washington what will they report? They will say that Jeb Stuart and his cavalry are fourteen miles from the capital. It will cause mayhem. They will bring troops to capture me and defend the capital. That will mean that General Lee will have fewer enemies to deal with."

Despite what was said about Stuart later on, that he was a glory hound, I believe that he did what he thought was right for the southern cause. Some of those decisions, like the one to take the wagons and the mules with us, were flawed but the sentiment behind them was sound.

We left in high spirits and began to move, for the first time, in the right direction. It seemed that the 1st Virginia Scouts were the vanguard again. Colonel Boswell loved it. This was what he had dreamed of in the early days of the war. He was with the most famous Corps in the Confederacy and it was his regiment which had the honour of leading. The road to Westminster was straight and true. We did not need to push our horses for the wagons and mules slowed us down quite dramatically.

I sent Sergeant Ritchie and ten troopers down the pike towards Frederick when we reached the crossroads. I was relieved when he returned without sighting a single Union flag. I thought that we could have taken that road to reach Frederick. It would have brought us closer to General Lee but General Stuart was keen to march north. We were in Union territory and moving further north than at any time in the war. There was an infectious air of exultation amongst the senior officers,

Colonel Boswell included. It seemed that we were on the brink of success. We had not seen any force which could stand up to us.

It was late in the day when we came upon the Union cavalry. There was no warning. They suddenly appeared from the direction of Baltimore and the woods which lined the road to our right.

"Take cover!"

I dismounted my troopers and we crouched behind the fence. Colonel Boswell suddenly yelled, "1st Virginia Scouts! Charge!"

We tried to hit as many of the troopers as we could before our men joined the fray. "Mount!"

We gathered our horses as quickly as we could but by then the Yankee cavalry were fleeing down the Baltimore road with Colonel Boswell in close pursuit. We were just about to follow them when General Fitzhugh Lee galloped up. I knew the general, General Lee's nephew, and he smiled as he recognised me.

"Hello, Captain Hogan. The general has sent me to find your colonel and see what this is about."

"We were ambushed by some Yankee cavalry and the colonel is chasing them back to Baltimore."

He nodded and then frowned. "The general had a task for him." He appeared to make up his mind. "You will have to do it in his stead. The general is concerned that General Lee has no idea where we are. We are assuming that my uncle will have sent messengers to us but by the time they reach us this may be too late. Take your men and find the army. Here is a report for General Lee." He handed me a leather document case. "Give it to General Lee only. He will give you further orders I daresay." He pointed to the north west. "I would hazard a guess that he will probably be somewhere close to Gettysburg or possibly York. An area I know you know well."

"Yes sir." I paused, "Will you tell the colonel?"

He gave me a wry smile. The news of my court-martial was legend. "Do not worry, sir. I will personally tell him that you were acting under my orders. Good luck, Jack."

With thirty troopers I headed down the road towards a date with destiny. We were heading to Gettysburg where we would witness the battle which decided the fate of the Confederacy of the United States.

Part 3

Gettysburg-The First Day

Chapter 13

I set off for Gettysburg in good heart. We were free from the shackles of the Corps and Colonel Boswell. However, we were the wrong side of the Union forces as we soon discovered. Despite our small numbers I still had scouts out and they galloped back in an agitated manner. This was not like them and I immediately halted the small column.

"Sir, there is a huge Union army ahead!" Trooper Drake pointed behind him. "There are artillery on the road and cavalry in the fields guarding the flanks. It must be Corps strength at least."

I was in a pickle. I had to get the message through but short of back tracking to Westminster I could not see how we could manage it. I examined the map. The two sergeants rode next to me to see if they could offer any advice.

I pointed to a small ridge, "This ridge runs south and it looks like there is a small trail running beside it. If we ride along the ridge then we can drop down the other side and get ahead of this army corps."

They both nodded and Sergeant Jones said, "At least it proves we are heading in the right direction. I don't think they would be marching this way if General Lee wasn't ahead."

"Right. Keep eyes and ears open. There may be scouts out. We aren't the only cavalry who are good at hiding."

We cut across country to begin to climb the hill which rose behind the small farm. As we rose we could see the long blue snake heading west. It was at least an army corps. I hoped that their attention was on their front and not their rear. It was with some relief that discovered the track which led along the ridge. It was not well worn but it was easier than picking our way across rough ground. When we reached the top of the ridge I dismounted and crawled to the sky line to get a better view. The lead elements of the Corps were almost at Littlestown. I glanced at the sun. I suspected they would camp nearby as we were still some way from Gettysburg. That decided me.

"Right boys, we'll drop directly down and ride parallel with the road." I pointed to the woods to our right. "Once we drop from the ridge then we will be hidden from view and we can move much faster than they can. I reckon that we can make Gettysburg by dark. We best ride single file."

Trotting down the slope we felt cocooned from prying eyes. I could see the outskirts of Gettysburg in the distance. It was still some seven miles away but barring an accident we should be there by nightfall. Trooper Wilson was on point, some four hundred yards ahead of us. Suddenly he whirled and drew his pistol. Although I could not see what had made him do that I trusted his judgements. "Ambush!"

His gun cracked and he turned to ride back to us. There was a ripple of fire and he fell from his horse. "Follow me!" I headed away from the danger but still down the slope. A line of horsemen appeared. There were only ten of them and, when they saw us, they halted. They were too far away for us to guarantee hitting them and we did not want to waste ball and powder. They fired at us with their pistols but, as the range was still two hundred yards they did no damage. I could now see that they had been travelling on the road which ran parallel to the pike and they were alone.

"Wildcats! Charge!" I suddenly wheeled Copper and it took the Union horsemen completely by surprise. We covered the ground so quickly that they had no chance to react. They appeared to be disordered and the corporal with them did not take the decision that was needed. He died in the first volley. A second and a third man fell and the survivors decided that they could now retreat. My men galloped after them as I dismounted to check Trooper Wilson. He was dead. I collected his gun, valuables and horse as my men returned. The enemy patrol all lay dead but I could hear the bugles from the main column. They would soon send cavalry to investigate.

"Grab any ammunition. Sergeant Ritchie, take the rear. We are going to find it pretty hot, real soon."

I left the troopers to retrieve the ammunition as I mounted Copper and tied Wilson's horse to my saddle. I checked the map. We would have to head to the south of Gettysburg if we were to lose the chasing cavalry. I could now see the cavalry. They were a mile away. It was at least three companies. Whoever led them had a sound military mind for they were coming in three columns and they would cut us off if we tried to deviate from a straight line.

"Let's go now."

I kicked Copper on and the chase began. The ground soon levelled out as we crossed the Frederick Pike. I briefly contemplated heading along it but that would take us away from our destination. I was resolved to stick to my plan. I did spy a road which led to the south of Gettysburg and I took that. I did not intend to become trapped on the road but it would cause confusion for the three pursuing columns. I noticed that the ground was falling away quite slowly and I remembered that there was a creek which ran to the east of the town. A waterbed meant places to hide. I veered from the road at a farm entrance and we galloped through the farm sending squawking ducks and chickens flying in our wake.

I heard Sergeant Ritchie shout and the message was repeated until Sergeant Jones received it. "They are gaining sir."

"Don't worry sergeant. Gettysburg is just a mile or so ahead."

"What if the Yankees are there too?"

"Then we are in an even deeper hole. Tell the boys to be ready to dismount quickly and hide their horses when I shout."

I saw two round-topped hills rising to my right. I veered closer to them. Suddenly the ground almost fell away. There were huge rocks and a mass of scrubby undergrowth. It was a perfect place to hide. We plunged, recklessly down the bank and then turned left to ride up the other side of the shallow creek we later found was called Plum Run; we came to know it well. I saw an enormous rock, seemingly planted by giants and I rode behind it. There was enough space to hide us all.

"Dismount. Horse holders."

The designated men grabbed their horses as we all cocked our carbines. "Find somewhere to hide let's hope that they lose our trail."

I was trying to picture it the way that they would see it. They would reach the side of the hill and see nothing before them save the creek and the mass of rocks and undergrowth to their front. They would have to stop unless they were as crazy as I was. Perhaps they would assume we had headed directly for Gettysburg. We would soon find out.

I took off my hat and began to climb the rock. There were enough smaller rocks to facilitate this. When I neared the top I paused and raised my head inch by inch until I could see across to the two round-topped hills. A solitary horseman appeared and halted. He waved to the others to join him and soon there were forty horsemen on the opposite side of the valley. I saw that one of them had a looking glass and was scanning our side of the valley. I remained perfectly still. Had I ducked down there was a risk he would have detected the movement.

Two of the troopers were ordered down to investigate the creek. If they went to where we had crossed then they would see the tracks and the muddied water. To my relief, they went right and not left. They went to the creek and rode in opposite directions for thirty yards or so.

They rode back up the slope. The looking glass kept scanning the undergrowth and then, to my relief, they left.

I slithered back down the rock and retrieved my hat. "We have lost them but let's just wait to make sure."

"Where are we, sir?"

"As near as I can make it we are a mile and a half due south of Gettysburg. We will head east and try to find the Emmitsburg road." As we waited I wondered about the cavalry we had seen. They could mount a search for us the next day and we still had no idea where General Lee was. I had hoped to come across some of our own scouts and it was worrying that we had found none.

I was about to lead us out when I heard a noise. I climbed back up the rock and saw, to my horror, that the cavalry had returned and were executing a more thorough search. They would find were we had crossed the creek. I slipped back down.

"We are going to try to find a way out of this warren of rocks. The last two men try to hide our tracks. The rocks will help us."

I watched as Sergeant Ritchie got handfuls of rocks and spread them out on the earth where we had stood. I led the men and our horses through the rocks. It was difficult to judge direction in this jungle of rocks, trees and scrubby undergrowth but that aided us as it would make pursuit difficult. The land began to climb and I saw another ridge rising before us. The rocks gradually petered out and then we came across an open area, a wheat field. We had to turn left and follow the slight indentation on the land covered with bushes. Ahead of us I could see the Emmitsburg Road but, as it ran along the ridge we would be highlighted. Then I saw a small orchard. If we lay the horses down we might escape detection.

"Quickly men, get into the orchard and lie the horses down." I waited until they had passed and then I followed with Sergeant Ritchie. "Any sign of them?"

"No sir but I can hear them in the rocks. They are still there."

I looked at the sun which was beginning to set. That would be our only hope. Copper lay down easily enough but Wilson's horse was a bit skittish. I wished that Sergeant James was with us for he would have calmed her down. Eventually, when all the rest had settled, so did she. There was total silence, save for the sound of the crickets and the fire flies dancing in the wheat field. We heard the troopers as they came up the slope. The creaking of their leather and the jingling of their equipment marked their progress. They crossed the wheat field and I could hear them talking on the other side of the wall.

"Well you had better report to General Buford that there are Rebs on this side of the road as well as to the west. Tell him we can't be certain how many. We'll return to the column."

After they had left us I was in an even greater quandary. There were cavalry ahead of us and General Lee or at least elements from Lee's army. I decided, after a short wait that we would risk crossing the road and heading west. We led our horses across the road into the woods on the other side. We all kept a close watch on both sides. Fortunately we saw no one and we plunged into the woods.

We mounted and headed as close to west as we could get. "Sir, where do you think the army is?"

"The Yankees believe it is to the west of us but it could be to the north or the south, sergeant. I take it as a good thing that the Union army doesn't know where the general is. With General Stuart's cavalry on the loose I have high hopes that we can win."

As we trudged through the woods I was optimistic. I just hoped that I would meet some of our men sooner rather than later. I had the feeling that the Yankees were bringing their army up and were already fortifying the hills. As we went downhill I tried to imagine how hard it would be to attack troops who were dug in on the hill.

I suddenly heard a noise and I held up my hand to halt the men. I could see a camp fire in the distance. I left Copper with Trooper White and, with pistol drawn I headed towards the sound. I smelled tobacco and caught the glow of the cigar the sentry was smoking. Was he a Reb or a Yankee? I moved a little closer and caught sight of a butternut trouser leg and a bare foot. That could only mean one thing, a Reb.

I did not want to be shot by frightening the guard and so I said, "Captain Hogan of the 1st Virginia Scouts with a message for General Lee."

He stepped towards me with musket levelled. We were just a yard or so apart. "Where the hell did you come from?"

I shook my head, "A long way from here, my friend." I whistled and the rest of my troop appeared. "Where am I?"

"This is the 3rd Alabama and General Hill is the commander." By now the officer of the day had arrived. "Sir I have despatches from General Stuart and they are for General Lee."

He nodded. "Follow me."

"Sergeant, see to the men."

We trotted off through the lines of tents to a glow at the far end. I had never met General Lee but I had seen him before and I knew him to be a gracious gentleman. He beamed at me, "Ah Captain Hogan I believe. My nephew speaks well of you sir."

I held out the leather pouch. "I have despatches for you sir; from General Stuart."

As he opened them General Hill came towards me. I recognised him from other campaigns. "Tell me Captain Hogan, where is General Stuart?"

I pointed east. "Between Westminster and Hanover and there is at least two Union Corps between him and us."

The general stopped reading. "Are you sure?"

"We passed one Corps of infantry, artillery and some cavalry close to Littlestown. I think there is a Cavalry Corps on that ridge yonder."

Hill looked at General Lee and said, "Seminary Ridge." General Lee nodded. "Damn Pettigrew, he should have occupied it when he had the chance."

"It is no use worrying about what might have happened we will have to deal with the situation in which we find ourselves." He finished reading and then looked at me. "Are there guns on the ridge?"

"Not that I saw general."

"Well that is a relief." He turned to General Hill. "We will not see General Stuart today general. We will have to deal with the men on the ridge without his aid. Captain, when your men are rested I would appreciate it if you would act as scouts. I believe you know the area?"

"Yes sir."

"Good." He put his hand on my arm, "Well done sir. You have done well to breach their lines. Tell me, did you lose many men?"

"Just one sir."

He shook his head sadly, "And that is one too many. Make sure you eat too. We may not have much but we will share what we have."

I smiled, "Don't worry sir, we bring our own. We always take from the Yankees. They are very generous."

Even the dour A.P Hill smiled at that. He nodded, "You'll do captain, you'll do. If you would care to join me in my tent in an hour or so I will give you your orders."

I returned to my men. They waited expectantly. As I had expected Sergeant Jones had arranged for food. He handed me a mess tin with some hot food."It seems the Alabama boys had heard of us and when they heard that you were one of the men with a price on your head they insisted on sharing their food with us. They had been hunting."

I greedily devoured the welcome food. "We are now attached to General Hill. I think it means that we will be used as scouts. Sergeant Jones, divide the men into three. I guess we will be in great demand." I pointed to the east. The first job will be to find those Yankee cavalry for the general."

We left almost immediately. I did not see the point in being briefed and then finding my men. We would need to get down to action immediately. General Hill came out to see me with a map in his hand. "I want to know numbers of men on these three ridges: Seminary, Herr and McPherson. We are blind at the moment without General Stuart's cavalry." He added bitterly.

I felt honour bound to defend my commander. "He is trying to get here general but the whole Union army is in his path."

The general snorted. "Make sure you keep me informed of what you discover."

I turned to my sergeants. "Sergeant Jones head north and scout Herr Ridge. Sergeant Ritchie, go with him and scout McPherson Ridge. I will take Seminary Ridge. Don't risk the men unnecessarily. The General needs to know the enemy numbers." I looked around. We will make our camp over there in the woods there. Good luck."

I looked at the eight troopers with me. Troopers Lowe and White were the most experienced. "You two, as of now you are corporals."

They both looked pleased, "We thank the captain."

I smiled, "Don't thank me yet. We are going to have to get really close to over five thousand men."

General Pettigrew's men were already rushing towards the east. I could hear the ripple of rifles and muskets firing ahead of us. I rode down the creek known as Willoughby Run. It hid us from the men on the ridge and I hoped to get behind them. I remembered that there were two creeks before the ridge and then the tangle of the rocks behind. That would be our observation point. We could hear the guns but we saw no one as we were cocooned in the shallow valley. After the small rise I headed east and crossed Pitzer's Run.

I saw, in the distance, Union troops marching in column. I wondered if they would form on Cemetery Ridge. I could see no one on Seminary Ridge as yet. Wheeling Copper north I led my patrol towards the ridge. We slowly climbed up and I constantly expected to see blue uniforms but there were none. I halted the troop and took out my pencil and paper. "You boys try to see where the enemy are."

I could see that, towards the west, they had dismounted cavalrymen and they were desperately trying to hold back General Hill's leading brigade. Away to the north I could see that there were infantry. I wrote it all down.

"Sir it looks like a Corps is heading from the east. I think it is the one we saw yesterday. "

"Well done Lowe." That was valuable information as it meant we knew its rough numbers.

I turned to Trooper Grant. "Ride back to General Hill and tell him that it is just cavalry to his fore but there is a Corps on its way." I pointed due west. "Try to get there the quickest route. We will come with you part of the way and see if we can help clear a path for you."

I turned to the troopers. "Right boys, here is where we earn our pay. We are going to clear a path so that Grant can take the message to the general. Follow me."

We headed down the hill towards Pitzer's Run. Ahead of us were the troopers holding the horses of the dismounted horsemen. It was too good a target to miss. "Grant, ride like the wind! Open fire!"

We blazed away with out Colts. Two of the men holding horses fell and another two went for their weapons. The noise of battle meant that we were in a private little war with these men holding their horses. They made the mistake of trying to use their carbines and we closed with them, firing at almost point blank range with our pistols. One trooper tried to grab Copper's reins and he was rewarded by a bite on the arm. He fell screaming to the floor to be trampled by Corporal Lowe's horse.

"Drive those horses!" There were enough loose horses now to cause a panic amongst the troopers who were busy fighting General Hill's attack from behind the wooden fences. Finally an officer saw us and turned his men to fire at the new target. I emptied my gun and drew my second. I contemplated dismounting until Corporal Lowe shouted, "Sir! On the ridge behind us!"

To my dismay I saw that the leading elements of the Corps we had seen were forming up on the ridge. "Let's get out of here!"

We had done all that was asked of us and now it was time to escape the two rocks which threatened to crush us. I saw a trooper fall but I had no idea which one it was. This was no time to stop. A blue coated trooper ran from the woods with his rifle aimed at me. He pulled the trigger and I expected a flash and then my demise but his gun either misfired or he had forgotten to load it. I grabbed the end of his rifle and pulled him towards my boot which crunched against his chin. I spun the rifle so that it was like a lance. It still had the bayonet attached. We galloped down the creek. General Hill's men must have been pushing the vedettes back for blue troopers streamed down the slope to cross the creek. I slashed the bayonet across the face of one trooper and speared a second. My men were still firing as we galloped away from the fray and soon the creek bed was filled with dead Yankees.

We rode until our horses slowed with exhaustion. I turned in the saddle. I had six men left. We had lost two troopers. Climbing the bank I headed for our own lines but I kept a good watch; General Jackson had not been killed by our enemies but our own men. Soldiers would be more than a little nervous this day.

We reached the headquarters without incident. General Hill strode towards me. "Captain Hogan. Have you news?"

I knew then that Trooper Grant had perished. "I sent a trooper sir. The force in front of you is nothing more than a dismounted Cavalry Corps but the Yankees have reached Cemetery Ridge and are digging in."

"Damn Pettigrew. Thank you sir. When you have rested could you ride to the Chambersburg Pike. Your men have not reported yet from the north."

"Gladly sir."

I made sure the men dismounted and watered their horses. The nearby creeks were a godsend but soon they would be brown and salty with men's blood. I had now lost three men and it was barely eleven o'clock. General Hill had been correct; had General Stuart been on hand then the battle might already be over. A handful of troopers had caused a near collapse of part of the line. I imagined the effect of the best Confederate Cavalry.

"How are we for ammunition?"

The two sergeants went around the men. "We still have twenty or thirty rounds apiece."

"Corporal Lowe, take two men and see what you can get from the dead Yankees." While they were gone we reloaded our weapons and made sure we grabbed something to eat and drink. This promised to be a long day. I could not remember the last time I had slept. I could see stretchers returning with the dead Alabama men. I watched each one in case my men were amongst them but they were not.

Corporal Lowe came back with a healthy supply of balls and powder. We shared them out and then I mounted the men. "We are heading north. Keep your eyes open for our men."

We had to navigate through brigades which were hurriedly being sent to shift the Union cavalry. They had sharpshooters who fired at us as we passed. Bullets and balls zinged around us. When we reached the Chambersburg road we could see heavy fighting. A major from a North Carolina regiment grabbed my reins. "Who are you boys with?"

"We are General Hill's scouts, the 1st Virginia Scouts sir."

He pointed to an unfinished railway line. "There are some Yankee cavalry holding us up there. Could you and your boys get around them and flank them?"

I almost laughed at him; seven men to make a flank attack? It was ludicrous but I could see the pleading in his eyes and the dead men lying on the Pike.

"Yes sir, we will do our best. Follow me." I led the men down the Pike away from the battle. It would have taken infantry much longer to cover the same distance. I could see the ridge ahead and I took us towards the railroad line.

I was about to begin to move down it when there was a sudden movement from our left. All hands went to our guns until I saw it was our men. It was Sergeant Ritchie and seven men. "Thank heavens it's you, sir. We were knocked about a bit. "

I gestured with my thumb. "As was I. Come on Sergeant Ritchie, we are going to make a flank attack on the cavalry."His eyes widened in surprise but he said nothing.

We approached in single file. We passed the bodies of the men killed in the earlier encounter. I held up my hand and slipped my carbine out. I dismounted and gestured for horse holders. Two men took the animals and I crouched as I led the men forwards. The men to the right of the railroad were firing at the major's men and they were exposed. I knelt and took aim. When I was sure that we were all in position I shouted, "Fire!"

We were only a handful of carbines but the shock of that volley on an unprotected side was devastating. "Pour it into them boys!"

We were either kneeling or lying down and the uncoordinated rifles did little damage as the Union soldiers fought back. Suddenly my carbine jammed. I slung it across my back and drew my Colt.

"How are we doing, Sergeant Ritchie?"

"Trooper Wainwright is dead and Trooper Dunn is wounded, otherwise we are doing well." He paused, "Considering our asses are hanging out in the wind here."

"Don't worry, we'll move as soon as we can."

I was contemplating pulling back to the horses when the troops before us ran back to form a new line. I heard a bugle sound the advance and knew that they had reinforcements. We had done enough here. "Pull back."

As we passed the dead Yankees we took their weapons and ammunition. I hoped that my carbine could be repaired but our master gunsmith, the Sergeant Major was many miles away. We rode back the way we had come. The major swept his hat off. "Thank you very much Captain. You bought us just enough time to bring up some fresh troops."

We waved and galloped back to General Hill. Even as we rode I could see that we were advancing, albeit slowly. There was no one taking pot shots at us this time. The camp appeared devoid of any senior officer and I was directed towards Willoughby Run.

"Sergeant Ritchie, get the camp organised and find some food." Although we could still fight our horses were so exhausted that another patrol might result in a serious injury and we had no way of gaining remounts. I stood patiently while the general spoke to his colleagues. He gestured me over when he had finished.

"Sir, we now have a continuous line to the north. When I left the Chambersburg Pike the Yankees were throwing in their reserves."

He clapped me around the shoulder. "That is excellent news. Now if General Ewell can do as General Lee has ordered and take Cemetery Ridge then we can win this battle tomorrow." He suddenly seemed to see me for the first time. "Captain you get some rest for you and your men. We will need your eyes and ears tomorrow. I can guarantee that."

I was dog tired and I think the general's words had made me realise just how tired I was. Walking Copper back to our lines I heard the crump of the cannon as they added their firepower. This was no longer a skirmish. This was the battle which would decide the war and the future of America. The Confederacy had their best generals and their best men. If we could not defeat them now then we never would. It was a sobering thought.

Gettysburg- Day Two

Chapter 14

Sergeant Jones and his men had arrived and, like us, had lost men. We had lost men before but never so many and in such a short space of time. I hoped that the rest of the regiment was faring better.

We had food and we sat around our fire as the afternoon drifted towards evening. We had no tents but it had been a hot day; it was still warm and we would sleep beneath the stars. As Sergeant Jones pointed out, we were better off than our dead comrades.

After we had eaten I fiddled on with the carbine but it stubbornly remained broken. It would have to wait until the Sergeant Major returned for a repair. The whole company sharpened swords and cleaned weapons while there was still light. I berated myself for allowing the carbine to become damaged. It had been a lack of care which had caused it. I knew that I could pick up a single shot carbine but I would stick with my three Colts. Perhaps I would pick another up the next day anyway.

Just then we heard some soldiers marching and singing as they came towards us. The song was the '***Mountains of Mourne***' and the voices were Irish. I looked up and suddenly realised that they were Union soldiers. They still looked aggressive and full of fight. It made me wonder what had made them surrender. When they saw our badges I saw them halt. The guards with them looked confused.

"Come on you Micks move on now."

One of them, a sergeant, tried to lurch towards us. "It's them murdering bastards. The ones who killed our boys!"

The corporal guarding them tried to hold the big sergeant but he broke free and swung a haymaker at me. I moved my head out of the way and as he lumbered he lost his balance and I hit him on the side of the head. He fell like a sack of potatoes. My men had their Colts out, trained on the rest in an instant.

Sergeant Jones' Welsh voice sounded in the silence which followed. "Listen you bog Irish. One more move and we will save the Confederacy the trouble of feeding you! Pick up your thug here and in your words, feck off!"

There was a rumble of discord and suddenly twenty Colts were cocked. The corporal in charge shrugged apologetically, "Come on boys, its Andersonville for you." They picked up the unconscious sergeant and trudged sullenly off.

Sergeant Ritchie lowered the hammer on his Colt and said. "Next time I see a Union Irish man I shoot first and ask later."

The last guard escorting the prisoners said, "Well there are thousands out there. This is the Irish Brigade and they are the craziest fighters in the whole Union army."

I was almost shell shocked when they had gone. They had not even known my name and yet they were willing to kill me, or die trying. I had to do something about this. I had to find Sergeant Mick Callaghan and end this.

I ached when I awoke the next day. I was as tired as I had ever been. The guns had awoken me before dawn as the first cannons fired over the field of Gettysburg.

General Hill had secured Seminary Ridge and the cannons were arrayed along its top. Across the valley, along Cemetery Ridge, we could see the bristling Union guns. Ewell had not removed the threat and now the Confederate grey would have to rid the hill of the blue by its red blood. We now held the high ground to the west but the crucial ridges were held by the Union. I also heard that they had control of the rocky land in which we had hidden a couple of days earlier. It would be like getting a winkle from its shell to remove the Yankees from there.

General Hill summoned me to his early morning meeting just before dawn. I was grateful for the good nights sleep and felt more refreshed than I had for some time.

"Ah Captain Hogan, you are refreshed I hope, for today we will need you and your invaluable scouts even more than we did yesterday." He lowered his voice and put his arm around me. "General Stuart, it appears, is stuck close to Hanover where he and the Union cavalry are fighting their own battle. You are our only eyes and ears. I need you to infiltrate their lines and find out their numbers." He saw the look of horror on my face. "Oh, come sir. I know you have been behind enemy lines before now."

I had but then I had been with Dago Spinelli, a man I trusted implicitly and whom I knew would get me out of any jam I might find myself in. Of course I could not say that. "Of course sir. What are your instructions?"

"I wish you and one of your comrades to get to Cemetery Ridge and ascertain what their dispositions are."

I bit my tongue. Had General Ewell done as ordered we would know that already. "Very well sir. Give me an hour to make my preparations."

I took a detour to the medical tent where the Irish prisoners who had been wounded were being treated. I saw the orderly at the entrance and I waved him over.

"Yes sir. How can I help you?"

"Those Irish boys who were just brought in have you any who have head wounds?"

"A few of them sir. Why?"

"I need to ask one a couple of questions." He gave me a questioning look. "Listen orderly the general has asked me to go behind the enemy lines. If I am to return than I need all the information I can get." He still hesitated. "I promise that I will not endanger the man's life."

He nodded. "But I will be with you."

"Very well." I pointed at his white coat. "Have you a spare one?"

He went into the tent and brought one out. "There is this one but it is a little bloody." He smiled at me as though he expected me to baulk at the sight of blood.

I put it on over my uniform. "I have waded through blood. This is nothing."

Once inside I was pleased to see that the interior was dark and it was difficult to make things out. He led me to a bed where there was a soldier with a heavily bandaged head. It covered his eyes. I knelt down next to the bed. I put my mouth close to his ear.

"Listen friend, I am Mick Geraghty from the 28th. I have just found those boys Mick O'Callaghan is looking for."

I heard him start. "The Wildcats?"

I was putting the accent on heavily. "Aye. I'll split the reward with you."

I heard suspicion in his voice. "I don't know you and besides how will you get to him?"

"I promise that if I get the reward I will share it with you. You have my word on that." I was not lying for I had no intention of getting any reward. "As for how I can get away, well they thought I was dead and left me with the corpses."

He reached up and grabbed the bloody white coat. He rubbed the sodden material with his fingers. Seemingly satisfied he laid back down. "He is with the gunners at the southern edge of Cemetery Ridge. Just before the Devil's Den."

"Thank you son. Now you rest."

I stood and left. The orderly followed me. As I handed him the bloodied coat I said, "Satisfied?"

He nodded, "But why are you looking for this man?"

"He has put a price on the head of a couple of friends of mine and I want to make sure that he isn't around to pay it." I realised how cold and hard my words and voice sounded when the orderly shuddered.

"I wouldn't want you to be on my trail."

"Nor will this sergeant either."

When I reached my men they gathered around expectantly. I felt that I was letting them down but I had no choice, I had my orders."I have been ordered by General Hill to go behind enemy lines." There was a collective gasp from my men. "I need a volunteer, a foolish volunteer, to come with me. I am not certain if either of us will return."

Every hand went up. I caught my breath. I was touched as never before. "Thank you for your support. Sergeants and corporals, I cannot take you for you will need to lead the rest of the men. I cannot take the married men, that would be unfair and I cannot take a recruit. That leaves Trooper Duffy."

Trooper Duffy had been with us for a year and had come from the 2nd Virginia. He was quiet but I had noticed that he was both reliable and never panicked. He was also single. His wife and child had died of the influenza. However the other factor in his favour was that he was Irish and that would help with our deception. He was my only choice.

I saw the disappointment on the faces of the others, especially my two sergeants. "Trooper Duffy, go to the medical tents and see it they have two uniforms from dead men. Try to get us a couple of Irish regiments."

Duffy nodded. "Any particular rank sir?"

"Not an officer; we don't want to get noticed."

I turned to the two sergeants. "You two will need to take the rest of the company and scout for the general. Do the same as you did yesterday. I should be back by late afternoon."

"If you aren't sir then we will come looking for you."

"No Sergeant Jones. Your job is to keep as many men alive as you can. If I don't return then the colonel will need as many good men like you as he can get." I paused. "Sergeant Ritchie, watch Copper for me. I'll be on foot today."

Duffy came back with two uniforms, a corporal and a private. "I had little choice for you sir. This was the only one big enough to fit you. He handed me the corporal's jacket. I could see blood on the chest and a small cut. I shivered. I was stepping into dead men's shoes. The kepi fitted well. I did not need to change my gun as Colts were used by the Union.

Sergeant Ritchie handed us our muskets. I noticed that they were smoothbore. He saw my look. "The Irish Brigade uses these with one large musket ball and four smaller ones. It makes them like a shotgun."

General Hill's aide appeared and nodded his approval. Then he saw our guns. "That won't do. Your uniforms are for the 28th Massachusetts; they use Enfield rifles. Wait here I'll get a couple."

I handed them back to the sergeant. "Keep these close they may come in handy."

By the time the aide returned with the guns dawn was breaking. "You had better get off captain. Good luck. Have your men escort you through our lines. We don't want your head blown off by our own side, do we?"

With that grim thought we headed east. We reached the Emmitsburg Road and saw that there were no Union forces before us. The gunners looked askance at us as we were escorted by our comrades. We could see the early light in the east and we said our farewells.

One of the artillerymen said, "You letting those Yankees go?"

As Duffy and I ran down the slope I heard Sergeant Jones say, "Those are our boys. You see them later and mind that you don't shoot them."

That thought had worried me. How would we get back? I could see how we could infiltrate their lines before the battle started but not when it was in full swing and we would have to return to our own lines when the battle was at its fiercest. We would cross that particular bridge when we had to.

There were still bodies littering the ground. Reb and Yankee lay in grotesque piles showing where they had fought and died. Instead of heading directly up to Cemetery Ridge I headed down the valley and along Plum Run. I deemed that it would be easier to cross the lines in the tangle of rocks and undergrowth that lay at the southern end of the Federal lines.

The rifle was far heavier to carry and I contemplated ditching it but that would have made the Union soldiers suspicious. There was much to be said for having a horse. We moved as swiftly as we could down that stream. When we heard horses we threw ourselves to the ground and feigned death. The Union horsemen passed us without reacting. We rose and moved on.

As we neared the spot where we had hidden from the cavalry I saw, to my dismay that it now bristled with guns and barriers. This would be a hard place from which to dislodge the enemy. I could see that an engineer had worked at that. I remembered how formidable it had been before they had done their work. It would be as a fortress now.

"Let's cut left. They look to be on the alert here. Let's try further up."

The going was a little easier towards the end of Cemetery Ridge but we had to move slowly for fear of alerting the sentries who would, no doubt, be watching for a Confederate attack. We were now behind the lines for the Union forces still held part of the Emmitsburg Road.

Suddenly we heard a voice say, "Halt, who goes there?"

"Corporal Geraghty and Private Duffy of the 28th."

Duffy and I had decided to accentuate our accents. "What the hell are you Irish boys doing here? You are supposed to be on the Emmitsburg Road." The sergeant who had appeared narrowed his eyes, "You ain't deserting are you?"

I snorted, "And who the hell ever heard of an Irishman running away from a fight. We have been sent to get some more ammunition. There's a mess of Rebs just raring to attack us and the colonel sent us to get some more .69 calibre balls."

"And who is the colonel?"

The sergeant was still suspicious. Luckily the general's aide had told us that the colonel of the Irish Brigade was Colonel Kelly. I decided to be bold and aggressive. "Why, Colonel Kelly of course. Listen sergeant, if you want to take us back to the colonel for you to confirm who we are I would be delighted. I like nothing better than watching him chew out sergeants."

"Ah get away with you. You'll find the wagons a mile or so yonder."

And with that we were through and able to do our job. I could see, as soon as we left the forward areas that they were bringing up many cannon. These were not the outdated smoothbore we had seen in our own lines. Some of these were breech loaders and others still had the factory grease on them. I dared not risk making notes as I would normally do.

"Keep a note in your head of what we see eh Trooper?"

He nodded, seriously, "Yes sir."

I decided to head for the wagons containing musket balls as it would aid our escape and also make us less conspicuous. We trudged, as though we were weary soldiers, towards the wagons which were close to the Baltimore Pike. The soldiers in charge of them were cooking up a breakfast and we could smell the ham sizzling in the pan. I felt hunger pangs even though, until then, I had been too nervous to eat. Bacon will do that to you.

A lieutenant came out of one of the tents. "Yes corporal, what can I do for you?"

"Colonel Kelly's compliments and he would like some .69 calibre musket balls."

A sergeant wandered over as the lieutenant, who looked to be barely old enough to shave said, "Where is your supply chit corporal?"

The grizzled sergeant laughed, "Let's get rid of that old ammo sir. They are the only ones mad enough to still use the old smoothbore."

"And sir, the colonel was too busy fighting Rebs to have the time to write anything down."

I saw the lieutenant colour at the implied criticism. "Oh very well. The sergeant is right. It will clear space for more useful ammunition anyway."

The sergeant winked at me as the lieutenant returned to his tent, "Will you have a bite to eat with us corporal. We have plenty."

As much as I wanted to head back to our lines I knew that it would be odd to refuse the food and so I grinned back at the sergeant, "Of course. We have been on iron rations for the past two days and that ham smells mighty fine."

He led me over, "We have some eggs too. There was a little farm we passed and it would have been pure wrong to leave the eggs for those civilians." The men made a space around the fire. They had cut logs for seats and Duffy and I sat next to each other. We held our mugs out and the hot steaming coffee was poured in. It seemed like weeks since we had had decent coffee.

"You boys help yourselves." I noticed that they used their bayonets to spear the ham. A private flipped the eggs on to slices of fried bread. I almost forgot there was a war as the yolk and bacon grease ran down my chin. The fried bread reminded me of home in Ireland. That was a rare treat. When we had managed to get a piece of bacon Caitlin and I would have bread dipped in the bacon grease while my father enjoyed the bacon.

"What is it like at the front, corporal?"

"Those Rebs might not have the best of weapons, sergeant, but they are mad buggers. They keep coming at you when a normal man would give up."

"Aye, we heard that." He pointed behind him. "Don't you worry we have plenty of cannon. If they try to cross that ground then they will be slaughtered."

One of the privates shook his head. "Even the Rebs wouldn't be stupid enough to do that."

We had finished our food and I was keen to get back to General Hill with the information we had gleaned. "Well thank you for your hospitality. Now if we could have those musket balls we can get back into this war."

There was a large case of them. We could barely lift it. "It's a pity there are no mules. We had a whole bunch of them until Jeb Stuart and his boys stole them."

I hid a smile. That had been us. "Don't worry, besides this is easier. Those Rebs have sharpshooters."

We turned to head back west. I took a slight detour to the southern end of the ridge. I wanted to examine the earthworks more closely. From close up they were even more formidable. As we headed down the slope I noticed the white flag with the green shamrock on it and the men sleeping by the cannon. It had to be Mick O'Callaghan and his men. The description had been too accurate for it to be any other. The thought flitted across my mind that I could end the threat to the colonel and the major there and then. My sense of duty and the presence of Trooper Duffy dissuaded me. I now knew where the sergeant was and I could return, if I survived this crossing.

We hurried down the slope a little to enable us to cross the valley. I was just trying to work out when we could ditch the ammunition when a general and some staff officers rode in the same direction as us.

"Colonel I don't care what General Meade says, my men have nothing to fire at here. Now, that Wheatfield down there looks much better."

"General Sickles, we have our orders."

The general suddenly noticed us. "Hey you two men. Stop." I almost panicked. Had we been discovered? "Are you boys with Colonel Kelly and the Irish Brigade?"

"Yes sir, we are that!" I laid the accent on with a trowel and gave him what I hoped he would take as an Irish smile.

"And you boys are dug in on the road yonder? Just past the wheat field and the orchard we can see?"

"We are indeed sir; right in the Reb's faces."

"Then I am decided. We can support the front line. We will not win this war by hanging back. We need to strike with purpose. The Third Corps will move in that direction." He pointed to the wheat field and as he did so he flipped me a silver dollar. "Here's for your trouble sir and tell your colonel that soon he will have the finest Corps in the army to support him."

"Thank you kindly sir."

I had to get back now. The general had just negated the effect of the cannon. They would not be able to fire at an advance from our forces for fear of hitting their own men. When we reached the sergeant who had stopped us earlier he grunted, "Well you weren't deserters then. Next time make sure you have written orders. If not you might get shot."

"Thank you for your trouble sergeant." We descended towards Plum Run. Once we reached the dead ground out of sight of both sides I halted. "I think we can get rid of this."

"It seems a shame to waste these musket balls, sir." Trooper Duffy looked ruefully at the US Army packing case.

He was right. "Break it open and we will carry what we can. " We both had haversacks and they could carry a fair weight of musket balls. Once we had taken as many as we could we emptied the rest into Plum Run. I wondered if they would ever be discovered.

It was much easier to move now but, unfortunately the attacks had begun and we heard muskets popping away occasionally punctuated by the boom of a cannon. "Well Duffy we are now in the lap of the gods. I don't know how we are going to get across the Yank lines."

We moved up the slope towards the Emmitsburg Pike. I could see the blue coats of the Irish Brigade. Their backs were to us. I saw that the line ended some hundred yards to our left. I pointed up the slope and we crabbed our way across the hill. We were just beyond the last man. "If we move down there we can ditch these uniforms and cross into our lines." Although we were not wearing Confederate uniforms, we would not be marked as Yankees by showing blue uniforms.

I found a dell and we crouched down to take off our jackets. We had barely done so when I heard a voice behind me. "Are you two deserting?"

There was a patrol of five men. They were five yards away, no more. Our disguises would not work now and I had to take the offensive. I nodded to Duffy and raised my Enfield. I knew it was loaded but I would only have one shot. The bullet slammed into the sergeant and I thrust forwards with my bayonet at the man behind him. He was taken by surprise and the blade slid into his side. He was a strong man and he wrenched the rifle from my hands. Duffy had killed one man but a second was raising his gun to shoot. I picked up the haversack containing the musket balls and hurled it at him. The lead missile smashed into the side of his skull. I drew my pistol and shot the soldier who was pointing his musket at me. It was a smoothbore. If he had pulled the trigger then I would be dead. I just managed to fire it before he did and his face disappeared.

I heard a cry from behind me and saw Trooper Duffy being bayoneted in the arm. I swung the Colt and killed his assailant before he could give the coup de grace. I slung the haversack over my shoulder and then picked up Duffy. The wound was bleeding but not heavily. I threw him over my shoulder.

"Leave me sir."

"Not on your life. We don't have far to go." I had just stood when I heard a pistol sound behind me. "I expected the thud of a bullet but there was nothing. "What the hell was that?"

"The man you bayoneted tried to shoot you."

"Thank you, trooper. You have just saved both of our lives."

We were not out of the woods yet. The firing had alerted both the Irish Brigade and our men. I struggled up the hill. The added weight made it doubly difficult. "They are chasing us sir."

"Keep firing. It may keep their heads down."

I could not see our men but I knew they must be close. I yelled, in desperation, "1st Virginia Scouts coming in. I have a wounded man."

The silence ahead was ominous until suddenly a line of muskets appeared and they fired. I heard the cries from the Yankees following as we crashed into our front lines. As I lay, with Duffy still draped across my shoulders I heard a familiar voice say, "Well sir, you are still Lucky Jack."

I looked up at Sergeant Ritchie. We had made it. While he and the other troopers took Duffy to the doctor I hurried to headquarters. General Hill was outside of his tent and was conferring with his senior commanders. His aide looked up as I approached, "It's Captain Hogan!"

Every face turned towards me. "Well Captain, what news for me?"

I went to the map. "Here they have built barriers to protect their flank. Along the ridge they have eighty guns at least." I ran my finger along the Emmitsburg road. "Here they are thinly defended but the Third Corps is about to march here," I pointed to the wheat field.

"You are certain?"

"I heard General Sickles himself give the order. Their cannon will not be able to support him."

General Hill slapped his hand, "Order General McLaws to sweep the Third Corps from the field." As the messenger galloped off he turned to me, "Well done, Captain Hogan. That may be the turning point that we needed."

I reached the camp when Sergeant Ritchie was returning from the infirmary. "How is Duffy?"

"He might lose the arm but at least he is alive. If you hadn't carried him back then he might have died, sir."

I felt exhausted but it was barely past mid morning. There were men dying out there. "Get the men mounted; we'll see what we can do to expedite matters."

By the time I had donned my uniform my men were ready to ride. The day already seemed to have lasted a lifetime and yet the first attacks against Cemetery Ridge were just beginning.

We headed for the Emmitsburg road. Already General Hill's men were pushing the blue coated regiments back to Cemetery ridge. I could see General McLaws infantry driving towards the Third Corps who were isolated between the Peach Orchard and the wheat field. This was where General Stuart and his cavalry would have been invaluable. They were not there and we were. We would have to do the job.

"Sergeant Jones, we will ride down Plum Run and see if we can surprise them on their flank."

We passed the first casualties who were returning from the attack on the ridge. The cannon might not be able to support General Sickles but they still turned Plum Run into a Valley of Death. I forced myself to ignore the carnage. We could do little about that but we could ease the pressure at the southern end of our line. The smoke had filled the valley and made it easier for us to move in the dead ground without being seen. We must have been the leading Confederates in this area. When we reached the wall lining the road I halted the company. "Dismount, horse holders!"

We crouched behind the wall of the road which dissected the wheat field from the orchard. The troopers took up a position behind the wall. As I peered over I saw the men of the Third Corps trying to form lines to face the advancing infantry. They were being decimated by the fire from the cannon. They might have been old fashioned smooth bore cannon but they were close enough to be able to use canister.

"Ready! Fire!"

My handful of men rose and began to fire into the flanks of the soldiers who now found themselves assaulted from two directions. When they tried to turn to face us we had the wall to protect us. This was where I missed my carbine. My pistol would be ineffective at this range and the Enfield I had had still remained with the dead Irishmen.

A company of infantry were ordered to charge us. "Stand to! They are charging." I drew my Colt and began firing at the infantry who ran with their bayonets towards us. I holstered my empty gun and drew my second. They were so close now that I could not miss but there were so many of them that I soon had an empty gun. I drew my sabre and retained the pistol in my left hand.

"Hold them boys!" A private thrust his bayonet at me; I struck the deadly blade away from me with my Colt and slashed him across the neck with my sabre. He fell dead. A second private climbed the wall and prepared to stab down at me. I swung my sabre sideways and it sliced through his leg. He fell screaming on to four men on the other side. I used the small lull to put my empty pistol in my belt and draw my last loaded gun. I leaned over and emptied it into the huddle of men who were struggling to rise from the other side of the wall.

I saw Sergeant Ritchie trying to fend off three attackers with his sword. He was isolated. I threw myself bodily at them with my sword held before me. We fell in a heap. My sword had impaled one of them but was stuck. I let go of it and drew my knife from my boot. I stabbed blindly in the direction of the blue uniform before me. I felt it strike something and I heard a scream and I twisted the blade. The scream became higher but I was able to withdraw my knife. I sensed something from my left and I swung my empty Colt. It crashed satisfyingly into something solid and I saw a private lying, holding his head. Sergeant Ritchie thrust his sword into his neck and we stood. His side was bleeding but he could, at least, stand.

"Thank you sir. I guess I owe you my life."

"We have no time for that now." I looked along the line. We had held but only just. The infantry were falling back in disorder. Suddenly I heard the rebel yell and General McLaws men fell upon the disordered Third Corps. They could not stand and they either fled or surrendered.

"We're done here. Let's see the butcher's bill."

As we rode back along Plum Run and then up the ridge I reflected that we had done our duty but there were five troopers who would lie forever in that charnel house of the Valley of Death.

We had some good news when we returned to General Hill's camp. His aide greeted us warmly. "Well done Captain Hogan. I heard that you helped to destroy their attack. The general thanks you. And we have some good news for you too. General Stuart and his men are in Gettysburg."

My smile must have shown my feelings. "I am afraid you will not be able to rejoin them just yet. General Hill has another task for you first. Your men can return to their regiment but we need you to slip behind their lines again tonight."

Sergeant Ritchie's face fell, "That's not fair sir. The captain needs some rest."

The major did not know what to make of it and he looked at me for help. "Sergeant, that is enough. If the general needs me again then I will oblige him. We all obey orders don't we?"

His face assumed the look of someone who has just sucked a particularly sour lemon, "Yes sir."

"Ready the men but wait until I have been briefed before you return to the regiment."

As we walked to the general's tent the major mused, "Are all your men as loyal as that one captain?"

"Most of them sir. We tend to operate outside of the main army and it breeds a familiarity which might appear unusual. I apologise for the sergeant. He means well."

He shook his head, "No, I find it refreshing. Here at staff we see too much politicking. I would prefer to be as you are with men who fight for you and not merely with you."

I remembered how near the sergeant and I had come to death not more than two hours earlier. "Believe me sir, the politicking will not get you killed!"

He laughed, "You are probably right."

"Captain Hogan. I am sorry to call upon your services again but I need someone to go behind their lines and find out how much ammunition they have for their cannon."

I frowned, "But sir, I told you this morning; they have plenty of cannon and more than enough ammunition to fire all week. I can go back but I will be bringing the same message."

General Hill looked over to General Anderson, "This appears to contradict what you believe General Anderson."

General Anderson shrugged. "All I said was they did not fire their guns as often as I expected them to. I believe they were conserving their ammunition because they were running out."

General Hill stroked his beard and went to the map. "It could be that they were conserving their ammunition because they intend to launch an attack. Captain Hogan, are you sure about what you saw?"

"I had breakfast with the men and the supplies. I clearly saw the ammunition for the cannon."

"I trust your judgement. You and your men may return to your regiment sir. Thank you for your valiant efforts. I will go and see General Lee. This changes things."

As I walked back to my men I heard the battle still raging at the southern end of our lines where General Longstreet and his men were still trying to winkle the Yankees out from the warren of rocks known as the Devil's Den. This battle had already lasted two days and I wondered how long men would bleed for this desolate piece of land.

"Sergeant Ritchie, you will be pleased to know that I am no longer required to go behind the enemy lines. We return to the regiment."

He must have told the men of my impending mission for they all gave a huge cheer. I shook my head and mounted Copper.

Gettysburg- Day 3

Chapter 15

We took the Emmitsburg Road to get to Gettysburg. I knew that General Stuart would have the grandest house in Gettysburg for his headquarters. We found it quickly. Dago was outside enjoying a cigar when we arrived. He yelped his delight.

"I knew it; I told the boys that Lucky Jack would still be alive."

I shrugged, "What else did you expect? Where are the men camped?"

He saw Sergeant Jones behind me, "Half a mile north of town, sergeant."

I dismounted, "Take Copper with you sergeant and I will report to the colonel."

I strode up the steps as my depleted troop trotted off. I watched them as they departed. "You had it rough eh Jack?"

I nodded, "Yeah. We were chased all the way to Gettysburg and we have been doing the job of a regiment since we got here. And you?"

"I think the Yankees have the measure of General Stuart. They held us at Hanover and at Hunterstown today. They have a golden haired general who is the model of Stuart with bells on." His face became serious. "We lost Jed and some good men the other day."

I could not believe it. Jed was one of the last of the original Wildcats. Now there were just five of us left, the colonel, Harry, Danny, Dago and me. All the rest littered Virginia, Maryland and now Pennsylvania. I had thought that Jed would survive this war and I wondered about the rest of us.

"And I found out where that Irishman is who put a bounty on our heads." I pointed to the south. "He is less than two miles away."

"And that might as well be on the moon. There must be fifty thousand men on this battlefield. At least that's what the colonel said."

"You had better take me to him so that I can report."

The senior officers Wade Hampton, Fitzhugh–Lee and the colonels of all the regiments, were all gathered in the dining room. It was crowded and smoky and smelled of stale alcohol. They had all been drinking and bottles littered the floor. I couldn't help comparing this with the men who had just fought to try to take Cemetery Ridge and making do with stale bread and salty pork. There was little justice in this world.

Colonel Boswell saw me and walked unsteadily towards me, "Its Lucky Jack! Now we know we can win this battle!"

Everyone cheered and I felt sick to my stomach. To these men it was a game but to the poor troopers like Trooper Duffy, this was life and death. If he lost his arm Duffy would be crippled and would not be as lucky as old Stumpy. He would have to eke out a living. If any of these officers lost a limb he would be rich enough for it not to affect him.

"Sir, Captain Hogan reporting. General Hill has no further need of me."

"Excellent, Jack." Give the general your assessment of the battle thus far."

The room went silent and I realised that Dago and I were the only ones who were still sober. I sighed and explained what we had done. I told them of the Union resources I had discovered and the good defensive position the Yankees had created. None of them seemed at all put out by that.

"Don't worry Captain Hogan. We will strike tomorrow and defeat these damn Yankees. This upstart Custer will learn who the better general is!"

I wanted to leave that instant. This was all about egos. It was not about the south or the war; it was like Ireland all over again. The rich ruled and the poor suffered. Here the officers prospered while ordinary men died. Many of the generals I knew did not survive the war but it galled me that even incompetents like General Sickles, who, although he had lost a leg that day, had a great political career ahead of him. The men who lay in the wheat field had nothing.

I went outside with Dago. "How did Jed die?"

"It was at Hanover. We ended up charging and their horse artillery scythed into Jed and his troop. There weren't many survivors."

"How did Danny take it?"

Dago pointed to the north. "He's not here is he? He is in the camp with Harry and the men. Colonel Boswell spends more time with the other colonels than with us."

I looked at him. "And why are you here?"

He looked hurt for a moment then his shoulders sagged. "All the other colonels have an aide. I am only a lieutenant. I got the short straw." I could hear the bitterness in his voice.

"Never mind, Dago. I will keep you company." I looked to the south were we could still see the flashes of muskets in the Devil's Den. "We don't know how many more of these moments we will have." I sat on the stoop. "I never even got to say goodbye to him."

"Neither did I. That is a luxury we don't have." He pointed upwards. "He is up there and he is watching us."

"You believe that?"

Dago looked at me seriously, "We don't talk about God and stuff like that but I know that you believe that your mom is watching over you." I could not deny it and I nodded. "Then Jed is up there too and that gives me some comfort. He'll be watching our backs tomorrow. The battlefield is no place for an atheist."

We carried our drunken colonel back to our camp. The general's aide, who had not drunk as much as General Stuart, told us that we would not be operating with the Corps the following day but we had a special mission. My heart sank as we dragged our leader home. Special missions normally meant that my friends died.

We were up before dawn the next day. Harry threw his arms around me. "I couldn't believe it when Jed got killed. I thought we were special and nothing could touch us. The Wildcats are becoming fewer in number."

"I know. Listen Harry; let's not take as many chances now. I am not sure that it is worth it."

He laughed, "It never was. Remember Jack, that the colonel, when he was plain Mr Boswell, took us and gave us a life when we had nothing. You would still have been aboard the Rose, or drowned; who knows. Me? I would be either a drunk or dead in some bar fight. Jed and Dago are the same. So long as the colonel fights then we have to as well, because we owe him. Not the Confederacy and not General Jeb Stuart but James Boswell." He shook his head. "We can do nothing about that. Danny and I talked about this last night before you and Dago came back. Life is a great adventure. Don't over think it. We do this job and then you go and find your sister Caitlin."

I smiled and nodded and then I told him about Mary. "You are truly Lucky Jack. You have more reason to live than any of us. You have two women now in your life. That is twice as many as the rest of us put together. You will survive of that I have no doubt and the rest of us will watch down on you."

I was shocked, "Harry! This is not like you! You are not usually maudlin."

"No, but I am a realist, and I don't have your luck."

I headed for my tent and Sergeant Major Mulrooney strode over to me beaming from ear to ear. "I heard that you made it sir!"

"And I am glad to see you too." I handed him my carbine. "This broke a few days ago. You couldn't look at it for me could you?"

"Sir, I would be delighted."

The colonel was still a little hung over when the courier brought our orders. Danny read them. We were not to be with Stuart. We found out later that he spent the day fighting the Union cavalry at East Cavalry Field. Instead General Hill had requested that we support the attack of General Longstreet. We headed south to a date with destiny. We were to guard the right flank of General George Pickett's division as they attacked the heart of the Union lines at Cemetery Ridge.

We left as the first thin light of dawn peered over the eastern horizon. As we headed down the Emmitsburg Road we could see the fires of the Union pickets flickering on the skyline. The supply sergeant was probably beginning to fry his bacon and brew his coffee as we passed the Confederate troops who were making do with stale bread and watered down coffee dregs. The men we passed were, however, in good spirits.

"Yee haw boys, you give 'em hell!"

We cheered them back. They probably thought we were going to charge the lines. Artillery men always liked the thought of their own cavalry hurtling across a field with guidons fluttering and sabres shining. The reality was different. Danny waved me forward.

"Jack, you know this area well. The orders say that the attack will go directly east. Where does that place us?"

"There is a stream called Plum Run. We can leave the horses at Codori Farm and head down to the valley bottom while it is still dark." I looked at the lightening sky. "What time is the attack supposed to be?"

"Some time after noon."

"Then we better make sure we have plenty of ammunition and supplies."

Danny nodded. "Sergeant Ritchie, go and see what you can dig up. Do you know where the farmhouse is?"

"Yes sir."

"Then meet us there."

I nodded to Danny and pointed at the colonel's back. He was riding next to Harrison, the bugler and his shoulders sagged. "What is eating the colonel?"

"He enjoyed playing cavalryman; the charges and the fighting with sabres. It is what he always really wanted to do and now he is missing out on a cavalry battle. He doesn't like us being a supporting regiment. He wants us to be at the heart of the action."

"I have lost my appetite for action sir."

"I know what you mean." He smiled brightly, "Still if this attack works today and General Stuart can attack them in the rear then this war could be over. Abe will have to sue for peace if we are loose in Pennsylvania."

"I have seen their cannon sir. This will not be an easy battle. Those men will have to charge uphill into the teeth of a fierce cannonade."

"Well, Jackie boy, at least we will have a front row view of the whole thing eh?"

We left the horses with Sergeant James and four men. We should have left more but we had less than one hundred and twenty men left for this action. I was just pleased that Copper would be spared the fighting. I did not want lose my horse. Copper was worth more than a vainglorious charge. The colonel looked glumly at Major Murphy, "Well Danny, where to? You read the orders."

Danny deferred to me and I spoke, "Well sir, if we head down to the bottom of the valley we will be in dead ground. We can move forwards when the attack begins."

"You suddenly seem like an expert, Jack."

"I have been watching men attack across this valley for two days. The generals might have maps and know where the men are going but once the attack starts then anything can happen. I guess we need to be flexible."

Sergeant Ritchie and his men joined us. They had some sacks with them. "We managed to get some ham; it's none too fresh but it will be better than nothing. We managed to get some ammunition off the Yankee prisoners from the other day."

Colonel Boswell waved an impatient hand, "Come on then; Captain Hogan lead them off."

The artillerymen gave us a cheer as we marched in single file down the slope. "We'll blast a hole for you cavalry boys. You'll just walk right through them!"

Our troopers cheered but I was not so sure. Our guns were effective at close range but I did not think they would worry the Union forces too much. Cecil hurried to catch up with me. "Here sir," he handed me my carbine, "it sure was in a bad way. Lucky I kept some parts from bust up guns. It'll work fine from now on."

"Thanks Cecil, I don't know what we would do without you."

He glanced over his shoulder. The colonel was a good fifty paces behind us. "Between you and me sir, I wish I was your sergeant again. I am not cut out to be a Sergeant Major."

"You are Cecil but I am not sure that any of us are cut out for this."

When we reached the bottom I sent my company up the slope about a hundred yards. "Tell me what you can see."

When the colonel arrived I saw him pale as the dawn showed the bodies left over from the previous day. They were still littering the valley bottom. Reb and Yank were entwined in death. The smell would be atrocious once the July sun started to cook them.

"How come nobody moved these bodies?"

"I think they were more concerned with the living, colonel."

"They are going to stink when the sun gets up."

I looked at Dago and shook my head, "That's war sir. Men die and their bodies rot."

It seemed to me that the reality of the situation finally sank in. This was not the glorious picture of war envisaged by the colonel. His dream of leading a regiment behind Jeb Stuart in a charge to win the war was a pipe dream. He sank to his haunches.

Danny looked at him sadly. "Right, let's get the men organised. Sergeant Major Mulrooney, spread the men out below Captain Hogan's skirmishers. Tell them to rest while we can. Sergeant Ritchie, distribute those supplies." He looked at the stream. "I was going to say fill the canteens but I ain't going to drink that water."

I pointed to the north. "There are two good streams just the other side of the Emmitsburg Road." I saw Sergeant Jones on the hillside. "Sergeant Jones, collect some canteens and head for Pitzer's Run and get them filled with clean water."

While the sergeant and four men went back up the slope Danny and I slithered forwards to join my men. We could see, in the distance the ranks of cannon arrayed on the top of the ridge. Behind them we could just see the officers of the infantry regiments on their horses. I looked to the right and saw the Irish flag which marked the position of Mick O'Callaghan's guns.

"Those are the fellows who want us dead, Danny."

He looked in the direction I was pointing. "Where the flag is?"

"Yup. We know he is a sergeant but each gun will have one of those."

Danny looked at me; he had a wild grin on his face. "When the battle starts it would be nice and easy to crawl close to them guns eh? Mebbe end this once and for all." I nodded. Yes, I would like that too. I hated looking over my shoulder and wondering if they were just the enemy or murderers. But we would obey orders and follow the colonel.

It was just after noon when the one hundred and fifty Confederate guns began to roar across the valley. Soon the whole of the Emmitsburg Road was wreathed in smoke. We heard the whistling as balls and shells soared overhead. Strangely the Union guns remained silent. We could see nothing of our own lines now save a fog of smoke which rose in spirals. We knew that the men of Pickett's division would be assembling and preparing to charge the Union lines. I did not know how they would charge for if we tried it as cavalry we would have to pause before the final assault. They would be running uphill and I did not think they would move very fast. The temperature was soaring. Although I would not drink the polluted water of Plum Run I did soak my jacket in it to cool me down. Others followed suit.

The cannons fired for almost two hours and then they stopped. We all knew what that meant. The attack by the infantry would soon begin. Danny mobilised us. "Sergeant Major, get the men spread out. We will approach to within carbine range and harass the gunners."

I turned to Sergeant Ritchie, "Let's go sergeant."

I made sure, for the umpteenth time that my carbine was loaded and we began to move up the slope. The shape of the hill meant that we saw nothing until we crested a bump and we saw the guns. I could see they were ready to fire for each gun captain had his lanyard in his hand. We still had another hundred yards to go before we were in range. An officer saw us and I expected an order from them to fire but I suspect we were too few in number to worry about. I risked a glance back to our own lines and saw that the smoke had cleared. There was a line of men a mile long and they were marching resolutely towards us.

"Good God Almighty! Will you look at that?" There was wonder in Sergeant Ritchie's voice.

"Back to business, sergeant. We need to annoy these gunners and make them miss!"

We scrambled to a point some hundred and thirty yards from the guns. If they took it into their heads then we could have been brushed aside like flies but the mile wide column of men which was advancing was a much better target and we would be an annoyance only.

"Pick your targets and fire at will!"

I aimed at a gun captain who appeared to be ready to fire. I hit him and he fell. As he did so he pulled the lanyard and the gun went off prematurely. There was a ripple of carbines and then our sound was drowned out by the wall of noise and concussion as seventy nine guns belched forth flame and lead. Fortunately for me I had taken a prone position but I saw some of our troopers knocked down the hill by the concussion.

I saw that some of my men were staring up the hill, "Keep firing!"

I shot again and hit the artilleryman with the rammer. Others hit the crew as well and one gun, at least was out of action until they could man it again. Someone had had enough already and a line of skirmishers appeared at the ridge line.

Danny yelled, "Yankee infantry!"

We switched targets. The skirmishers had the Enfield rifle which was more accurate than our weapons. Our only advantage was that we could fire from a prone position. I aimed at a sergeant who was urging his men forward. He fell clutching his arm. I heard cries from around me as men fell. I kept firing until I had emptied my gun. I drew my pistol. The range was too great but the skirmishers were closing with us. All the while the guns behind them could not fire. We were, at any rate, still helping our comrades who were now almost at the bottom of the valley.

The colonel suddenly shouted, "Fall back!"

To my horror I saw some of the men with him turn and begin to run down the hill. It was the wrong decision to make. Our pistols would be more effective the closer the Union skirmishers came. The fleeing men were thrown to the ground by the volley from behind.

I turned to my men. "Face your enemy!"

I slung my carbine and fired four shots from my Colt in the direction of the blue uniforms heading for me. I stepped back a few steps and fired my last two shots. I changed guns. I could see the bodies of our troopers lying to the left of me. The skirmishers had now dropped to their knees and the cannon fired again. Glancing over my shoulder I saw that there were huge gaps appearing in the mile wide column. The men of Pickett's division were no cowards and they closed the gaps and relentlessly marched up towards the top of the ridge.

"My company! To me!"

I was on the extreme right and I did not want to become isolated. Sergeant Ritchie appeared with a handful of men. "Let's hold them here."

The ten of us knelt and began to fire as fast as we could reload. When I looked up the slope I saw that the skirmishers were falling back. I wondered why. When I looked behind me I saw the column had crossed Plum Run. It was now just half a mile wide but they were still marching relentlessly up the slope. They were singing patriotic songs. I could see that they only carried single shot rifle muskets. When they charged it would be with a bayonet; they were courageous men indeed.

I began to reload my carbine. I had a terrible thirst but I had no time to drink. "Right boys, let's go back up and annoy them some more."

Just then Cecil appeared at my shoulder. "Do you mind if I join you, sir?"

"Shouldn't you be with the colonel?"

In answer, he pointed to his left and there was the body of Colonel James Boswell bleeding his life away on Cemetery Ridge. His grand adventure had come to an end. "And the major?"

"He's been wounded too I had the lads carry him back to the farm." He pointed to Harry and Dago who had a knot of troopers with them and were making their way back up Seminary Ridge. "That's all that is left, sir. The rest are dead or wounded."

I was as angry as I had ever been. What a waste of good men! "Right, lads! We are going up that hill and we aren't going to stop until we have that flag with a Shamrock on it!"

They gave the rebel yell and we began to dodge and duck our way up the slope. The infantry column was now less than six hundred yards from the guns and the canister was sweeping all before them. Everyone in the Union lines was firing at Pickett's men. They had forgotten about us. They would pay for that error.

"Don't fire until I give the order." We got to within a hundred yards of our target. We were looking directly at the guns operated by Sergeant O'Callaghan and his men. "I want both of those gun crews killing! Fire!"

There were eleven of us and we fired our carbines at the two crews. They stood no chance. We were aided by the fact that, even as they died they fired their guns and we rushed the last few yards through a wall of smoke which hid us from view.

I found myself close to the limbers. A major rushed at me with his sabre. I fired my Colt at point blank range and his head disappeared. I saw blue everywhere and I fired until my gun was empty. I took my carbine and used it as a club. I had battle madness within me. Every face in a blue uniform was someone for me to kill. I was afraid of no one. I felt my arm being tugged and heard Cecil say, "Sir. We have done enough. Let's get back!"

I nodded. I saw a charge lying on the floor next to me still in the gunner's hand. I picked it and threw it towards the limber some forty yards away.

"Irish, shoot the bag and then drop to the ground!"

He laughed, "Sir, you are a mad bugger. Go on then!"

I picked up a second one and hurled it after the first. I threw myself to the ground. Cecil followed its arc and fired. He dropped almost immediately. The explosion deafened me and a wall of air knocked other gunners from their feet. I groggily stood as quickly as I could. I helped Cecil to his feet. "Get the men back to safety. I'll be right behind."

158

I was lying for I had one more job to do. I ran to the sergeant of artillery who was lying next to the flag with the Shamrock on it. He was barely alive when I reached him and was trying to push his guts back inside his body. He looked at me strangely

I put my face close to his, "Are you Mick O'Callaghan?" He looked confused but nodded. "I am one of the Wildcats you have been hunting. I guess I will claim my reward now eh?"

I reached inside his jacket but I found no wallet. Instead, I found a bundle of paper. I took them anyway. "Rot in hell, O'Callaghan!"I turned and ran. As I ran down the ridge I was forced to witness the slaughter of the men of Pickett's division. They were enfiladed by muskets and cannon and their flanks were filled with their dead and dying. I saw that it was enough for one Virginia regiment which fled down the hill. I did not blame them.

As I ran I passed familiar faces; they were the dead troopers we had led towards the guns. I felt balls and bullets buzzing around me but I led a charmed life and they all missed me. I almost fell in Plum Run but I managed to stumble across and up the other side. Suddenly there was a blinding light as a shell exploded above me. I found myself lying on the ground and looking up. Was this what death felt like?

I briefly closed my eyes for some peace and, when I opened them, there was Sergeant Ritchie and Sergeant Major Mulrooney standing over me. "Come on sir. I think you have just about used up all of your luck."

They half dragged and half carried me back to the farm. There was David, our doctor, seeing to our wounded. I looked for the faces of my friends. There was Dago, having his head bandaged and Harry lying on a cot looking white. At least two of my friends had survived.

I turned to look back at Cemetery Ridge; the survivors of the failed charge were flooding down the hill. Lee's gamble had failed. We would now lose this war. Of that I was certain.

"You had better lie down sir."

"It is alright Ritchie; I just had the wind knocked from out of me. Sergeant Major, see what the butcher's bill is."

"Sir!"

Ritchie handed me a canteen. "What were you doing at the end, sir? With that sergeant?"

"I was laying a ghost to rest. That was the man who put a price on our heads. He won't be paying it any more." I suddenly looked around the farmhouse. "Where is the major?"

"He didn't make it, sir. We passed his body in the bottom of Plum Run."

I suppose he would have wanted it that way. He had followed Colonel Boswell loyally and he had followed him in death. It was the end of an era.

The Sergeant Major's face was grim when he returned. "There are thirty men outside who are unwounded and these fifteen wounded sir. We have less than fifty men."

I looked at Harry and realised that I was now the senior officer. David wiped his hands on his apron and came over to me. "I hear you were knocked down. How are you?"

"I feel fine."

"Take off your jacket and let's have a look."

I reluctantly did as I was told and David examined me. He shook his head. "You will be black and blue in the morning but you appear to have survived intact."

"How are Dago and Harry?"

"Dago will be up and about by tomorrow. Harry? I am not sure. I took a ball out of his back but he has not regained consciousness yet." He looked sad.

I patted his arm, "I am sure you have done your best. Make sure you get some rest too."

"What now Jack? We are finished as a regiment."

"I know." I began to wonder what I would do. "I will put any decision off until we are back in Virginia."

There was an air of severe depression along the whole of the Confederate line. We had not lost but that was not enough we had had to win and in that, we had failed. I took the remaining troopers down the hill to bring back our dead. We saw Union troops doing the same but it was not the time to fight. It was the time to bury. We laid the dead out in a line close to Codori Farm. Hopefully, Dago would be able to help me make decisions the following day.

Sergeant Major Mulrooney was a tower of strength. He organised food and tents and even managed to send Sergeants Jones and Ritchie to collect ammunition. As he said to me, "Well sir, it seems to me that the generals always seem to use you and this regiment to do its dirty work. We had best be prepared."

I must have dozed off for David woke me, "It's Harry. He's awake."

I went to Harry. He had been my oldest friend. We had been equals from the days of the Wildcats: both sergeants, both lieutenants and now both captains. He had been from England and I had come from Ireland but we had shared much in our lives. We had had an easy friendship with little need for words. It felt sad to see him laid so low.

He gave me a brave smile. "Still Lucky Jack eh?" I nodded; too full for words. "You did well today. Your attack saved a lot of lives." He tried to shake his head but failed. "The colonel made some bad decisions today and the boys paid with their lives. I should have stayed with you. Well he has paid the final price. It's a shame about Danny. He should have been colonel. He knew how to look after men."

"You know he never would. He was the colonel's man through and through. He lived for James Boswell. He couldn't have lived in a world without him."

He coughed I noticed gobs of blood on his chest. David dabbed them off and gave me a sad look. "What will you do now Jack?"

"What will we do more like? We will wait until you are fit to travel. I daresay the army will be moving south soon. We weren't licked but we can't stay here."

"You'll be going back without me then." He gestured to David. "I know the laddo here is a good doctor but he is no miracle worker. I'm dying; it's just that there are bits of my body that don't know it yet." He closed his eyes briefly. "David says you got that Mick who was trying to kill us."

"Aye, well we got him. I knew which guns he was working and I found him when he was gut shot. He would have died slowly."

"Good. It's bad enough fighting without someone trying to collect your head as a bounty." He closed his eyes again and was quiet for quite a time. He opened them again. "I think I'll sleep for a while. Give me your hand Lucky Jack." I gave him my right hand. "You have been a good mate and I am proud to have had you for my friend. Don't waste your life on a lost cause. Find that girl and get yourself a life."

"I will and you will come to the wedding." He smiled and then closed his eyes.

David and I stood and went outside. The air was marginally cooler than it had been but I needed air. "He's dying. He knows it. That was goodbye." I felt choked up and I found I could not speak. I nodded and fought for control. I was now the senior officer in the regiment and it would not do to break down. But I wanted to.

A messenger arrived just before midnight. It was a sergeant and he looked at the handful of men before him. "Sir," he said looking at me, "General Hill wishes Colonel Boswell to report to him at headquarters."

I said, flatly, "The colonel is dead. I am the senior officer."

The sergeant face looked crestfallen. "I am sorry sir. Would you…"

"Of course sergeant." I turned to David. "Until Dago is awake I am afraid you are in charge."

He smiled, "You really mean Sergeant Major Mulrooney; well we are in good hands then."

I went to pick Copper up from Sergeant James. Sergeant James had not been the same since his wounding. "I am sure glad the horses weren't used today sir. It's bad enough men died but at least they have a choice. These dumb animals are too brave for their own good." His voice broke a little. "Ask the general if we can go home sir."

"I will do sergeant, I will do."

Copper and I endured a dispiriting ride through broken men. They appeared to shamble as though in a trance. I saw grown men crying on the side of the road. They were without wounds but inside their spirits had been broken. As I reined up outside the headquarters tent I heard three shuffling soldiers moaning. "If Tom Jackson had been here today it would have been the Yankees who would have been whupped!"

The sergeant gave me a lopsided smile as he rode off on his next errand. "It's what a lot of the boys are thinking sir. Good luck sir."

General Hill was sat at his table when I entered. He was alone and he looked ill. I had heard that he had not been well. He was a good general but perhaps his illness had prevented him from being able to influence the battle as he would have wished. He looked at me in some surprise.

"Colonel Boswell?"

"Dead sir, along with Major Murphy."

"Damn shame. They were fine officers." He took a deep breath as though dreading the answer. "How many men do you have left who are fit for duty?"

"Thirty sir and another fifteen or so who are wounded."

"Dear God! That must be hard to bear sir."

I nodded. "Sir, most of us joined Colonel Boswell when he was Captain Boswell and we fought as the Wildcats. We just sort of ended up as the 1st Virginia Scouts. The men are broken sir. They want to go home."

I expected a reprimand but he nodded. "I can see that. I'll see General Lee but I will recommend that the 1st Virginia Scouts be disbanded and any men who wish to join another regiment can do so."

"Thank you general."

"There are many of us who would hope that you would do so Captain Hogan."

"It is too early to say sir but at the moment I am not inclined to fight any more."

"I see. Well I have another task for you." He held up his hand. "It is not a hazardous task; at least I don't think it is. I want you to go to

Williamsport and ensure that we can cross the river. The army will be retreating soon."

Inside I sighed with relief. We could do that. "Yes sir. How long will it take to get the army across the Potomac?"

"That depends upon the Yankees and what they do here but I reckon no more'n ten days."

"Very well sir and you will make our case to the General?"

"Of course Captain Hogan. It is the least I can do. I will send the wounded with General Imboden and they will go a longer route to avoid the enemy. We must get our wounded home and you have to hold the bridge."

I nodded, "You have my word sir. I will not leave the bridge until I am relieved."

"That's all that I can ask."

I returned to the farm in higher spirits than I had left but soon I was plunged into despair. As soon as I dismounted I knew there was bad news. David and the Sergeant Major were waiting for me with grim expressions.

"It's Harry isn't it?"

"Yes Jack. He died half an hour ago. He just slipped away. I think he only waited to say goodbye to you." Lieutenant David Dinsdale looked on the brink of tears himself. "I am so sorry."

I was unable to speak. My eyes fell upon Cecil who nodded. "Leave it to me sir. I'll see to his body with the lieutenant here." He took a bottle of whiskey from the table. "Here sir. It won't be a true wake but have a drink to the captain. He was a lovely man."

I went outside and sat watching the battlefield and remembering my friends who had perished that day at Gettysburg.

The Road from Gettysburg

Chapter 16

I gathered all the men the next day outside the farm. Two more men had died during the night. "We have been given one more task. We have to ensure that Williamsport remains in our hands until the wagons with the wounded cross over the Potomac. I believe that General Lee will then allow us to be disbanded. Any man who wishes to continue to fight will be able to join one of the other regiments. There are many vacancies to fill." I looked at David. "I would like to take as many of the wounded who can ride."

He nodded, "There will be ten who can accompany you." He paused. "I will join the medical department. I'd like to save lives."

I shook his hand, "And we all applaud that sentiment."

"All of you can leave with your heads held high. No one in the whole Confederate Army could have fought better or achieved more than you did." I noticed that it had begun to rain. I looked up at the sky. "In Ireland we believe it is a good thing if it rains when you are burying those you have loved. It is God crying with you. This morning our last act will be to lay to rest all of our comrades and then we head south."

The graves had been dug already; the Sergeant Major had seen to that. Dago stood by me as I named each man as he was laid to rest. We buried them with their weapons. It was the right thing to do. David and Cecil had dressed the officers in their best uniforms. They would meet their maker looking like soldiers. We had few troopers left to say goodbye but, after we had all fired our guns we passed by each grave and said goodbye in out own way. It was the most sombre day of my life. I had not buried my mother and father; I felt like I was burying them now for this had been my family since I had come to America.

We left David to leave with the wagons which were being loaded with the wounded. They would be escorted by General Imboden and were taking the Greencastle route. It would be easier on the wagons and the wounded. We would be talking the shorter route to Hagerstown. We said little as we bade farewell to the wounded and David. We had no doubt we would be seeing them again in Williamsport.

As the rain pelted down and the two armies watched each other from their respective ridges we left Pennsylvania. We were like the tide which had reached its high water mark and was now ebbing. We ebbed south.

Our losses meant we had spare horses. We saw others looking enviously at them as we headed south along the rain sodden roads. Each man led two horses. This would be the pay off for men who had received no pay for many months. Most of the men had money we had acquired during our raids and all of the kept it well hidden about them. The horses could be sold for, when they returned to their homes, they would all find such beasts in great demand.

Dago rode next to me while the three remaining sergeants rode with Cecil at the rear. I knew that they would be doing as we were and talking of our dead comrades.

"It doesn't surprise me that you survived Jack. You were born to survive but I feel lucky too. I never thought I would see the war out and I definitely did not expect to ride away from Gettysburg."

"It was hell; quite literally."

"When the colonel ordered us to fall back I felt relief and then when that ball slammed into me I thought my world had ended." He looked at me, wiping the rain from his face. "You didn't fall back did you?"

I shook my head. "No. It was just the wrong thing to do. Those gunners weren't bothered about us. They had over twelve thousand Rebs marching towards them. We were like fleas on a dog. I like to think that when we took those few guns out on the ridge we saved a few men's lives."

"No, don't get me wrong. You were right. More of your men survived than those who fell back." We rode in silence for a while. We were constantly passing soldiers heading back to the south. Some were patently deserters. We saw the furtive looks they gave us and their hands hovered close to pistols. Others were the ones wounded early in the three day battle. Those too weak to walk would already be heading west in the wagons. We were passing a broken army. I recognised men from the famous Stonewall Brigade, his foot cavalry. They had followed Jackson blindly but now they shuffled home betrayed and broken.

We crossed Monterrey Pass and I could see why the wagons had taken the longer northern route. It would have been a painful and difficult journey for the wagons filled with injured men. I had already decided to stay for the night in Hagerstown. This was largely a selfish move on my part. I wanted to find Mary. However I also wanted my men out of the rain and I knew that there would be shelter there. Unless, of course, the Union held it.

We reached the railroad line in the late afternoon and early evening. I gathered the men around me. "Lieutenant Spinelli, stay here with the men. Sergeant Ritchie and I will scout out the town and make sure there are no nasty surprises."

"Sir, let me come too."

I smiled, "No Sergeant Major. Lieutenant Spinelli will need your help here. We have a responsibility to all the wounded. I can promise you that I will be careful."

Sergeant Ritchie smiled, "Don't worry, Irish, I want to get home. I'll keep the captain out of trouble."

The troop huddled beneath the canopy of trees adjacent to the woods. It kept some of the rain from them. We rode down the railroad tracks. The rain was easing and becoming the misty mizzle that seems to permeate your bones. For July this sure was wet up here in Maryland. I did not expect any trains. They would be coming from Chambersburg and that was too close to Gettysburg to make it safe for engineers. The station was deserted as we clip clopped along the rails.

"Sergeant, cut the telegraph wire to the station. Just in case."

With that done we rode through the houses just off the main streets. I was looking for signs of occupation. There would be flags or sentries. We saw none. I took us south to the outskirts of the town. I knew that Williamsport was just a few miles to the south. We could have reached it in a few hours but I wanted a day to scout it out. At least that was what I told myself. Besides which I knew that the wagons would not reach it for a couple of days at least. The real reason was I wanted the morning to find Mary.

"Right sergeant, let's sweep to the east of the town and approach the railroad from that direction."

"Sir."

As we rode we talked of our plans after the war. "What will you do when the war is over?"

"Go back to South Carolina. I have a little money saved. I thought I might earn a living teaching guitar." My surprised look made him smile, "I know it's as different as can be from what we do now. I'd just like to make something instead of destroying it. I find peace playing the guitar."

"You could always earn a living playing for folks."

He shook his head, "No sir. I am too shy. I don't mind playing for the boys. They are kind enough to like me but strangers? No sir. That's why I will teach. And you sir?"

"I suppose I will head back to Charleston and see if I still have a home there." I shrugged. "I owe it to Colonel Boswell to find Jarvis and

166

tell him what happened to his master. And I will look up the lawyer fellow who invested my money for me." I patted my saddlebags. "Like you I am not poor but I had a whole bunch of money tied up in the house and in investments. The colonel seemed to think it was a good idea."

"Yes sir, that was back when we thought that we could win."

I vaguely recognized the track we were taking. It led to the railroad and was the spot where I had had a run in with the Union troopers. I was alert and, thank goodness, so was Copper. The neigh and the whinny told me there were horses nearby. I held up my hand. Sergeant Ritchie halted and drew his Colt. I did the same. We waited. The rain had stopped but droplets still continued to fall from the leaves and branches. I heard what sounded like a shout. I spied a sort of narrow trail leading from the green road we were on.

We dismounted and led our horses down it. I saw a glow ahead which indicated a house of some description. The track twisted and turned until it eventually emerged at a clearing and farm house. It was a well made house and not rustic in any way. There was a stoop and a veranda which ran around the house. At the foot of the steps was a pair of hitching rails; attached to one there were four Yankee horses. We tied our mounts to the other hitching rail and I drew my second Colt. We went to the door where we could hear voices from within.

"Now listen you dumb bitch. We know there is gold in this house. Your husband and your son were too stupid for their own good which is why they are lying there dead. Now stop your blubbering and tell me where it is or so help me I will slit your throat too!"

I heard a woman wailing, "Oh please, I beg of you. We have no gold."

"You live in this fine house and you have a servant girl and you say you are poor! Do not take me for a fool."

I then heard a second voice. "Mrs Delancey is speaking the truth you have done enough. Leave us alone. Where is your officer? He would not want you to treat civilians like this." It was Mary! I recognised her voice. Suddenly everything changed. We had to rescue her.

"Our officer? He was the first one who we killed. We have had enough of this war so don't think we will worry about killing a couple of women. After we have had some fun with them."

I heard a wail. We had to move. These were deserters and as such would be unlikely to surrender. I gestured for Ritchie to head around the back. He nodded. I holstered one gun and tried the door. They had not locked it. I moved it ajar so that I could peer inside. There was a large hallway and a central staircase heading to a landing. A massive grandfather clock ticked away. To the left was a door which was slightly open with a shaft of light shining on the hall floor. That had to be the room. I stepped inside and closed the door. I didn't know how long it would take the sergeant to gain entry but I could not wait forever.

"Strip the girl! That might make the old woman talk."

I could wait no longer. I had to act. I had no idea where they would be in the room. I could only hear the two voices. I cocked both Colts and kicked the door open. It flew back. I saw a blue uniform standing by the fire and I let him have my right hand Colt. He slumped to the ground. I saw two men holding Mary; I dare not fire at them. Suddenly a knife sliced down from my right. I just reacted and fired both Colts as I fell backwards. The corporal who had tried to knife me was thrown backwards by the force of the shots.

One of the men holding Mary let go of her and drew his Colt. I rolled to my right as his first bullet struck the oak floor recently occupied by me. As I brought my gun up to fire I saw that Mary was biting the hand of the fourth soldier. It seemed to take an age for me to raise the Colt. I saw the deserter's gun swinging around to shoot me. I fired a second before he did. He fell clutching his arm and I heard a scream from behind me. I fired a second shot and hit him between the eyes. He fell dead.

The last man had thrown Mary to the floor and was drawing his gun. I pulled the trigger of my right Colt and it fell on an empty chamber. I saw the look of joy on his face as he took a bead on me. My left hand was swinging my second Colt up but it would not be able to save me. Lucky Jack's luck had just run out. Then I heard Ritchie's two guns boom from behind me and the last man was thrown through the window.

The room was filled with the smell and smoke of gunpowder and the crackling of the fire. All else was silent save the ticking of the hall clock. I saw Mary's look of horror. I turned and saw the old lady they had been threatening. Her head had been blown almost clean off and her body lay draped over that of her murdered husband and son.

I saw Sergeant Ritchie in the doorway at the far end of the room. "Sorry it took so long, sir. I had to break in."

"You made it and that is the important thing."

Suddenly Mary threw her arms around me and began sobbing on my chest. "You came back! I can't believe it, you came back!"

I holstered my gun and put my arm around her. I did not know what to say. "I said I would. And I am not letting you out of my sight."

The only sound that could be heard was the regular ticking of the clock. Sergeant Ritchie coughed. "Er sir, Captain Hogan..."

"Yes Sergeant Ritchie. You are quite right. Go and fetch the rest of the troop." I pulled back from Mary. "Is there anyone else in the house?"

"No, I was the only servant." She pointed to the three members of the family. "They were all murdered."

"I know, I heard. Off you go, sergeant."

After he had gone she kissed me again full on the lips. "Thank you for returning." She broke off and looked at the bodies.

"You go in the kitchen and put some coffee on. I'll deal with the bodies."

She nodded. "You get rid of that scum and when I have made a pot I will look after the Delanceys. They were good people."

After she had left I searched the four bodies and collected their weapons, their papers and their money. They had a lot and must have been in business for themselves. I dragged the bodies out one by one and laid them in a line well away from the horses. We might bury the family but I would leave these jackals for the other harbingers of death who feasted on corpses.

I had just moved the last one when I heard hooves behind me. I whipped around with my gun in my hand. Dago grinned and held up his hand, "Steady Jack. We are on your side."

"Sorry Dago."

Sergeant Ritchie said, "There is a barn around back. We can put the horses there."

"You do that and then come in the house."

By the time I returned to the house Mary was trying to move the bodies. "Leave that Mary, I have men. They will dig the graves."

She shook her head. I can't leave them like this. Don't let your men in until I have covered them with a winding sheet." Her eyes pleaded with me. "Please."

"Very well." I went out of the door Ritchie had used earlier. There was a short passage and it emerged in a large kitchen. I could smell the coffee. The back door opened and Sergeant Major Mulrooney and Dago stood there.

"We thought that the men could sleep in the barn sir. Sergeant Ritchie told us...."

I smiled, "I can imagine what Sergeant Ritchie told you Sergeant Major. Get some men to dig three graves out back for the dead family and get some men who can cook in here to prepare food. The coffee is made. Help yourself."

Dago went and poured three mugs. He gave one to me and left one on the table for the Sergeant Major. "Lucky Jack eh? I take it this is the woman you were talking about?"

I nodded. "For once I agree with you. This must have been luck. I have no intention of losing her. She is coming with us."

He laughed, "Of course."

When the men came to the kitchen to prepare food I went to find Mary. She was just finishing sewing the last body into a shroud. "There. I don't mind your men seeing them now."

It was at that moment that I realised I had found a jewel. She was both loving and yet practical. "My men are digging graves and I have some others preparing food."

She suddenly changed, "In my kitchen! They will make a mess." She hurried off like a miniature tornado. I looked down at the three white sheets. This was a family who thought the war was just passing them by and yet they had been destroyed by their own soldiers. That was what war did to people. There were no bystanders. You were in it even if you tried to hide from it.

Mary supervised Cecil's cooks. She seemed satisfied with their work and Cecil seemed at ease with her. He caught my eye at one point and gave me a cheery wink.

"I think we should lay the Delanceys to rest before we eat Mary. What do you think?"

She nodded and went to get a coat. Just five of us went to bury the family destroyed in the aftermath of Gettysburg. Having just buried so many of my comrades I hoped that this would be the last burial I had to attend. Mary said a few words and gave her goodbyes. The rain had stopped but tears flooded down her face.

"We came from Virginia to avoid the war. Mr Delancey never thought that this part of Maryland would be in any danger."

We walked back into the kitchen. "Were there any others in the family?"

"No. This had been Mr Delancey's brother's farm and he died of the fever."

There was a pause and Mary began to lay out dishes. "Seems to me ma'am, like it belongs to you."

She looked at Dago as though he had sworn in church. "I want to leave this place as soon as possible."

Dago was always practical. "I'm sorry ma'am. As soon as this is empty someone else will come along; deserters likely or not. They might be Rebs or they might be Yanks. It won't make any difference. They will tear through this place like pack rats."

"He's right Mary. I would just take those things that the family would like caring for. Does that make sense? I didn't know them."

"They were good people. And you are right." She looked at the plates. "We haven't got enough fine china for all our men I'm afraid."

Cecil burst out laughing. "The boys'll not mind eating off the floor they are so hungry. Ma'am if you would serve up the food for you and the officers me and the lads will take this out to the barn."

"No Sergeant Major, you eat in here with us."

"That's kind of you but it will be easier if it is you and the two officers. My boys won't have to mind their cuss words."

She laughed, "I've heard them before."

Cecil said, in all seriousness, "That doesn't mean you should have to hear them again."

When he had gone the three of us sat around the table with an oil lamp burning in the middle. It was the cosiest meal I had had in a long time.

"I like your men, Jack. They are gentlemen."

Dago laughed, "I don't think they have ever been called that before but the colonel taught us well."

"The colonel?"

We told her, as we ate, of James Boswell and his Wildcats. By the time the tale was finished so was the meal. She rose and went into the dining room. She returned with a decanter and three glasses. "Mr Delancey was very partial to port. He decanted at lunchtime ready for this evening. Let's drink it and remember a fine man and a lovely family."

The wine was delicious and we did not spoil it with unnecessary words. She looked at me as I drained my glass. "And now what?"

"Sorry?"

"What happens now?" She looked at her glass and swirled the dregs in the bottom. "To me."

Dago coughed and began to rise, "No Dago, you can stay. You know my thoughts as well as I do."

He shrugged and sat down. Pouring himself another glass of port he said, "Besides there is still port to finish."

"You will come with me... with us. We have been given the task of holding Williamsport until the wagons come through and then we go home. You shall come with me. If you will."

Her eyes lit up. "Of course I will. That was a proposal was it not?" She giggled and was suddenly a girl again.

Dago laughed, "I believe it was ma'am and I am a witness."

I felt myself colouring. "Well yes, I mean I would ..."

"Then I accept. And where is home?"

"We all came from Charleston although I don't know how it stands now."

"Is that the place you said you had a house?"

"I did. I bought it a year or so back and I have a man who looks after it for me but I don't know if it has been taken, destroyed or what."

She nodded, eminently practical. "Then we shall take a wagon with some of the nicer things from this house. You shall have a fine home."

"And I will escort you there too. It's the least I can do. Besides there may be people who have not heard that there is no longer a bounty on your head."

I glared at Dago as Mary put her hand to her mouth, "A bounty?"

"Sorry Jack. I blame the port."

I explained to her about the threat from O'Callaghan. "But he is dead now. I left him on Cemetery Ridge." I suddenly remembered the papers I had taken from his dead body. "That reminds me." I patted my pockets and found the packet. It was slightly wet. I put it on the kitchen table. "I took these from him. I don't know why." I began to separate them. There was a handbill, crudely printed with the bounty for Hogan, Murphy and Boswell and any Wildcat. I gave it to Dago and Mary.

There was a wad of damp Yankee money which I put to one side and there was a letter. I felt a chill as I took the letter from the envelope. I recognised the hand.

Dear Mick,

I am sorry to have to write like this to you but I have become afraid of you. You have changed and you are not the man I fell in love with. The death of your cousins and the hate you have for those men in the Wildcats means I cannot live with you.

I have sold the bar. I have left $100 with Father Dolan. I think that you should have something from our time together but it is over between us.

I am going to leave here and go to Charleston. I have heard that my brother once live d there. If I can find him then my life might make sense. I once thought that I had that with you but I can see that I was wrong.

Your friend

Caitlin

Mary and Dago looked at me aghast. "What's up Jack? You look like you have seen a ghost."

"I have Dago." I thrust the letter across the table and they huddled together to read it.

Mary looked up. "Who's Caitlin?"

Dago shook his head, "It's his sister."

Mary put her hand on mine and said to Dago, "But this Mick, wasn't he the man who was trying to kill Jack?"

"He was but from the letter I don't think he knew that Jack was Caitlin's brother. Caitlin must have been unaware as well." I was just shell shocked. This was too much information to take in at once. "Well Jack, I think that means we definitely all go to Charleston."

The Sergeant Major was summoned before we turned in for the night. "We need a wagon for Miss Malone's things. We can use the Yankee horses to pull it. Put some guards out. We wouldn't want to be surprised tonight would we?"

"No sir, we wouldn't and congratulations to you and your lady."

I threw an irritated look in Dago's direction as I said, "Thank you." Dago just shrugged in a good natured fashion.

I took the money I had collected from O'Callaghan and the deserters and divided it between the men. They tried to refuse but I was in no mood for an argument. It meant each man profited by $40. With the two horses they had I knew that they had done well.

Mary sat on the wagon and one of the wounded men drove it. I took Cecil and Dago to one side. I want her safe and I want the wounded men safe too. "I want the wounded men and you, Dago, to guard her. We have enough fit men to do what we have to. I will have no arguments in this."

Dago laughed, "You'll get none from me sir. Mary is a sight easier on the eye than the Sergeant Major here."

"And no arguments from me either sir." Irish looked positively happy which was a rarity.

We left the tragic farm and headed south to complete our service to the Confederacy.

The Road to Charleston

Chapter 17

Sergeant Ritchie took our four best trackers to scout out Williamsport. To my great relief there was no one there to oppose us. The pontoon bridge still stood. I sent Dago with Mary, the wagon and the horses to the safety of the southern bank of the river. No matter what happened I wanted them safe. Dago nodded when I told him to make sure that Mary would be kept out of harm's way.

"I want to be with you Jack."

"No Mary. I have one last job to do and I cannot be worrying about you. It might get my men and you killed and I couldn't bear that. When we are married you can order me around all that you like but for the moment I still command here." I gave a half smile. "You can get to know Copper while you are waiting."

The men cheered as they crossed to safety. "A wise move sir." The Sergeant Major rubbed his hands together. "Now what sir?"

I pointed at the pontoon bridge. "That is the only way across the river. Our orders are to protect that until the wagons with the wounded arrive. I want this bridgehead fortifying. Get anything you can, wagons, lumber, tables, chairs, anything to build a barricade. I want a wagon putting in the middle so that we can open it for our wounded when the wagons finally arrive. Get Sergeant Jones to organise that. Put a man at the far end of town to let us know of any enemy movements. Get food and water. We may only have to be here for a day or so but at least we can eat and drink. Send Sergeant Ritchie to me."

"Yes sir." He strode off to give his orders. I had thirty troopers; I only hoped that would be enough.

"Sir?"

"Right Sergeant Ritchie, we have to make this like a fort. We need to have ammunition and guns ready to hand. Go across the river and ask Lieutenant Spinelli for the spare ammunition and any spare carbines from the wounded."

We had brought the weapons of our dead friends and spare ammunition. We might only be thirty men but we would fight like three hundred. I looked out from our little fort. We had a clear killing zone and we had the height advantage. It was the best we could do.

By late afternoon everything was in place. There was a sentry in the top of the tallest building and we had our fort. Sergeant Jones laughed, "It's just like the Alamo sir."

"I just hope, sergeant, that we don't end up the same way."

Every trooper had his own carbine and two spare ones already loaded. With our pistols loaded and ready we could lay down a heavy rain of lead on any attackers. We saw the sentry signal at dusk. He soon came running towards us, although we already knew he had sighted the enemy. Had he stayed there then it would have been the wagons.

"Get ready men."

Trooper Cooper threw himself over the barricade. "Sir there is a troop of cavalry heading from the direction of Boonsboro."

"Well done Cooper. Everyone stay hidden. No one fires until I give the order."

We had cleared our line of fire so that no one had any cover for a hundred yards in any direction. The nearest buildings which overlooked our positions were two hundred yards away. Unless they had sharpshooters we would be safe. I was just grateful that it was cavalry and not infantry or artillery. Our weapons would be equally matched but I was counting on the mettle of my men. They would not let me down.

The cavalry troop rode in a column of twos. I suspect they had anticipated that the army would still be at Gettysburg. They would be in for a rude surprise. I now had a future wife to fight for. They would not cross the river. I wanted them as close as possible before I fired to create as many casualties as possible. I waited until they were eighty yards from the barricade. I think that the captain leading them was duped by the poor light and did not recognise the barricade for what it was.

"Fire!"

Thirty carbines tore into them; hurling men from saddles and throwing horses to the ground. We fired until our guns were empty and then picked up our second weapons.

"Cease fire!"

We could hear the moaning of dying horses and wounded men. The smoke hid all.

"Sergeant Ritchie, take four men and bring back any guns and ammunition. We will cover you."

I was guessing when I issued my orders. I knew that we must have killed the officer, bugler and sergeant. I assumed that any survivors would have panicked and raced back some way to the safety of the buildings. They must have thought that we were battalion strength. In addition there were no longer any shots being fired back at us.

The five men leapt over the barricade and I peered down my second carbine, looking for danger. As the smoke cleared I saw a few horses standing forlornly next to dead masters and the rest of the ground was a graveyard of dead horses and troopers. When it had cleared completely I saw the survivors gathered at the edge of town. They were disorganised and that pleased me. Sergeant Ritchie and his men brought back guns, ammunition and horses. We wasted nothing.

"Sergeant Major, any casualties?"

The cheerful voice sounded back, "Just Yankees sir." The men all cheered and I felt better inside. This was the first time I had commanded the regiment or what was left of it and it had gone well.

I watched as the troopers regrouped. Would they attack? There were less than fifty of them remaining and they had no idea of our numbers. All that they saw was a barrier and all that they had experienced was a solid wall of lead which had cut them down. I guessed that they would send for help. When they did not move for a while then I was convinced.

"Sergeant Major, I want one man in three on watch. Wake the next team in three hours." I wanted them to be tired and my men to be fresh.

A short while later Cecil approached me. "I have assigned the men. Will you sleep now or later?"

"We have four sergeants, you do the watching."

"Three sir, Sergeant James was wounded again. I sent him over the river with the other wounded."

Poor Carlton, he had no luck. "Well share the duties between the three of you."

He seemed relieved and started to walk away. "And you sir?"

"I will sleep when I need to." I smiled at him. "You will have to be my mother now Irish; I will soon have a wife to worry about me."

He laughed as he walked off and I reloaded my gun. I had no intention of sleeping. My future depended upon my defence of this pontoon bridge; what was one night without sleep? In the end I did catch an hour or so of sleep although I tried not to. Sergeant Jones shook my shoulder and held a mug of coffee for me.

"Where the hell did you get coffee?"

"Mistress Malone brought it from the farm and she told me to make a pot." He nodded sagely. "She's a keeper sir."

I drank the hot steaming mug gratefully. I expected that General Imboden would arrive some time in the morning. We had just a few hours to hold on. Trooper Dawson brought round the ham sandwiches soon after the coffee. I had found a full stomach made a man fight well.

I heard a cavalry bugle sound 'Boots and Saddles'. The Union cavalry were coming. "Stand to!"

The men went to their allotted positions calmly. These men had fought with me for two years. There would be no panic, no matter what the Yankees threw at us. I issued no unnecessary orders. They would have all reloaded and checked their weapons; no one would need to pee and they would obey every order calmly. They were my men.

This time it was not a troop, it was a brigade. This time it was not a captain in a brand new uniform, this was an experienced Brigadier General and he halted at the end of the street to assess the situation.

"Just like yesterday, wait for your orders before you fire." Even as I said it I knew I had not needed to but I felt I ought to command. Sergeant Major Mulrooney appeared at my shoulder. "Tell me Cecil what will you do when we are discharged?"

He looked appalled. "I have no idea sir. Boswell's Wildcats gave me purpose in life sir. The 1st Virginia Scouts made me more important than anyone I had ever known. I just don't know."

"There is more in you than you realise. You have the most gifted hands of anyone I have ever met. You could make guns or machines. Anyone can kill but only a few have the gift to make or repair something."

He looked at me as though I had said the most profound statement ever. "Thank you sir. I will think on that." He cocked his carbine, "Of course that is after I have escorted you and your good lady to Charleston. When we reach your house then my job will be done."

Whoever was in charge of the cavalry had a wise head on his shoulders. He dismounted two troops of his cavalry and they began to sprint across the open ground. He had them fanned out to make it harder for us to hit them. I saw him looking through glasses, at us. He was counting our guns. Soon he would know how few we were.

"Fire when you are sure that you can hit something." I aimed at a sergeant in the middle who was approaching carefully whilst watching his troopers. He was a veteran and he knew what he was doing. My shot struck him in the upper thigh and he went down on one knee. I moved my carbine an inch and fired at the trooper who stood and looked down at the wounded sergeant the force of the impact of my shot threw him around and he lay writhing on the ground.

All of my men were firing. This was not the continuous fire of the previous night. This was a measured attack. Gradually their numbers thinned. They knelt and began to fire at us.

I heard Cecil yell, "Fire and move!"

The enemy would fire at where we had been. By constantly moving we minimised the risk to ourselves. The smoke from their guns partly obscured them but their shapes were still visible and men fell. I heard the retreat sounded and shouted, "Cease fire." I wanted our ammunition conserving.

The troopers carried back their wounded although there were still six bodies left littering the street. There was a hiatus as the gaggle of officers discussed their options. "Anyone hit Sergeant Major?"

"Smith had his cheek nicked sir but other than that we are in good shape."

"Make sure you drink plenty, men. This will get hotter than hell soon."

I was proving to be a prophet for the Brigadier General sent in a whole regiment and they ran hard at us. They were trying to overwhelm us. I think he had worked out how few we were.

"Fire at will!"

There was no point in moving our positions for they were not firing. It was an old fashioned charge and I was reminded of those veterans of Pickett who had charged up Cemetery Ridge. Sadly we did not have the numbers to do the same to the blue coated cavalrymen. I kept firing until my gun was empty and I picked up my second. Our front was wreathed in smoke. I heard the screams and yells as men fell before our barricade. When my second carbine was empty I drew my Colt. A rifle and a face appeared below me and I blew both away. I drew my sword and held it in my left hand.

Another rifle with a nasty looking bayonet was levelled at me and I ducked just as it fired. I stood and shot the man who had just tried to kill me. A corporal was clambering towards me and I slashed at him with my sabre; it sliced across his face and he fell screaming to the bottom of the barricade.

Once more we heard the retreat sounded. "Keep firing!"

I stood on the top and fired at the fleeing men. When my gun was empty I stared at the scene. Below me was a pile of bodies. The Union cavalry had not lacked courage but our fort had held.

"Sergeant Major, take the roll."

As the smoke cleared I saw the survivors stumbling down the street. The officers disappeared. We would have a respite for a short time.

"Sir?"

I turned to a grim faced Sergeant Major. "Yes Cecil?"

"We lost Sergeant Jones and ten troopers. Another five are wounded."

I nodded. "Can they still fight?"

"Not well sir."

"Then get them across the bridge. I think the next attack will finish us. I want as many of our men to survive as possible. Keep their weapons."

"Yes sir." He paused. "We aren't finished yet. Not while Lucky Jack still stands."

Their belief in my invincibility was terrifying. I reloaded all my weapons and took a long drink of warm stale water. It tasted like nectar.

The wounded men gathered just behind the barricade. "Captain Hogan, we can still fight."

I waved at them. "I know but if you stay here then the others will worry about you. We will all fight harder knowing that you are safe on the other side of the river and, if we fall, then it will be your job to hold them on the other bank."

They cheered and waved as they trudged across the pontoon bridge. It shifted and moved alarmingly but it was our only lifeline to home.

We were afforded a respite. It wasn't until eleven that we heard movements. Cecil brought over some stale bread and ham. He pointed as he chewed. "More cavalry sir?"

I shook my head, "I reckon either infantry or," the ugly shape of a horse cannon appeared at the end of the street, "artillery! Get the men down from the top of the barricade. They will blast at us first and then charge."

"Everyone down!"

I stayed at the top while I watched them load the gun. It was not a large gun but it didn't have to be. At four hundred yards it was almost point blank range. I saw that they were not loading ball but canister. That was a relief. They hoped to sweep us from the top before they assaulted. When I saw the gun captain raise his arm I dived to the bottom of the barricade and covered my ears with my hands.

There was a wall of flame which lit the sky and then a crack like lightning. Finally there was a whistling as the small, deadly balls scythed across the top of the barricade. I hurriedly climbed to the top. Were they attacking? I saw that they were reloading. The Brigadier General wanted us dead. This time I didn't wait for the signal but found a place at the bottom of the barricade which had a couple of iron bars and a barrel. I hunkered down in as small a ball as possible. This time there was a shout as the balls whipped into the wooden wall. They had lowered their aim. Someone had been struck.

I heard a cheer. They were attacking again. "Back to the barricades!"

I leapt to the top. The dismounted cavalry were racing across the open ground. Most of the top half of the barricade was wrecked; we had lost some of our cover. To my dismay I saw blood soaked grey uniforms marking the place where my men had died. It was frustrating to think that my future happiness lay across the river and I would die here following my orders. The last of the Wildcats would perish in Union Maryland.

"Open fire!"

There were fewer of us but we fought like twice our number. They had launched a full attack with a regiment and our barrier was gone. We would die like the men at the Alamo. I picked up my second carbine and fired at the advancing men. They were falling like wheat to a scythe but the gaps were filled by other troopers eager to get at us. They were less than one hundred yards away when I drew my Colt and my sword.

"Come on you Yankee bastards! Jack Hogan and the Wildcats stand here yet!" I gave the rebel yell and heard my men echo it. Balls flew around my head but I cared not and I fired until my Colt was empty. I was just drawing my second when I heard the bugle sound the charge. It took me a second or two to realise it came from my left and it was the Confederate call.

The first the Yankee troopers knew of the disaster about to strike them was when Brigadier General Imboden's men crashed into them. They stood no chance. They were in the open and facing the wrong way. We continued to fire as fast as we could until our guns were empty.

A captain rode up to the barricade. "Sorry we were late boys but thank you for holding out as long as you did." He peered along the line as my men stood. "My God! You were facing a regiment with twelve men?"

I looked at the handful of survivors and said, proudly, "There were more captain." I saluted with my sword and he returned the gesture.

As he rode off I looked for the survivors. I saw Sergeant Ritchie who gave me a wave and I saw a handful of men gathered around Sergeant Major Mulrooney. I ran to him. "He caught one in the leg sir."

I took off my bandana and tied it around the top of his leg to stop the bleeding. He gave me a pale, wan look. "Looks like my luck ran out."

"Don't talk daft man. It is your leg and not your hands. You still have your luck."

I heard hooves behind me and a doctor appeared, "Have you any wounded here captain?" He smiled. "I thought I would see to our boys before those damned Yankees."

"This one is the most serious sir. Do what you can please. He is a good man."

Cecil smiled, "Thank you captain." Then he passed out.

"Sergeant Ritchie, get the unwounded men and the weapons across the pontoon. We will follow as soon as we can."

"Sir." He paused. "That was a glorious moment sir. I shall never forget you standing on top of the barricade waving your sword. It made me proud to be a Wildcat."

I shook my head, "Just don't tell Mistress Malone. It was a daft thing to do."

"No it wasn't sir. Me and the lads were all scared but seeing you defying them all it put steel in our backbones."

I waved him away. What had I done? I looked at the bodies of the men who had fallen. We had done our duty but at what cost? I heard the recall sounded and walked across the wagon. Two of its wheels had been shattered and we would need to manhandle it.

The Brigadier General and his staff galloped up to me. They all saluted. General Imboden dismounted, "Well done Captain Hogan." He pumped my hand as though he was trying to draw water from a well. "This will go down in the annals; a handful of men holding off a brigade of cavalry and cannon. Well done sir."

"Sir, thank you. Have I your permission to rejoin my men across the river? We sent our wounded there to safety."

"Of course." He pointed behind him. "We have the wagons with the wounded and we will start them across too."

I reached the doctor who had just finished with the Sergeant Major. "How is he doctor?"

"The ball took a chunk of muscle from his leg but it missed the bones. He will limp but he will live." He pointed to the others. "The rest are less serious."

"Can I take them across the river then sir? We are anxious to join our comrades. There aren't many of us left."

"Of course. Orderly. " Two medical orderlies ran up with a stretcher. "Take this wounded man across the river with the captain." He saluted. "After the war I will dine out on this story."

My wounded men formed up in twos behind me and we followed the orderlies as they began their precarious walk across the wobbly pontoon bridge. I noticed that some of the stray balls had damaged one end. It was a lucky thing that General Imboden had arrived when he had or the wounded would have been trapped in Union territory.

All of us were glad when we were safely across. Mary and Dago ran to meet us. Mary threw her arms around me and my men all gave a huge cheer, as though we had won the war.

"I was so frightened and when the men came back and told me what you faced, I feared I would never see you again."

"I was in no danger."

Dago laughed, "Not even when you stood on top of the barricade defying the Yankee cavalry?"

I glared at Sergeant Ritchie who shrugged, "What you gonna do sir? Take away my stripes?" He and the rest of the men all laughed. Mary linked me and we headed towards the large house which stood a little way back from the road.

"We found this empty house and we have been using it." She looked up at me. "Your men are very civilised you know; not like those deserters. They took their boots off and went outside to spit and smoke. They are a credit to you."

"No my love, they are a credit to themselves. The south will never see their like again. These thirty or so men are all that remain from a regiment of three hundred. They owe the south nothing more."

Dago had given Mary and me a room of our own. I took my boots off and sat on the bed. Before I knew what was happening I was asleep. I was awoken by the sound of cannon. In my semi-conscious state I wondered if I was back in the battle but then I saw the curtains and felt the soft bed. I jumped to my feet and ran downstairs. The others were all gathered on the stoop.

Dago pointed to the river. "Look Jack, the Yankees have damaged the pontoon bridge. Lee is trapped on the other side."

I watched as half of the bridge floated east. "Did the wounded get across?"

"Yes, thank God." Dago pointed to the tents behind the house. "David is over there with the wounded."

I was wide awake and the three of us watched dawn break and saw the grey masses that were precariously perched on the north bank of the Potomac. I wondered if this would be the end of the war. If General Meade or Hooker, whoever was commanding the northern forces, came south now and attacked then it would be all over. General Lee had nowhere to run.

David Dinsdale walked over to us in the mid morning, he looked tired. "How is it going David?"

"We lost another couple of men last night."

"Irish?"

He laughed, "No he is a tough old bird. He keeps trying to get up and says you will need him."

"I think our days of fighting are over now."

David nodded and then said, "I nearly forgot. General Hill sent this by messenger. I only received it just before we crossed the river. You were asleep."

I tore open the letter. Was this a sentence of death and further fighting or was it our freedom. Dago and David looked at me anxiously while Mary had a puzzled expression on her face. I almost cheered when I read the letter.

"The 1st Virginia Scouts is disbanded. We can all go home."

Dago slapped me on the back. "I'll go inside and tell the boys."

The cheer from the house told everyone that we could now forget the war and find a new life.

The Road Home

Chapter 18

I told the men they could go home but they all insisted on waiting with me while the pontoon bridge was repaired and the rest of the army crossed the Potomac. I gave each man a letter showing that they had been discharged from the army. I wanted none of them shot as deserters. That would the final irony. Sergeant James offered to lead them. He was a good man.

"Sir, do you want the Appaloosa?" I had captured the horse from the Yankees but I preferred Copper.

"No Carlton, call her my parting gift to you."

He shook my hand firmly. "Sit it has been a privilege to serve with you. If you are ever in Winchester then look me up. I intend to own a stud farm and breed horses."

"That is wonderful news and the same to you if you ever make Charleston."

When the first of the wounded crossed then they began to depart. Most came from Virginia and they had the short journey to the Shenandoah Valley ahead of them. The rest of us faced the much longer journey to Charleston. It was over five hundred miles due south but we faced it in good heart.

Dago and I said goodbye to David who was staying with the army. We were the last three officers from the regiment and I would miss the quiet man who had saved so many lives. Sergeant Ritchie and Cecil came with us to Charleston. Ritchie to find his family and Cecil had promised himself that he would see me home and safe. I think Dago came with us because he enjoyed our company.

Cecil drove the wagon. It was easier for him than riding. His leg was healing but it was an ugly wound. He was philosophical about it. "Like you said sir, I still have my hands and I don't need to walk to fix things."

We had our string of horses behind us. It was like a walking bank. There was a desperate shortage of horses in the south and, if we needed money, then we could just sell them. The first three hundred miles helped Mary and Me to get to know each other. I rode next to the wagon and we chatted. Cecil would have a wry grin on his face when I told her some of our adventures. The war seemed to be forgotten. We were not passing soldiers and we heard no fighting. We avoided Richmond and stuck to the back roads.

The first major town we passed through was Raleigh. There were munitions factories and more evidence of a military presence. We paused only to buy supplies but we were challenged by the town marshal. He was a portly looking man who looked remarkably well fed considering the blockade of the coast. He had the smug look of someone who had a little power and abused it.

"I see you boys are wearing the Confederate grey. How come you aren't at the front? You ain't deserters are you?" His face told us he thought that we were.

I smiled at him. That was the best way to deal with officious officials. "No marshal. Our regiment was disbanded after Gettysburg and we were discharged."

"Seems to me you look young enough and fit enough to still be fighting."

Cecil snorted. "A little fighting might be good for you marshal. Get rid of that gut of yours."

"Cecil!"

"Sorry sir."

The marshal's faced was red and angry. "You got any papers?"

"I could say that as a captain in the 1st Virginia Scouts my word should be enough."

"Well it ain't. Papers or else."

"Or else what?"

His hand slid down to his waist band and his gun. Dago had his Colt out even faster and it was pointed at the marshal who went from red to white in an instant. "You boys don't want to start any trouble."

I stepped from Copper and strode over to him. "No we don't and we don't need any from someone who has never fought for the Confederacy and lived by the grace of the blood of others." I reached into my jacket and he flinched. I pulled out the letter from General Hill. I thrust it under his nose. "Here are our papers. Now you read them… if you can."

He unfolded the letter and read it. He still had hold of it. I held out my hand. His fingers tightened on the paper. "How do I know this is genuine?"

Dago snorted, "Captain let me kill him. This is wasting our time."

I grabbed the letter back. "He's not worth it." I reached into his waistband and took out his pistol. I emptied the gun and gave it back to him. "Now marshal, we are going to leave your town. Believe me we are never coming back but if I ever see you again you had better reach for that hog leg or I will shoot you myself. It makes me sick to think of the brave men who have died to keep you and the other people of the Carolinas safe. You sicken me."

As I climbed back on my horse he said, "Go on! Get out of my town!"

A small crowd had gathered. "If you folks elected this man then you made a big mistake. He has abused brave soldiers who have just come from the slaughter of Gettysburg."

We all turned to look at Mary. Her words, coming from her tiny body seemed to make the crowd shrink back far more effectively than my threats. We left the town and the marshal. None of us ever returned to that town. There may have been good people there but they had a poor choice for a marshal.

We camped some fifteen miles south of Raleigh and discussed what had occurred. Dago was the most depressed, "How come good men like Jed die and scum like that live? There is no justice in the world."

Ritchie added another log to the fire. "I guess it's always been that way. The bravest and the best volunteer and go off to fight for their country. The cowards and the selfish ones stay at home."

"It isn't right though."

"No Cecil, it isn't but you can't change human nature can you?"

Our good humour from the early part of the journey disappeared as we headed south towards Charleston. What would we find there? In my mind I had a picture of finding Aaron and my home intact; setting up house with my new wife and finding Caitlin. I now knew that life didn't always work out the way you wanted it to.

We decided to skirt all the towns from now on. Ritchie or Dago would ride into towns and buy whatever we needed. I was regretting retaining my uniform but we had all wanted to wait until we reached our destination before we became civilians. Part of me also thought that we were honouring the dead by wearing our uniforms.

We found it easy to camp and just have our own company. It was as though we were all getting to know each other as people and not as soldiers. We were outside Lafayetville, camped by a small creek. Cecil and Mary were preparing food and Dago and I were trying to catch some fish.

"You know there is just Ritchie and me who have homes in Charleston and yet for the first year and half of the war we recruited all our men from there. It gives you pause for thought. All those young men born in Charleston and they will never return."

Dago nodded. He had been in Charleston but he had not been born there. "I know. I guess I don't have any home to go to."

"If the colonel hadn't persuaded me to buy a house there then I wouldn't either. You know his house doesn't belong to anyone now."

"Hey you are right. What do we do about that?"

"I guess we start with Mr Abercrombie, he was the colonel's lawyer. He will know what to do. He handled my investments for me and he seems like an honest man. We will ask his advice."

Ritchie rode into the camp. His face was filled with frowns and it was not like the cheerful Ritchie who had left a couple of hours earlier. "What's the matter Ritchie?"

"It's probably nothing but when I bought the supplies there was a bunch of no accounts hanging around and they looked mighty suspicious to me. They started to follow me." Dago stood to get his gun. "Don't worry sir, I lost 'em but I figure they may be looking for us." He pointed at the horse which was laden with supplies. "They seemed interested in our gold and the supplies."

"I think we will all take a turn at watching tonight." Mary was still at the fire and had heard nothing. "Best say nothing to Mary eh? We don't want her worrying over nothing."

The next day dawned and our fears had been without foundation. As we continued our journey south, keeping well to the west of Lafayetville, Mary said, "So why were you boys keeping watch last night?"

I thought about lying but I could not think quick enough and her eyes laughed a smile at me, "Don't try lying Jack. Let's not go down that route. Tell me to mind my own business but don't lie to me. Never lie to me."

"Sorry. Ritchie thought some ne'er do wells might have tried to steal from us last night. We just took precautions."

"Good. Next time tell me. I can fire a gun. Maybe not as good as you fellows but well enough."

I nodded to Cecil, "Pass one to her then Cecil."

He reached under his seat and brought out a Navy Colt. It was not as big as an Army Colt but it was still an effective weapon. "There you are. You might as well practise loading and cleaning it." I pointed to Cecil. "You have the best armourer in the Confederacy riding next to you." Cecil blushed but I could tell that he was pleased with the compliment.

In the early afternoon I rode ahead to find our next campsite. Bearing in mind Ritchie's words I was more alert than at any time since Williamsport.

This was flat farmland with small streams criss-crossing it. It made easy travelling but it would also be an easy place to be ambushed. I found a small knoll. It was barely higher than the land around it but it would give us a better view of anyone approaching us. Satisfied I turned Copper around and headed back.

Once again it was Copper who saved me. The pricked ears and the whinny warned me of horses that were alien. I slipped my Colt from its holster. Now that I was no longer an officer I had removed the flap and was wearing it lower on my hip. I found it easier to take out quickly. I stopped Copper and listened. I could hear raised voices. I slid from Copper's back. There was a wall running down the road. I ran along the field side keeping as low as I could. The voices became clearer and I heard Cecil shouting.

"You boys better move on. We don't want any trouble."

"You ain't gonna get no trouble. All we want is your gold your horses and your pretty little woman here."

I heard Dago shout angrily, "You'll get neither you thieving bastards."

I heard a crash and a cry from Dago. I had to hurry. I saw the top of the wagon. Before it were three men holding shotguns. On the far side of the wagon there were two more with pistols. These were the men Ritchie had mentioned. I could see neither Dago nor Ritchie. This was no time for thinking; this was the time for bold action. I put my spare Colt in my holster. I took a deep breath and stood up. I could not bring myself to shoot a man in the back even if he was trying to rob me and hurt my woman.

"Reach, I have you covered!"

They turned and I emptied my gun. I felt the blast of the shotgun as it took off my hat. I threw my gun to the ground and drew the second so quickly that the two men with the pistols were still trying to see where I was. As I pulled the trigger Mary and Cecil both fired their guns and the two men fell dead.

I picked up my spare gun and leapt over the wall. "Are you all right Mary?"

She was pale but she smiled, "Yes. See to Dago and Ritchie."

I could see that they had both been cold cocked and were lying on the ground; blood was seeping from their heads. I knelt next to Dago, he was still alive. I remembered David telling me that you never leave an unconscious man on his back and I turned him to his side. Ritchie was also alive but his breathing was more irregular.

Mary appeared at my side with a wet cloth. "Cecil, keep a watch. These bushwhackers might have friends."

She cleaned his wound. "That's a deep cut. I have some cat gut and a needle. It will need sewing. You clean Dago's wound while I go and fetch them." As she stood she kissed me on the cheek. "Thank you. That's twice you have saved my life."

Dago started to come around while I was wiping the blood away. His eyes were wide with terror until he recognised me. "The bandits?"

"Dead."

"Sorry Jack. They got the jump on me. I must be slipping."

"Not to worry. Copper's nose saved us again."

Mary returned and she sewed Ritchie's wound. "Better lay him in the back of the wagon." She looked at Dago. "Do you want to ride in the wagon?"

He shook his head and regretted it immediately. "No ma'am. I'll ride and try not to get caught again."

I retrieved Copper and we set off again. "What happened, Dago?"

"We got tricked. It was my fault. I should have seen the ambush. One of them was lying on the ground. We stopped and Ritchie went to see him. When he rolled him over the man hit him with an iron bar and the others had us covered with shotguns." He shrugged apologetically, "If we had tried anything then we might have got Mary hurt." He suddenly stopped, "Hey Mary, you better get here. Jack got shot."

As Mary ran to my side I said, "What the hell are you talking about? I feel fine."

Mary was pale as she said, "He is right. You have shotgun pellets in your face. Dago, get some whiskey." She ran to the wagon and her bag. Cecil looked frightened. I put my hand to my face and it came away bloody. Then I remembered my hat being hit. Once again I was lucky.

Mary washed my face with water and then dabbed whisky on my face. I frowned. "Don't frown it will make this harder. The whisky is to numb your face a little." She then picked each pellet out one by one. When she had finished she wiped more whiskey on my face. "You might smell like a distillery but you look better and it will stop an infection. The sooner we get to your house in Charleston the better."

Ritchie had recovered by the next day but we took no more chances and kept a guard each night as we camped. I had thought that the ending of the war meant less danger for me. There was more in this apparently peaceful Carolina.

The peace ended as we approached Hanahan. Union ships were firing at Fort Sumter and the harbour. We halted and watched the smoke from the burning buildings and ships. I turned to Mary. "This may not have been such a good idea."

"Not a good idea to find your sister who travelled here to look for you?" She looked at the map she and Cecil had been using. "Where is your house?"

"It is to the south of the city close to the colonel's plantation."

"Then let us get there and get there quickly."

As Dago and I led the way he said quietly, "Not the kind of woman you get the wrong side of eh Jack?"

"So I am learning."

We took the ferry across the Ashley River. The ferryman was grateful for our business and our dollars. He was quite garrulous as he pulled us across. "How long have the Yankees been bombarding the city?"

"Oh some months. Folks keep on working. Course there's no ships coming in, leastways not during daylight. Our guns keep 'em away and we have sunk some of them but there's little business around here. You folks passing through?"

"No, I have a house further south and we are heading there."

He nodded sagely, "You might be alright there. You are the other side of the river and they just seem intent on making the city uninhabitable. Damn Yankees."

I liked the ferryman and gave him a healthy tip. He had a better attitude than the town marshal at Raleigh. Even though it was late afternoon, we kept going. I was determined to sleep under my own roof that night.

The house was in darkness when we approached. It was however still standing. I wouldn't have blamed Aaron if he had deserted it. I had not been a particularly good employer. He had not heard from me for over a year. For all he knew I might be dead. We left Mary and Cecil in the wagon. Bearing in mind our recent experiences the three of us took loaded weapons with us.

The front door was locked. I frowned. I didn't blame Aaron for deserting me but how was I to gain entry to my own house?

"Let's try the back." We moved around the side of the house. Dago rattled the back door but it too was locked. Suddenly, from behind us we heard the unmistakeable sound of a gun being cocked.

"Now I told you white trash before, this house belongs to a soldier fighting in the war now skedaddle before I cut you all in two."

I raised my hands and turning, said, "And that soldier has returned now, Aaron. Thank you for watching out for me."

I saw his white teeth as he grinned and lowered the shotgun. "You come back! Thank God you come back."

I strode up to him and shook him by the hand. "You know Dago Spinelli."

"I sure do. Good to see you again Corporal Spinelli."

"I finished up a lieutenant but that is behind me. Good to see you again too. This is Ritchie, he was with the Wildcats too."

"Aaron we have a wagon and a lady out front. Can you open the house for us?"

"I sure will."

We returned to the front of the house to get Mary and Cecil. We watched as lamps were lit in the rooms and then the door opened. "I would have had the fires lit if I knew you was coming sir."

I led Mary forwards, "We didn't know. Aaron this is Mary, she will soon be my wife and we will be living here."

I thought he was going to burst into tears. "What a wonderful day. I'll go and get the beds aired." He started to run upstairs and then stopped, "We ain't got any nice food for you folks. Just what me and the missus eat."

Mary laughed, "Don't you worry Aaron. We have food. You air the beds. Cecil get the wagon unloaded and Jack, you show me the kitchen."

Dago laughed as he left, "Like a tornado Jack, a veritable tornado!"

Aaron and his wife had kept the house immaculate and Mary was delighted with the kitchen. She hugged me, "My first ever kitchen and it is wonderful!" She kissed me. "Now go and help the boys to bring in our things."

By the time we had seen to the wagon, its contents and the horses, food was ready. Cassie, Aaron's wife had appeared, fearful at first, and the two women had knuckled down to the task of providing food. As ever, Sergeant Major Mulrooney organised Ritchie and Dago so that everything was put in its proper place.

"Jack, ring the dinner gong."

There was a gong in the hall way. I had never noticed it but my sharp-eyed Mary had. I rang the gong. Aaron came down the stairs and we went into the kitchen. "Now let's get this food into the dining room."

I had a blazing fire going. It was not cold but it made the room brighter and cosier at the same time. "Now everyone sit down and help yourself."

Aaron and Cassie started to back out of the room. "And where are you two going? We are all eating together here tonight. This is a celebration that the house is still here and we are all alive!" Mary had her hands on her hips and a look which brooked no arguments.

Aaron looked to me for help and I smiled and, putting my arm around him, led him to a chair. Mary did the same with Cassie, "You will soon learn, Aaron, that when Mistress Mary speaks, we all jump."

Their embarrassment lasted no more than two spoonfuls of the superbly cooked food. We chatted away and I discovered how hard life had been. "Lots of slaves ran off and there was no one left to work the fields. We weren't as badly off as most for we had free men working for us. Colonel Boswell's place, well that suffered. My pappy couldn't stop the boys from running. We had to help him out."

"Well Colonel Boswell is dead now so I will have to go into town tomorrow and see Mr Abercrombie."

"It sure is good to have you back Captain Hogan." He lowered his voice. "She sure is a fine lady. When did you get married?"

"We haven't. I'll need your help to organise that." He seemed delighted at the prospect. "How many workers do we have now then?"

The worker's quarters were some way from the main house. "We are down to ten, sir; six men and four women. But they are all hard workers."

"I'll see you all get the pay you have coming to you."

"That don't matter, sir."

I remembered my father in Ireland scraping a living together and I knew that it did matter. "You will get your pay." I was not certain if I had any money to pay them but I could see the horses I had brought back with me. Somehow they would get paid.

"You thought we were white trash. Have you had trouble?"

"Yes sir. Some of the poor white folks see this big old house and don't like a nigra living here. That's why I had the shotgun."

Just then a stone was thrown through the window and a voice shouted, "Come on out nigger! We don't like it that you live in the slave quarters but we ain't having you living in white folk's homes."

Cassie looked terrified but I winked at her and put my finger to my lips. I gestured for Ritchie, Dago and Cecil to get their guns and go out of the back door. I fastened my holster around my waist.

"You better come out quick or we'll whip your black skin off'n your miserable black back."

I nodded and pointed to the door. He gave a half smile and went. I was pleased to see that Mary was not put out by this at all. When we reached the door I stood to the side and Aaron opened it.

"That's better now..."

The leader got no further and I stepped out next to Aaron. I saw that there were about fifteen men with wooden staves and shotguns. There were a couple of cheap-looking women at the back too.

I stepped in front of Aaron. "Now before you are thrown from my land, which one of you threw that stone through the window?"

The large man at the head of the crowd said, belligerently, "Me and what will you do about it?"

He was just four yards from me and I covered it in a couple of heartbeats. I had my pistol out and I smacked him across the face, hard. He fell screaming to the ground. "I will do that and I trust you to speak a little more politely to me. I am used to my orders being obeyed. Now tomorrow you will arrange to have my broken window repaired."

He laughed and I was pleased to see teeth come out when he did so. "You talk mighty big for one man." He stood. "You wouldn't talk so big without that hog leg."

I nodded, holstered my gun and then hit him in the stomach with my left hand before punching him on the side of the head with my right. He fell to the ground and I picked him up and head-butted him. He lay on the floor this time he was still.

"Apparently I can talk that big without a gun."

His cronies moved forwards and a smaller version of the man I had felled yelled, "There's just one of him and his gun is in his holster."

He rushed forward and I pulled the Colt out. It was aimed at his face and he was less than two yards away. "Now my gun is out of my holster and you are about to die."

I then heard Aaron cocking his shotgun. "And my two barrels will take a whole bunch of you others out."

Then I heard the guns of my comrades being cocked and Dago's voice called out. "And I am pretty certain that we can kill the rest."

They turned to run and I, firing my gun in the air, yelled, "Stop! I need reparations." I pointed to the broken glass. "I want the money for that before you leave, or you ain't leaving."

They went to their unconscious leader and took money from his pocket. They handed it to me. One of them said, "That enough?"

"It'll do. Now if I ever see any of you around here again I will shoot first and ask questions later and if any of you insult my estate manager, Mr Jarvis, again, I will horsewhip you. Do you understand?"

They all nodded dumbly. As they carried their fallen friend one asked, "Who are you, sir?"

"I am Captain Jack Hogan formerly of Boswell's Wildcats and me and my friends are here to stay so spread the word."

When they had gone we returned to the dining room. The glass had been cleared and Mary said sweetly, "Dessert anyone?"

"I'm starving," I said.

Cecil laughed, "Well it looks like it could be fun around here."

Chapter 19

The next day I left Dago to watch the house while Aaron and I rode over to see his father. Mary, of course objected as she didn't think there was any danger.

"Ma'am, I am still tired after that long journey and my wound is playing up. You wouldn't object to an old soldier resting up for a day on the front porch would you?"

She was not taken in but she smiled sweetly and said, "Of course."

Cecil and Ritchie rode into Charleston. We needed supplies but they also needed somewhere to stay. Both had jobs they wanted to start as soon as possible.

Aaron and I set off on the few miles ride to the old Boswell plantation. "How is your dad these days?"

"Not so good. He remembers it from the days of Colonel Boswell. He complains it needs a lick of paint and some loving sir."

I was not sure that it would get that. I had hoped that it would have ridden the storm of war but then I remembered that the colonel had spent little time there and he had put all of the money into, men, horses, uniforms and weapons. Most of those lay on the field of Gettysburg. He had wasted his money.

When I rode up the long drive I saw that the white paint on the fence was flaking and the grass was longer than I remembered it. It was sad to see the faded beauty of a once beautiful building. From a distance it looked as though nothing had changed but closer up you could see the boards which needed repairs and the broken windows which needed fixing.

We tied our horses to the metal negro jockeys which stood on either side of the colonnaded portico. One of the steps was loose and creaked alarmingly as we walked up. Aaron looked at me and shrugged. "It's sad isn't it captain?"

"It sure is and it seems we came back none too soon."

Jarvis' hair was whiter and his eyes seemed to have sunken back into his head. He beamed a smile at me. "It is good to see you, sir." He noticed my uniform, "Captain Hogan!" He looked beyond me, "Where is the colonel, sir?"

Aaron put his arm around his father as we led him into the house.

"The colonel won't be coming back Jarvis. He fell at Gettysburg."

It was fortunate that Aaron was holding his father or he would have fallen. We took him to a chair and Aaron scurried off. "He fell bravely Jarvis, leading his men." It would do Jarvis no good to know that he had been leading them in a disastrous retreat.

"But the end result is the same Captain Hogan. He won't be coming back." The old servant swept a hand around the room. "What will happen to his lovely home?" The words, 'and me' remained unsaid but hung in the air like an early morning mist.

Aaron brought a glass of, what smelled like whiskey. The old man was going to refuse it but I said firmly, "You will drink that Jarvis and then we can begin to plan a way out of this predicament."

He nodded and drank the whiskey. Aaron and I sat on two of the other chairs. I thought back to when I had sat here and planned the purchase of my own home in those hopeful early days of the war. That was a different world and those dreams were dead. We had to be practical and plan for a different future.

"Now the first thing I will do is to see Mr Abercrombie. We need the legal niceties of the colonel's death tying up. If things do not turn out the way we hope then you, your wife and your family will come to live with us at my place." Aaron's eyes filled with gratitude.

"What do you mean sir?"

"I do not know what debts the colonel left. It may be that the lawyer needs to sell the house to pay his debts. He may have left the house to one of his family."

"No sir!" Jarvis' voice became harsh. "He would never do that. He said that you boys were his family." He suddenly remembered something. "Mr Murphy?"

"He died too, and Harry and Jed." A name suddenly came into my mind. "What happened to Jem?"

Jem had been invalided out of the Wildcats early in the war. Jarvis shook his head. "He died last year when the Yankees raided the town. He was walking down the street and he got killed by a shell from the Yankee ships."

It was a shame. I liked Jem. "We have to carry on without these good people. It's the living who will need our help." I stood and rubbed my hands. "Now I will go to Charleston. Aaron here will stay and give you whatever help you need. I have men getting some supplies in town and we will bring some here." I turned to Aaron, "Make a list of what needs doing eh Aaron?"

He nodded, "Thank you captain. You are a good man."

I shook my head, "I am repaying the debt I owe to the colonel. He saved me when he came aboard the Rose that day and gave me a life. I will try to save his home for him."

As I rode Copper along the road to town I wondered how I would achieve that. I had some money with me but I would need that for my own plantation. I dreaded to think what had become of my investments. In a way I was dreading this meeting with Mr Abercrombie.

Charleston shocked me as I rode along its once graceful avenues. The random shelling by Union warships had destroyed many fine buildings, including churches and torn up beautiful trees and gardens. It was like riding through a war. We had never thought that Charleston would suffer so. Although when Colonel Boswell had returned, following his wound, he had been somewhat depressed. I could now see why.

Mr Abercrombie's offices were in the commercial district. This part of town looked to have escaped much of the damage. I hitched Copper to the rail and walked into the quiet white washed building. A diminutive figure was seated at the desk in the entrance. He looked up at me and scratched his nose with inky fingers.

"Yes sir, how may I help you?"

"I am Captain Jack Hogan formerly of the 1st Virginia Scouts and I would like to see Mr Abercrombie please."

"I will see if he is free."

I smiled as the tiny man scurried away. He was the clerk version of Sergeant Major Mulrooney. He served Mr Abercrombie well. He was only away a few moments and seemed disappointed as he said, "You may go in. Can I offer you a drink? Mint tea perhaps?"

"That would be kind."

I entered the office. I had never been in here before for Mr Abercrombie had come out to the plantation to deal with my paperwork. I had only visited the office when I had been guarding the colonel. We had always waited outside with the horses. It was an opulently furnished office with fine leather chairs and a magnificent mahogany desk. The shelves were lined with neatly arranged books. My spirits rose as I hoped that Mr Abercrombie might have good news for me.

He held out his hand. "Good to see you er..." he peered at my collar, "Captain Hogan. Please sit."

He waited until his clerk had brought in my tea and then asked, "Is this visit to Charleston a brief one?"

He came straight to the point and I liked that. "No sir, I have been discharged from the army." I took a sip of my tea. There was no easy way to say this. "I am here with bad news sir. Colonel Boswell died at Gettysburg."

The old man took off his glasses and pinched his nose. He was silent for a few moments and I sipped my tea. He coughed and replaced his glasses. "Did he suffer?"

"No more than the many other men who fell on that day."

"I am sorry, Captain, that was crass of me. You and the other fine young men... were many killed?"

"Almost all of them."

He shook his head. "There will be a time for grieving but I can see that you are a practical man." He suddenly looked at me. "Quite remarkable. You have business of your own to conduct with me and yet you wish to deal with the estate of a dead man first. You are indeed a loyal friend." There was little I could say to that. "Hargreaves, bring me in the Boswell file."

Outside I heard the crash of the guns as they began their daily bombardment. "Is that hard to bear Mr Abercrombie?"

"Compared with what you boys have to put up with in battle no but it is petty. It serves no purpose and does nothing to destroy the Confederacy, if that is their aim. It is like a small vindictive child breaking a toy for no reason at all." The file was brought in. "Thank you Hargreaves. No visitors, until Captain Hogan has left us."

He untied the string which bound it together and laid some documents in a line before him. He scanned them until he seemed satisfied. Colonel Boswell came to see me on his last leave whilst he was convalescing. He wrote a new will out." He peered at me like an owl. "The wound disturbed him somewhat?"

I smiled grimly, "He nearly died at the battle of Kelly's Ford. He was lucky to be saved."

"Quite. Well he rewrote the will. I should read this in the presence of all the interested parties but, as you will hear when I read it to you that might prove difficult."

He then read the will out to me. It was written in plain English so that there would be no ambiguity. Jarvis and the other slaves were given their freedom. As far as I knew that would only apply to Jarvis and his wife now as the other slaves had run off. They were allowed to live their lives out at the plantation. The plantation was left to those members of the Wildcats who survived the war. The colonel's investments were placed in trust to pay for the upkeep of the estate.

He leaned back in his chair and removed his glasses. "So you can see my dilemma. Apart from yourself how many Wildcats remain?"

"Dago Spinelli, Cecil Mulrooney, Carver Ritchie; they are all here with me now. Carlton James and David Dinsdale, they are in the Shenandoah Valley. They are the only ones who remain alive."

Mr Abercrombie looked genuinely upset. "How immeasurably sad, that virtually a whole generation has been wiped out." He shook himself. "This maudlin attitude will get us nowhere. I will write to Mr James and Mr Dinsdale and tell them of their good fortune. You say the others are here with you?"

"Yes sir. They are staying with me until they can find their feet."

"You learned much from James Boswell. I shall miss him. He was like the son I never had. He was a fine young man, who was badly treated by an uncaring family. I will come with you and we can give both them and Jarvis the news."

"Might I ask about the investments, sir?" I waved an airy hand. "Charleston does not seem prosperous and the plantation looks to be run down."

"Charleston is no longer prosperous and as for the plantation; I apologise. That was remiss of me. I should have made funds available to Jarvis to continue its upkeep. No, Captain Hogan the investments of James Boswell and yourself are doing well for they are not based here in the Confederate States of America but in Liverpool."

"Liverpool? In Britain?"

"Yes. I believe your home was close to there."

"Just across the water."

"And that in itself is appropriate." He took off his glasses and sipped his own mint tea, "When the war began there were a few of us, here in Charleston, who realised that trade would dry up. We gathered investors such as yourself and James and we set up a company in Liverpool called the Dixie Line." He smiled. "It seemed an apt name for such a venture. We had ships built in Liverpool; the 'Richmond' and 'Jefferson Davis' were the first two. They began to trade with Spain as well as running the blockade. With the trade embargo they found many ports with which to trade. You are a rich man and James Boswell's heirs are also rich. The company is a British company although the major shareholders, apart from you and James' heirs are myself and two other lawyers here in Charleston. The only difficulty we have, at the moment, is cash flow but we have a few thousand dollars held in reserve here in Charleston. We shall call at the bank and draw some out for yourself and the others."

I was flabbergasted. I had expected to be impoverished by the war and, ironically, the war had made me rich. I wondered what Danny and Harry would have made of it all. Had they survived then they too would share in the good fortune. If only the colonel had held his nerve that day at Gettysburg then they might have lived.

It was early afternoon when we reached my home. I realised, as we rode up the drive, that I needed a name for it now that I lived here. I would leave that for Mary. I saw the horses tied up outside and knew that my men had returned. Aaron was still with his father and so Cassie took us in.

I smiled when Mary flashed me an irritated look. "You should have warned me that you were bringing visitors back Jack. The house is a mess."

Mr Abercrombie gave me a questioning look. "Mr Abercrombie this is the lady I am to marry, Mistress Mary Malone. Mary this is my lawyer Mr John Abercrombie."

He took her hand and kissed it, "Congratulations my dear." He nodded to me. "James always said you were lucky. He was right."

"Cassie can you ask the other gentlemen to join us. Mr Abercrombie is here to speak with them also."

Mary scurried from the room. She returned with a decanter and some glasses. "I could make tea if you prefer Mr Abercrombie."

"No, my dear. This is a celebration anyway. It is a celebration of the vision and thought of a man now departed."

My three comrades looked confused as they came into the sitting room. I reflected that I would need to spend some of my money on better furnishings now that I could afford it. I sat back with a smug smile on my face as the four of them heard the news. I knew what was coming and they did not.

Mary looked at me and was the first to speak. "So you share in the estate too?"

"No, I have given my share to the others." I had made this quite clear to the lawyer once I had discovered my own good fortune. Mary squeezed my hand and smiled at the gesture. "So, boys, that means that the three of you, Sergeant James and Lieutenant Dinsdale now have a home and an income."

"So we don't need to find our own home?"

"No."

Ritchie smiled, "Which is a good thing as we found nothing this morning."

Cecil laughed, "I wouldn't say that. We found a nice bar where they had a pretty young girl singing Irish ballads."

"Well there you go Irish. You can visit there as often as you like."

Mr Abercrombie stood. "And now my dear you must excuse us. We have to visit Jarvis and give him the news of his freedom too."

Dago said, "Do you mind if I come too? The boys here..." He nodded his head at Mary.

"Of course."

Mary grabbed me as I turned to leave. Dago and Mr Abercrombie left along with Ritchie and Cecil. "I knew when I agreed to marry you that you were a good man. I just didn't know how good. You have given a fortune to your friends." She kissed me.

"Before you have me canonised you should know that we are as rich as the estate of the colonel. You are marrying a successful businessman." I swept my hand around the room. "Begin to think now how you will spend it and what we shall call this house."

Jarvis burst into tears when we told him of his manumission and Aaron joined him. The lawyer handed over five hundred dollars to Jarvis. "This will enable you to make the house and grounds look as they used to. This is Mr Spinelli who will be one of the new owners. I think the other two will be over shortly."

Jarvis smiled and nodded. "I know the gentleman well." He looked up at the ceiling. "And thank you Colonel Boswell you were always a fine man and a kind master. Now I see just how kind."

That evening the dinner was a joyous affair. Cecil had acquired some good food and we all celebrated our success. As we sipped our brandy and smoked our cigars Dago said, "So when are you getting married Jack?"

I looked at Mary who smiled and touched my fingers with hers. "First he wants to find his sister. She was supposed to have come to Charleston."

Ritchie shook his head, "That will be like looking for a needle in a haystack."

"And I will start tomorrow. But Mary, we can marry whenever you wish. I may not find Caitlin."

"You will and I will wait. Besides I have some money to spend."

I laughed. "We all do. I shall buy some civilian clothes tomorrow."

We left Aaron and Cassie at the house while the six of us headed into Charleston. Mary was appalled at the wanton destruction. "Those damned Yankees. This must have been a beautiful city."

"And it will be again. The war cannot last forever."

After we had bought clothes I left Mary ordering furniture, dishes and the many other items I had not even dreamt that we needed. I went to the newspaper office where I put an advertisement in asking for news of Caitlin. I was not sure that, even if she was here in Charleston that she would read a newspaper but someone who knew her might.

Mary had still not finished her shopping. We left Ritchie as her escort while Cecil took us to the bar he had found. It was in the quarter of the town closest to the harbour. In the past it would have been bustling but the lack of trade meant that it had fallen on even harder times. The whores looked shabby and tired and the bar itself had fading, peeling paint. It was quiet.

"I thought you said they had music."

"They did. Perhaps we are early. They have good beer here but it is a bit rough."

Once inside I saw what he meant. It had low ceilings and was filled with rough men whose smoke filled the room. We squeezed through to the bar and Cecil ordered us four beers. The owner took in our uniforms as he served us. He had the leery look of someone who operated on the wrong side of the law and I disliked him the moment I laid my eyes on him.

"You boys wouldn't be deserters would you?" He nodded to Cecil. "I saw him yesterday and had him marked as a deserter but you are an officer."

I put my arm out to restrain Cecil. "No, we are discharged soldiers. We are not deserters."

"Oh don't get me wrong we don't mind deserters here." He winked at me. "I find them very useful if you catch my drift."

I did and his words confirmed my dislike of him. I threw a handful of coins on to the bar and then found a table.

Cecil was apologetic, "Sorry about this sir. I thought it was nicer yesterday. It must have been the Irish songs the girl was singing but this is not good. We'll just have the one and leave."

I swallowed a mouthful of the beer. "No you were right, it is good beer and we don't have to talk to the landlord do we? But we will just have the one and then get back to Mary."

As I looked around the room I saw that the men all had the same furtive look. These were the men who did not fight for the Confederacy but fought, instead for themselves. I was sure that I recognised some of those who had been around my home the previous night. Certainly some of them looked away as I scanned the room. These would be the ones who preyed on the elderly and the weak. My war might be over but that didn't mean I would not fight to protect what was mine.

We were about to leave when there was a little cheer and a number of men stood. "This is it Jack. This is the singer. Sit down and listen. Her voice will take you back to Ireland."

I sat down. Her back was to me as she was helped to the bar. I took my eyes from her as I finished my drink but when she began to sing I knew that Cecil was right. She did take me back to Ireland for it was Caitlin, my sister.

I stood, as she sang and made my way towards the bar. I was oblivious to the men who stood before me. Fate had directed me to this bar and nothing would stop me. I pushed past them. Caitlin was singing with her eyes closed. As she finished I stood beneath her. She opened her eyes and I held out my hand, "I have come to take you home Caitlin."

She burst into tears and threw herself into my arms. I held her as tightly as I could. I dare not speak any more for I was filled with emotion. I was suddenly aware of a hostile wave of noise and I saw the landlord, with a wooden stave in his hand. "Get your feckin hands off my singer!"

"This is my sister and we are leaving now!" I gripped Caitlin's waist with my left hand and slipped my right down to my Colt. The landlord took one step towards me and my gun was in my hand and pressed against his forehead in a blur of movement. "Now much as I do not want my sister to witness violence you either put that stave down or I will blow your head clean off."

"No Jack, it's alright."

Without taking my eyes from the thug I said, "No, it is not alright. I didn't fight for this land to be told what to do by a piece of filth like this. Dago! Cecil!"

The two of them appeared at my side with guns drawn in an instant. The landlord's look changed to one of terror. I let go of Caitlin and grabbed the stave. I hurled it at the bar where it smashed into glasses and bottles. I took a handful of the landlord's jacket in my left hand and began to lift him from the ground. I put my face close to his and said, quietly, "Now we are going upstairs so that my sister can get her things and then we are leaving. Then I would suggest that you get out of Charleston for the next thing I will do, will be to find the Provost Marshal and tell him of your deserters."

His face went white. "You wouldn't"

I cocked the Colt and the sound seemed to echo around the room. "Now move!"

The crowd parted as he walked before me. "Caitlin, stay close behind me."

We had just reached the bottom of the stairs when a man appeared from behind the bar with a wicked looking knife. As he slid it towards me I pulled my hips back so that the blade slid harmlessly by and then smashed the Colt onto his wrist. I heard it break and he dropped the knife. I swung the Colt to crush his face. He fell to the floor in a heap.

"The next man who tries anything will get you a bullet in the back!"

"Leave him be. For the love of God, leave him be. He's mad!"

Caitlin had a pitiful few belongings in the room. It was obvious to me that she had shared the room with this animal. She hesitated as she picked up her bag.

"What is it?"

"I had some money when I came here. Billy said he would look after it for me."

I almost rammed the barrel of the Colt up his nose. "Get it!"

"I have rights!"

"No, you don't. You don't even have the right to life. I will decide if you live or die. I hate men who prey on women. They are the lowest of the low. Now get it!"

He went to the bed and reached under. He brought out a box in his left hand. I caught the exultant look on his face and was ready as he pulled the hidden pistol out. I was less than three yards from him and I didn't miss. The bullet caught him in the wrist. The gun fell from his now useless, shattered hand.

I strode over and grabbed the box. "I would tie a tourniquet on that or you will bleed to death."I holstered my pistol and took Caitlin by the hand. "Come with me Caitlin. I will take you to a better life than this."

There was stunned silence as we descended the stairs. My two friends had them all covered with their Colts. I gestured upstairs. "Your friend tried to shoot me. I could have killed him but I didn't." My eyes searched every face. "If I ever see any of you again then you will regret it."

We walked from the bar and Dago and Cecil backed out, still covering the crowd. An elderly marshal walked up to us. "Was there some trouble, captain?"

"There was. The landlord tried to shoot me. He is wounded."

"It's about time someone stood up to Billy Bragg."

I looked at the marshal coldly. "And why didn't you?"

"There are only a couple of us and…"

I gestured at Cecil and Dago. "My friends and I are living south of the town. If you ever need help to get rid of scum like this then you come and find us."

I will captain…?"

"Hogan, Jack Hogan."

Mary and Ritchie were sitting on the wagon as we walked up to the house. She saw Caitlin and jumped down. "Don't tell me. This is your sister."

I nodded and Caitlin smiled, Mary continued, "And I am Mary. Jack and I are to be wed. We have a wedding to plan!"

The smile on Caitlin's face was in contrast to the tears which flowed from both women's faces. Dago looked bemused while Cecil also looked emotional.

"Come on let's get home." I had wanted to say that for years, ever since the home I had shared with Caitlin had been burned down. I mounted Copper and we headed south.

We had not left the city when Mary said, "I think I have the name for our home now."

"And what is that?"

"The Sanctuary; you have brought hope to all of us and that name shows what it means to us. Does it not sister?"

Caitlin nodded. "I have dreamed of this for all those years since you sailed west and I never dreamed that it would arrive. I feel lucky to have you as a brother."

Dago laughed, "And that is appropriate for he is Lucky Jack Hogan!"

The End

Historical background

My heartfelt thanks to the re-enactors at Gettysburg in July 2013 for all their help and advice. Any historical errors in the book are mine and not theirs. I realise that there were few Springfield carbines in the war but the nature of the business of James Booth Boswell meant that he would be rich and, like the chaps in Silicon Valley, would have ensured that he used the most up to date technology. The irregulars I described are loosely based on Mosby's Rangers and I used William S. Connery's excellent "*Mosby's Raids in Civil War Northern Virginia*", extensively. Mosby was called the Grey Ghost and I used that appellation as the inspiration for my title. Boswell is not Mosby and this is a work of fiction; however the incidents such as the charges using pistols, the wrecking of the trains, being mistaken for Union horsemen are all true. Mosby and his men carried three or four revolvers and I have used that idea for Boswell and his men. They used captured guns and that explains why they were formidably armed. I also used "*The American Civil War Source Book*" by Philip Katcher and that proved a godsend for finding who fought where, when and with what. I also used the Osprey Men at Arms book, "*The Army of Northern Virginia*" by Philip Katcher.

The Confederate cavalry preferred raiding to charging infantry and rarely used their sabres. They preferred to use pistols or carbines. This proved useful most of the time but, as Gettysburg showed, Stuart and his cavalry could let down his general at crucial times. It was said that the biggest supplier for the Confederate Army, and especially the cavalry, was the U.S. as they captured so many of the Union supplies.

The battle of Chancellorsville was one of the pivotal moments in the war. Hooker's original plan had been foiled by the weather. There were heavy rains in April 1863 and the rivers could not be forded until the very end of the month. Lee was not to know this but it could have affected the outcome if the weather had been better. Lee was outnumbered and Hooker had many more resources. Lee took the bold, Napoleonic move, to split his forces and he gave the majority of his smaller army to Stonewall Jackson who marched around the flank of the Union army. He was screened by Jeb Stuart's cavalry which prevented the Union from being aware of this threat. The down side was that a day or two after the battle Jackson was wounded by his own troops who mistook them for Union soldiers. Although the wound was not life

205

threatening Jackson had to have an arm amputated and he died of pneumonia. Who knows what the outcome of Gettysburg would have been had Jackson not died prematurely?

The Battle of Brandy Station took place almost exactly as I described it. Stuart ordered a mock battle on June 5th with 9,000 troopers. General Lee was not able to be there and so it was repeated again on June 8th so that he could see it himself. Both horses and men were exhausted. General Lee ordered the cavalry to move north of the Rappahannock on June 9th and clear the area of Union soldiers but General Pleasonton had ordered 11,000 Union horsemen to attack the camp at Culpeper. Although the Union lost more men and the Confederacy held the field at the end of the day it was considered that Stuart had lost the battle and from this moment on the rebel cavalry lost their invincible status.

General Lee's forward elements crossed the Potomac in the middle of June. The Federal army, now under Meade's command followed some days later. Meade was attempting to stop Lee from heading for Washington which left the Confederate general with the whole of Pennsylvania at his mercy. It was Brigadier General Pettigrew who first ventured into Gettysburg. His commander, Hethe, said in his memoirs, that he had ordered him there to get supplies, notably shoes. The south was desperately short of all manufactured goods. The battle followed that incursion. Buford and his cavalry occupied the town when Pettigrew withdrew.

General Sickles disobeyed orders and moved his Corps down to the wheat field where they were slaughtered and he did lose his leg.

As far as I know there were no skirmishers preceding Pickett's charge but I suspect that there were. There were many small units who had lost large numbers and this would have been a perfect place to use them. The Union Irish Brigade had lost so many men in the battles that there were only at regimental strength. The Union artillery did conserve their ammunition whilst the Confederate was short of ammunition. This was about resources and the Union had far more.

General Imboden did sweep the Union cavalry from Williamsport and the pontoon bridge was damaged by Union cavalry and Lee had to wait for it to be rebuilt before he and the army could cross. General Meade was heavily censured by both the other generals and Lincoln for not pursuing Lee more vigorously. Despite what history may say about General Lee the Union generals always feared facing him. Gettysburg was the high water mark of the war. Lee came within a whisker of victory.

The similarities between Gettysburg and the Battle of Waterloo deserve a book to themselves. In both cases they were very close run battles and could have gone either way at any time. The misuse of cavalry was also dramatic. A.P Hill, like Napoleon Bonaparte, fell ill on the day of the battle and subordinates took some poor decisions in their absence; Ney in the case of Napoleon and Longstreet in the case of Hill. It is interesting to note that the defensive side in both battles ultimately won. In addition the skirmishes leading up to the battle in both cases also had a major impact on the outcome. Had Stuart's cavalry been on the battlefield then who knows what may have happened?

The Dixie Line did exist. The ships were built in Liverpool and plied their trade between Britain and Spain but the profits went to the investors who had funded the line. Many of them also operated as blockade runners. Thanks to the online History Today for that information. http://www.historytoday.com/john-d-pelzer/liverpool-and-american-civil-war

Thanks to Wikipedia for these public domain maps made by Hal Jespersen. I used *Civil War: The Maps of Jedediah Hotchkiss* by Chester G. Hearn and Mike Marino for the detailed maps of the valley. (Thanks to Rich for loaning me his copy!)

Griff Hosker, January 2014

Glossary

Name- Explanation

Aaron - Housekeeper in Charleston for Jack

A.P. Hill - Confederate general

Barton - Boswell's Horse

Blackbirders - Slave ships

Caitlin Hogan - Jack's sister

Carlton James - Boswell's Horse/1st VA Scouts

Carver Ritchie - Boswell's Horse/1st VA Scouts

Cecil (Irish) Mulrooney - Boswell's Horse/1st VA Scouts

Colonel Cartwright - 1st Virginia Scouts

craich-Good conversation/banter (Gaelic)

Dago Spinelli - Boswell's Horse/1st VA Scouts

Danny Murphy - Boswell's lieutenant/1st VA Scouts

David Dinsdale - Boswell's Horse/1st VA Scouts

Gee jaws - Cheap barter goods

Harry Grimes - Boswell's Horse/1st VA Scouts

Jack Hogan - Farmer's son/1st VA Scouts

Jacob Hines - Boswell's Horse/1st VA Scouts

James Booth - Boswell-Colonel/1st VA Scouts

J.E.B. Stuart - Confederate Cavalry Commander

Jedediah Hotchkiss - Jackson's map maker

Jedediah(Jed) Smith - Boswell's Horse/1st VA Scouts

Jem Cartwright - Boswell's Horse/the plantation

Jimmy Stewart - Boswell's Horse/1st VA Scouts

Matty - Boswell's Horse

Mary Malone - a Virginia Servant

Poteen - Homemade spirit

Sandie Pendleton - Jackson's aide

Sergeant Major Vaughan - 1st Virginia Scouts

Small beer - Watered down beer

Vedettes - Mounted cavalry sentries

Wilkie Collins - Boswell's Horse/1st VA Scouts

Other books by Griff Hosker

If you enjoyed reading this book, then why not read another one by the author?

Ancient History

The Sword of Cartimandua Series
(Germania and Britannia 50 A.D. – 128 A.D.)
Ulpius Felix- Roman Warrior (prequel)
The Sword of Cartimandua
The Horse Warriors
Invasion Caledonia
Roman Retreat
Revolt of the Red Witch
Druid's Gold
Trajan's Hunters
The Last Frontier
Hero of Rome
Roman Hawk
Roman Treachery
Roman Wall
Roman Courage

The Wolf Warrior series
(Britain in the late 6th Century)
Saxon Dawn
Saxon Revenge
Saxon England
Saxon Blood
Saxon Slayer
Saxon Slaughter
Saxon Bane
Saxon Fall: Rise of the Warlord
Saxon Throne
Saxon Sword

Medieval History

The Dragon Heart Series
Viking Slave *
Viking Warrior *
Viking Jarl *
Viking Kingdom *
Viking Wolf *
Viking War*
Viking Sword
Viking Wrath
Viking Raid
Viking Legend
Viking Vengeance
Viking Dragon
Viking Treasure
Viking Enemy
Viking Witch
Viking Blood
Viking Weregeld
Viking Storm
Viking Warband
Viking Shadow
Viking Legacy
Viking Clan
Viking Bravery
The Vengeance Trail

The Norman Genesis Series
Hrolf the Viking *
Horseman *
The Battle for a Home *
Revenge of the Franks *
The Land of the Northmen
Ragnvald Hrolfsson
Brothers in Blood
Lord of Rouen

The Road to Gettysburg

Drekar in the Seine
Duke of Normandy
The Duke and the King

Danelaw
(England and Denmark in the 11th Century)
Dragon Sword *
Oathsword *
Bloodsword *
Danish Sword*
The Sword of Cnut

New World Series
Blood on the Blade *
Across the Seas *
The Savage Wilderness *
The Bear and the Wolf *
Erik The Navigator *
Erik's Clan *
The Last Viking*

The Vengeance Trail *

The Conquest Series
(Normandy and England 1050-1100)
Hastings
Conquest

The Aelfraed Series
(Britain and Byzantium 1050 A.D. - 1085 A.D.)
Housecarl *
Outlaw *
Varangian *

The Reconquista Chronicles
Castilian Knight *
El Campeador *
The Lord of Valencia *

The Anarchy Series England
1120-1180
English Knight *
Knight of the Empress *
Northern Knight *
Baron of the North *
Earl *
King Henry's Champion *
The King is Dead *
Warlord of the North*
Enemy at the Gate*
The Fallen Crown
Warlord's War
Kingmaker
Henry II
Crusader
The Welsh Marches
Irish War
Poisonous Plots
The Princes' Revolt
Earl Marshal
The Perfect Knight

Border Knight
1182-1300
Sword for Hire *
Return of the Knight *
Baron's War *
Magna Carta *
Welsh Wars *
Henry III *
The Bloody Border *
Baron's Crusade*
Sentinel of the North*
War in the West*
Debt of Honour
The Blood of the Warlord
The Fettered King
de Montfort's Crown

The Road to Gettysburg

Ripples of Rebellion

Sir John Hawkwood Series
France and Italy 1339- 1394
Crécy: The Age of the Archer *
Man At Arms *
The White Company *
Leader of Men *
Tuscan Warlord *
Condottiere*
Legacy

Lord Edward's Archer
Lord Edward's Archer *
King in Waiting *
An Archer's Crusade *
Targets of Treachery *
The Great Cause *
Wallace's War *
The Hunt

Struggle for a Crown
1360- 1485
Blood on the Crown *
To Murder a King *
The Throne *
King Henry IV *
The Road to Agincourt *
St Crispin's Day *
The Battle for France *
The Last Knight *
Queen's Knight *
The Knight's Tale

Tales from the Sword I
(Short stories from the Medieval period)

Tudor Warrior series
England and Scotland in the late 15th and early 16th century

213

The Road to Gettysburg

Tudor Warrior *
Tudor Spy *
Flodden*

Conquistador
England and America in the 16th Century
Conquistador *
The English Adventurer *

English Mercenary
The 30 Years War and the English Civil War
Horse and Pistol

Modern History

The Napoleonic Horseman Series
Chasseur à Cheval
Napoleon's Guard
British Light Dragoon
Soldier Spy
1808: The Road to Coruña
Talavera
The Lines of Torres Vedras
Bloody Badajoz
The Road to France
Waterloo

The Lucky Jack American Civil War series
Rebel Raiders
Confederate Rangers
The Road to Gettysburg

Soldier of the Queen series
Soldier of the Queen*
Redcoat's Rifle*
Omdurman*
Desert War

The Road to Gettysburg

The British Ace Series
1914
1915 Fokker Scourge
1916 Angels over the Somme
1917 Eagles Fall
1918 We will remember them
From Arctic Snow to Desert Sand
Wings over Persia

Combined Operations series
1940-1951
Commando *
Raider *
Behind Enemy Lines
Dieppe
Toehold in Europe
Sword Beach
Breakout
The Battle for Antwerp
King Tiger
Beyond the Rhine
Korea
Korean Winter

Tales from the Sword II
(Short stories from the Modern period)

Books marked thus *, are also available in the audio format.
For more information on all of the books then please visit the
author's website at www.griffhosker.com where there is a link to
contact him or visit his Facebook page: GriffHosker at Sword
Books or follow him on Twitter: @HoskerGriff or Sword
(@swordbooksltd)
If you wish to be on the mailing list then contact the author
through his website.

Made in the USA
Middletown, DE
10 September 2024

60730271R00130